GOLDENSEAL

GOLDENSEAL

A Novel

Maria Hummel

COUNTERPOINT • BERKELEY, CALIFORNIA

Goldenseal

First Counterpoint edition: 2024

Library of Congress Cataloging-in-Publication Data
Names: Hummel, Maria, author.
Title: Goldenseal : a novel / Maria Hummel.
Description: First Counterpoint edition. | Berkeley : Counterpoint, 2024.
Identifiers: LCCN 2023019028 | ISBN 9781640096066 (hardcover) | ISBN 9781640096073 (ebook)
Subjects: LCGFT: Novels.
Classification: LCC PS3608.U46 G65 2024 | DDC 813/.6—dc23/eng/20230505
LC record available at https://lccn.loc.gov/2023019028

Jacket design by Robin Bilardello
Jacket photograph of woman on balcony © Nikaa / Trevillion Images;
palm trees © Shutterstock / Lucky-photographer
Book design by Laura Berry

COUNTERPOINT
2560 Ninth Street, Suite 318
Berkeley, CA 94710
www.counterpointpress.com

Printed in the United States of America

1 3 5 7 9 10 8 6 4 2

For the godmothers

But the swan my sister called, "Sleep at last, little sister,"
And stroked all night, with a black wing, my wings.

—RANDALL JARRELL

GOLDENSEAL

1.

WHEN THE STRANGER RETURNED TO THE CITY for the first time in forty-four years, she fought to recognize it. The flattened blue sky was the same, the mountains ringing the horizon, the glaze in the air that suggested proximity to the sea—but the city had soared and spread. Its frontier atmosphere had vanished. Gone were the orange groves, the gingerbread homes, the oil derricks poking above dark canals. Ocean met pavement and pavement met packed blocks and high-rises. And dust, so much dust, and so many cars and trucks. And no end of people inside them, or cultures. The whole world, right here. Bright international neighborhoods flashed outside the taxi; this -*town* and that -*town*, they were named, as if filled with quaint shops instead of strip malls and apartment blocks. Many sign makers did not bother with English at all. The stranger's cab passed through entire corridors of foreign letters. She marveled at their slashes and loops, then grew embarrassed at her fascination. She knew she was illiterate in a way you could not justify anymore.

The closer the taxi got to downtown's skyscrapers, the more the traffic thickened, slowing her progress to the hotel. It was early afternoon, but she had been awake for twelve hours, having left the other coast and traveled back in time. She looked down at her small suitcase, crammed with clothes too woolly and warm for the city's beating sun. She had packed to stay the night. Maybe tomorrow night, too. She was too old to simply turn around and fly back, but it was what she longed to do. To arrive, to have the conversation, and to stalk off, spine straight and step sure, all the way to that gap between the airport's last tunnel and the flank of the plane, breathing her first gust of canned air. To head home.

The city had changed, but the hotel's name was the same. Its thirty-eight-story facade would be spiffed and scrubbed, but unaltered. She'd know it on sight: the columned entrance, the redbrick walls above, bordered by a lace of cream-colored stone. The texture of a castle, the shape of a fortress. The height of a spiraling hawk. An outdated tribute to human majesty, plunked among skyscrapers, like orchestral music suddenly piping through a rock station.

She'd know the hotel. On sight. She clung to the notion. In all this tarmac, this adobe and glass and paint, in all these structures rising up, falling down, and replaced again, the hotel would be the one fixity, the center of the clock, the pin that held the moving hands. Her friend had chosen it for this reason, and others. And because her friend had chosen it, because it was her domain, hers, always, the stranger would never sleep there. But she would have to stay somewhere. She was already exhausted. She leaned her head against her window and felt the hum run through her, until she fell into an uncomfortable doze.

* * *

Along the hotel curb, all the other guests trailed their suitcases like little pets, even the children, who yanked blue ones or red ones with the face of a mouse. Her small valise had no wheels, so she had to lug it herself, her stiff body tipped sideways against its weight. Twice, she refused help, once in the curve under the building where the valets stood, and once at the gold-rimmed door. The hotel men peered down at her, still in sober suits, still projecting the same restrained courtesy and city manners. Meanwhile, she had grown shorter and countrified, her shoes practically boots, her fabrics badly cut, and her face winter-pale and indistinct, unadorned by makeup. She knew she looked odd to them, like a candy in a plain, old-fashioned wrapper on a shelf of colorful bars.

With her suitcase thumped on the marble floor, she got in line for the front desk clerk and took in her surroundings. Now that the taxi driver had been tipped, properly she hoped, and she had huffed her way to the correct spot, she could breathe in her arrival. She *had* recognized the hotel on sight, three-towered, anchoring the block next to the public library. Inside, too, her eyes rested on familiar sights: The Austrian teardrop chandeliers. The braided columns. Insets of scalloped wood on the walls, and the skylight framing a fake sky. All the same. As decorative as a wedding cake, and as blazing as the barrow for the fairy dancers.

It surprised her, standing here, to feel a tug of homesickness, remembering old times. She thought she had put it all behind her, all but the essentials, all but the great losses. But now an ache began for the finer ones: the sight of the bar across the lobby, with its glittering bottles, an empty stool. The sound of Italian to her left, a man greeting a woman he clearly admired. The hotel's heady air of possibility, that you could step from one life into another, just by passing through these doors. *It's like breathing champagne,* she used to think, back when she believed that wealth could change her. The line to the clerk advanced. She would be next. She opened her purse and brushed ChapStick, her only cosmetic, across her cracked lips. Now they would look moist but still pale and bloodless. She wished she had considered her appearance more, standing in her bathroom at home, with its oval window on the pines and the retreating April snow. But her reflection in the mirror had looked like herself: white-gray hair bound back, green eyes bright, forehead mostly smooth except when she frowned. Her once full cheeks were leaner and foxier with age, and her mouth had pursed into an expression that suggested mild disapproval. She had become that woman who judges often, and is usually right, but doesn't say what she is thinking, not until the opportune moment. Shrewd. Direct. But not unkind. The headmistress incarnate. And she'd thought, *No, she should see me as I am, as what I have made myself, and not some painted version.*

The clerk smiled at her, perfunctory, and asked if she was checking in. She gauged him to be around twenty-nine and resigned to his job, which had been temporary once, a side gig to support his acting ambitions. He was handsome in a dark-haired, rugged way, but he moved his mouth too much when he spoke, and it delivered a clownish effect.

"Or how I can help you, ma'am?" he said.

"I'm here to see Lacey Crane," she said.

The clerk blinked. He took a breath and looked at the phone on his desk, then back at her.

"I'm sorry," he said. "Who?"

She repeated her statement.

He looked at the desk phone again. "That guest does not receive visitors."

The stranger had expected a reception like this. Lacey had not written back to her letter. In truth, she didn't know if Lacey would see her. But she also knew that Lacey had to see her.

"She knows I'm coming. Give her a call."

"I'm sorry, ma'am." He splayed his hands and looked beyond her at the line forming.

"Give her a call."

She did not raise her voice, but the clerk flinched as if she had. She could put force into her words without added volume. Thousands of times she had done it, speaking to squirming adolescents behind closed doors. It wasn't hard; it just took willpower.

"I have come a long way to see her," she added, standing erect.

"Ma'am, I have to ask you to step aside so I can check in the other guests," he said.

She remained there, stony, smelling her stale sweat after a long day of travel, feeling her greased lips. She resisted the impulse to rub them together.

"If you step aside, I'll get my manager to speak with you," he said, faltering. "Please."

* * *

The manager was a prim, efficient woman who barely listened to the stranger's request before cutting her off. She smoothed her blue pinstripe suit and returned the same stern gaze she was receiving. "That guest has given us specific instructions not to be disturbed. By anyone. You can rest here as long as you like today, but then you'll have to leave."

The stranger regarded her in silence, suddenly dizzy.

"I'm sorry, ma'am," said the manager, patting her arm. "You just let me know when you want me to call you a taxi."

"It's 1990," said the stranger.

The manager's benign expression did not change, but her body went rigid. "Yes, ma'am. It is 1990."

"That means Lacey's seventy. She was born Lucie Weber. In Prague. How would I know that if I wasn't her old friend?" She couldn't bring herself to say more, about how she'd once lived at this hotel, had traipsed through the ornate galleria morning and night, how sometimes she and Lacey had fallen asleep upstairs on the same exhale.

"But she's *our* guest." The manager rose. "Rest as long as you like," she repeated, and clacked away.

The stranger had expected some resistance upon arrival, yet faced with it now, she felt the precipice of her position. She had not counted on total failure. In all her struggles to buy the tickets, close up her home, board her plane, navigate the city's labyrinthine airport, and secure a taxi, she had envisioned innumerable delays and missteps. But once she reached the hotel, she'd thought, the doors would open and on the other side would be Lacey, waiting.

She sat in her plump chair and stared straight ahead. And stared. Afternoon faded, hour by hour, to evening, and people's clothing changed: jeans and T-shirts to dresses and tuxes. Hair-sprayed up-dos tucked with baby's breath. White bow ties and cummerbunds. Gangly boys and blushing girls: prom season at the hotel's ballrooms. Meanwhile, the bar filled with a chattering business crowd, all collars and pleats, sharp shoulders, teased bangs. Gorgeous, armored, aging creatures. They looked in a race to defeat their own insignificance. Watching them chuck back their chardonnays, the stranger grew immensely thirsty, but she didn't budge. If she got up now, it would signal defeat. Any movement would suggest she could be carted away. The actor-clerk left his post, and the prim manager took his place, occasionally glancing in her direction. But the manager didn't stride over again, and the stranger didn't rise. Only eye contact volleyed between them. *You need to let me see her* versus *You need to leave*. It was like that silly game with James Dean and the roaring cars and the cliff. What was it called? Chicken. The stranger didn't care to win Chicken. She didn't even want to play, but she couldn't think of anything else to do, anywhere else to go. Her imagination, always alight, always flying ahead, had abandoned her completely.

Instead, her mind soaked in the familiar permanence of the room, the way the dark wood and travertine expressed *always* and *ever*. The fountain still bubbled and murmured, spilling shimmer from a lion's mouth. The stone angels still posed on serpent tails behind the bar.

The skylight still spliced its glow to diamonds. Piano music from the last century played over invisible speakers. Had this chamber been the lobby so long ago? She didn't think so. This was the old Music Room, where they'd held afternoon tea dances, men and women, waist to waist and wall to wall, loafers skidding, tulle dresses spinning.

With each passing hour, it was getting harder to imagine that upstairs Lacey would finally relent and let her through. It was hard to imagine standing up, either. The stranger's legs felt sore and cramped. Her blue cotton skirt had wrinkled like a used napkin. How had it ever seemed sharp? It was the garb of a naive country matron. She detested the sight of her ankles these days, fattened in her early sixties, so she'd worn ankle-high sneaker-boots. They looked bloated now, blobs of shiny white leather.

When the shift changed again, and a neat, graying man took up roost behind the front desk, it came to her at last. The key. A piece to twist in the lock of the gate. The likeness wasn't close, but the clerk's posture had jogged her memory—he had a high but bowed stance, as if hung from a hook between his shoulders. Proud yet servile. No young people stood like this. They'd been taught to nourish their self-esteem instead of their sense of duty. It was the reason for so many teen suicides now: this insistence upon drawing happiness from the self's well. The self ran dry all the time. Or it spat up mud.

There was her imagination, finally returned. Jawing at her like a willful bird. She'd notice something about a clerk or a crewman and see his whole life arrayed in her mind, and then other lives, when she was supposed to be talking about how to pound her pork or plow her driveway. It had once been a useful skill, developed from years of analyzing her staff and students, guessing what they really wanted, finding it for them, but now that she was mostly powerless, the reveries got in the way, like a vestigial toe.

As the line came to an end and the clerk waited alone, she checked the outside pocket of her bag to make certain the envelope was still there. It was. Who could have nicked it when she'd kept her suitcase with her the whole time, on the plane, in the taxi? The white corner jutted, sharp to the touch. She pushed the envelope deeper, zipped it safe, then stood slowly, her head swimming. For a moment, it felt like time itself was spinning through her, all those lost years when she could have been . . . Then she lifted the suitcase again and walked on trembling legs to the counter.

The old clerk glanced up, guarded. He had been warned about her. His hands drifted toward the keyboard in front of him, as if he might need to type in a name.

"I'd like to speak to Bruno," she said.

2.

ALL DAY, LACEY HAD BEEN WATCHING THE YEL-
low taxis glide up to the corner, turn right, and vanish into
the porte cochere under the hotel. It was like watching a le-
viathan swallow fish after fish, she thought, first pleased by her image,
then disliking it. She was neither whale nor whale-swallowed, after all.
Inside her rooms, she was free.

Thirty-three taxis passed before she grew dizzy and her legs complained of standing, and she lowered herself to the little couch. She
picked up her novel and did not read. The novel was too new, too gripping and forgettable, but she wouldn't be able to focus on a classic,
either. Her stomach had already revolted three times. Her pulse raced
and stuttered. She laid out several outfits, but she was still in her house
robe at noon, a big ballooning thing that smelled of her cherry blossom
soap and shampoo. Its coziness was the only thing keeping her from
shaking all over, teeth chattering, as if she stood in a frigid wind.

This was not the calm, resolute appearance she'd planned for. Her
goose-bumped skin showed none of the gloss of two pots of beauty
cream, spread every day this week, over every inch of her body. Her
hair, dyed black to the roots just Tuesday, was still uncurled, un-
brushed. The desk had not yet been set like a table; the order for wine

and a seven-course meal waited by her phone. All the elegant ways she intended to impress her visitor were readied, but Lacey had stalled in the final steps. The problem, as it had always been, was that Edith wouldn't care for elegance. Not really. She didn't crave it. Some people watched a sunset and cherished every pastel hue of the horizon, while others preferred hailstorms and lightning. Displays of power. Well, elegance was power, too.

Lacey stared at the words of the book. They marched their ink across the page, meaningless. She looked at her walls, lined by bookshelves, and the trio of paintings that Cal had given her on their wedding day: a white flower, no stem, magnified, split across all three frames, so that the image abstracted and became something else, a broken vortex. You had to see all three artworks together to know there was a blossom behind it, and even then the image gestured toward an equation, a mathematical coldness at the heart of things. It was a strange gift for Cal, who'd often bought Lacey the exactly right camel coat or lambskin driving gloves, who dictated his own intricate bouquets to the florist. A man of taste, people had said about Cal. "They'll grow on you," he promised on their wedding night, seeing her look of surprise. "And if they don't, you can sell them in ten years and buy a Jaguar. This artist is on the rise."

Years ago, Lacey had them appraised, and Cal had been right, probably righter now, as the artist died young. By then, Lacey couldn't imagine what a day would be like without seeing the paintings, hating them a little.

At one o'clock, she bathed and, wearing a clean robe, made a phone call. A feverish will grew in her after the man promised to deliver what she wanted. Her head cleared. The nausea quelled. She hovered over her outfit choices: the ivory pantsuit; a forest-green blouse with velvet slacks; a midnight-blue dress with subdued leg-of-mutton sleeves. The dress was only an option because she liked its fabric, a creamy synthetic blend that would hide her flaws. She had always been a trousers girl: leggy, with a pert behind, a trim waist, and ankles to die for. Skirts made her ordinary, but once, wearing a snug pair of lime capris and a little heel, Lacey had made every man on set turn to watch her cross it. Women didn't seem to think it fun anymore, inviting the swivel, capitalizing on it to get what you wanted. Maybe they were right. It wasn't fun but thrilling. The thrill of a prey creature launching the chase.

The pantsuit was out. White was too guru. She wasn't a sage. That left the dress, and the blouse and slacks. The former would look too feminine, the latter too casual, like she hadn't fortified herself for this encounter. She went back to her wardrobe and ticked through her other options, most of which were too small. She had gained in the past two years, forgoing her dance exercises too often. She didn't seem to have enough breath for them anymore. Worse, her sweat had stunk up her suite—and the creaks her joints made! Like flea market furniture. Pants were probably a bad idea, after all. They revealed too much slump. She was better off shrouding herself in flows of expensive fabric. It wouldn't be hard to outdo Edith, but her clothing wasn't about Edith entirely. It was about armor.

Lacey scooped the cool weight of the dress, admiring its detail. The garment had been made by a Milanese designer who borrowed from opera for her drama: sleeves with puffed shoulders that went snug below the elbow, a skirt that would sway with the body. Lacey carried it to her bathroom, hooking the hanger over the towel rack, checking her hot rollers, her cosmetics. They were all in place.

She hadn't decided on exactly how long to make Edith wait. Not overnight, certainly, and not late, but until daylight faded, and night had truly arrived. Then they would dine and talk, and Lacey would say what she had waited decades to say, and Edith would go away. Edith's announcement that she would arrive at 2:00 p.m. on a certain date might have been thoughtfully intended, but it had come across as a decree. *I will arrive. You will open your door for me.* So Edith would wait, and understand, thereby, that she was welcomed by grace and not necessity.

And grace she would experience. Lacey had already mapped out the menu, chosen the beverages, and unearthed her mother's gold candlesticks. New white candles lay smooth in their box. Lacey slid one out, savoring the drag of wax against her skin. It had been a decade since she'd sat in firelight, the warmth and flicker of it—since she'd seen any fire at all, in a grate, on a hillside, anyplace. She would light the wick with Cal's silver lighter, one, two, that old hiss and click they both knew.

The Milanese opera dress. Hair softly lifted and bent by rollers. Silk hose. D'Orsay pumps in a navy leather. A lipstick that approximated the berry red of her girlhood lips. A sensation spread through Lacey, not nerves exactly, but the feeling you get when you're listening to a concerto and really hear it inside—each note—a terrible intimacy, one that makes you cry. All these years, and the hour had not come. Now it was here.

* * *

At 6:00 p.m., the phone rang, the low tone rippling in the quiet. She had been watching the windows darken, dressed now, coiffed, smelling of a musky sweetness she'd dabbed behind her ears.

"Miss Lacey." His voice had thinned with age, grown reedy.

"What happened?" she said. Bruno never phoned her, except once, last year, to announce he was a month into rehab for a stroke on his left side.

"It's Miss Edith. She is here to visit you."

"And they called you, not me?"

"You knew." He sounded surprised, disappointed with her.

"I had some idea," she said evasively. "They shouldn't have called you."

"She asked for me."

Oh, that tiny note of pride. They'd all been sweet on Edith. The delight in her husky voice over the smallest kindness. The pleased way she'd strolled the marble corridors downstairs, noting each detail. Edith had even found a way to tease Bruno, perpetually polite and grave, and he wore a special smirk around her. He lingered after bringing their breakfasts, gripping the cart, waiting for Edith's green gaze to land on him. Over the years, though, he'd never inquired about her sudden departure. Not once. Likely, he knew.

"It was Gary, wasn't it?" she said. "He should have phoned me first."

The other end was silent. Bruno was not a rat.

"How are you?" she said.

"Every day, a few steps," he said. "Then a few steps more. I walk a mile a day now."

"What did she say to you?"

"She said, 'Hello, Bruno. It's been a long time.' Then she told me she has been waiting in the lobby since the afternoon and you won't see her."

"I won't see anyone," Lacey said.

"Then she said, 'Bruno, I need to talk to her, can you please talk to her, and ask her to let me come up? I have to see her.'"

"They had your number, just like that?"

"Gary checks in on me. More than you, if we're to be honest."

"Did she say how she was?"

"How she was what?"

"How she's feeling. Her health."

"How she's feeling? She's traveled thousands of miles. She's waiting hours to meet you."

"How long did you talk?"

"Few minutes." Now he sounded evasive.

"You talked about me?"

"To cover the necessaries, yes. You may not know, but I have worked in a hotel for many years. I know how to be discreet."

"What necessaries? What would you be discreet about?"

"Miss Lacey," said Bruno heavily. "You have a guest. Your papi had a guest, he took the best care of him. He treated his guests like kings. What do they need? A whiskey with an ice cube cracking in it? The softest pillow? The right waltz for the wedding dance? He would find it."

Bruno had the same Prague German accent as her father, though his voice had always been lower, weighted by gravitas, while her father's smooth baritone could glide and glide. But the slow bite on the vowels, the blunting of English syntax, it always got to her. After all these years, a whole lifetime, in America, Bruno was still Old World. Still Papi's right-hand man. She felt her eyes water. She twined her finger through the black phone cord, letting it tighten and whiten her skin. The coils, they must have been designed to protect the line within. Or maybe they enabled the phone to stretch with someone who wanted to walk away from what she was saying. A coil reminded you to put the receiver back.

She tried to summon a calm voice. It came out tired.

"Thank you, Bruno," she said. "Tell her she'll be expected for dinner in one hour."

3.

FTER SHE HAD CALLED THE HOTEL KITCHEN AND made her precise orders, Lacey still had forty-six minutes to wait. She had dressed too soon, and she could feel her body betraying her, dampening her armpits, breathing out sour breath. She turned up the air-conditioning and sat close to its cool artificial breeze. Her parents had insisted on ceiling fans to the end. They hated the whir of anything newer, the tinny taste of the air. "I like to feel my summers," Papi used to declare, and then with widened eyes added, "preferably at the Overlook," naming his favorite resort. It was sometime after the war when Lacey realized that both her parents had stopped smiling for good. They still told jokes, they liked sitcoms and funny songs, they complained bitterly about humorless acquaintances, but her father's old flashing grin and her mother's trilling laugh had departed, and in their place a new language of shrugs and squints and mock-shocked gazes had become their norm. Their shoulders dipped, too, as if someone had placed a rock on their backs and they were glumly bracing against it. Her mother's steps, always light, developed a shuffle. Her father, who'd first taught Lacey that dancing was whirling together on an axis, grew a pronounced limp. Her mother had lost eight relatives total, including her parents, to labor camps and to the ovens. Her father lost her mother, bit by bit, then all at once.

Lacey's birth name was not Lacey but Lucie, *loo-tsee-yeh*, changed the day she arrived in America because her father did not like the floppiness of the English version. Lucy, *loosey-goosey*. Lacey's earliest memories were of leaving Prague in winter, when the coal smoke made thick soot on the windows of their old apartment and swans melted ovals in the ice of the Moldau. She remembered the cold gray air, the statues that lined the river bridge, and the ancient drafts from a plaster building that had stood on its corner since the time of Charlemagne. Mutti and Papi, shrouded in great fur coats, sat on either side of her in a rumbling black cab, the hood so long and pointy it looked like a raven's beak. She was seven, and it was 1927, two years before the stock market crash, and twelve before Prague would fall to the Nazis.

That morning, Lacey's favorite doll had been lost in the packing, and she was crying and begging to go back. Sobs burst from her. They seemed too large for her body, and wrong-way. Gulps that went up, not down. Her parents put their arms around her, engulfing her in the scents of animal skin and cigarettes, but they ignored her requests. They glanced anxiously at the passing medieval streets as if desperate for them to disappear and the flat coastline to replace them.

"Hush, darling," said her father, rare irritation in his voice.

"You have Astrid in your suitcase," said her mother, reminding Lacey of the care they had taken to nest her one porcelain figure in tissue and clothes. "She's your best doll."

"But she's not my favorite," Lacey said, hiccupping. "I can't hold her."

"You can hold her with your eyes," said her mother. "Sometimes that's all you get." Her voice trembled as she said this, and Lacey felt Papi look over at Mutti, and look away again. The statement and the look passed slowly, as if the family, all three of them, were submerged underwater and suspended there. For the first time in her brief life, Lacey wondered what someone else was thinking, and she stopped crying, because she realized that her father was sad. His black wavy hair, Lacey's hair, was carefully combed as always, his scarf knotted elegantly around his neck, but he seemed to have been invaded by a different man, a defeated one, who had an ashen complexion and a grim mouth, and who blinked at the mess his life had become. It all became clear years later: Papi's meaningless affair with a hotel receptionist, one of the principal reasons they'd left Europe. Her mother's lack of forgiveness, her refusal to accept America, her wish to return to her old life. Yet during that moment, Lacey, ever smitten by Papi, surmised only his grief, his ache, and tucked herself, consoling, against his side. She fell asleep there, secure under his arm.

Her next memory was at the train station: a cave of arches, the walls painted a caramel brown and tall as a cathedral. It was hard to know where to look. Each arch opened to a platform and track, but above the arches posed statues, mysterious stone figures that stared blankly down. Above the statues loomed the vast dome, crisscrossed by carved wood. And then there were the travelers below: gentlemen in herringbone suits, hurrying alone, and families with children, clustering on a platform, flushed, rumpled, and happy after a long journey. In and out, back and forth, groaned the trains, each the height of a house's first story. Lacey shrank from the engines' sinister faces, the long snaking bodies they dragged. She did not want to climb into one.

"What time do you see?" said Papi, pointing out over the tracks to the giant clock, its face so white and broad it could have been the moon.

When Lacey recited it correctly, he squeezed her hand.

"Exactly right. Time for our new life to begin," he said.

Her mother wasn't there, only Papi in his furs, his homburg hat perched on his head. "There's a dining car on this train," he said. "We can eat on china plates and watch out the window. Would you like that?"

"Yes."

A whistle shrilled across the station and a train rocked forward, departing. They regarded it in silence. A shadow crossed Papi's face.

"You must have manners, or they won't allow you to stay," he told her. His tone dipped, making his voice sound harsh.

Tears sparked in Lacey's eyes again. "I'll be good," she whispered.

Papi looked down at her, and then pressed her in a tight hug. "I know," he said.

Her mother had gone missing in the station, of course. That was why only Lacey and Papi were standing by the large clock, why her father focused so intently on the hour. Mutti had run off, perhaps intending to turn back, and when she returned they were late. They'd missed their train to the port city and had to take another. They hurried at the port, barely reaching the ship in time, earning the sharp rebuke of the bursar, who had nearly crossed them off the manifest. Only Papi's charm saved them, and by the end of the journey, he promised the bursar a job in his new Manhattan hotel, a new life where the man could live close to his family, but still inhabit the glamour and luxury of a traveler's world. The bursar was Bruno's father, and Bruno, already twelve by then, became Lacey's first real friend, and her first kiss.

* * *

But before Bruno's friendship, before the kiss, there was the New World, their new city like a brash country cousin to somber Prague, packed with honking cars, bootblack boys, and half-finished buildings crawling with workers. The New World was an apartment twice the size and brightness of the one in Prague, and a new school for girls only. And English. English was a sound Lacey's mouth had to make: *Hello* and *young lady* and *mister* and *missus*. English was also curly letters on the page: *Mother's sewing* and *Father's necktie* and *Tell me, what does bluebird say, when he sings at peep of day?* For Lacey, the reading came faster than the speaking, because she loved the ink and pictures, and most of all because the pages waited for her silently, patiently, instead of trying to interpret her like grown-ups, or moving on, like her classmates. "You are such a reader!" exclaimed Mutti, startled and slightly disapproving, whenever Lacey buried herself in a book. She made Lacey learn how to do embroidery and how to properly set a table, busying her so she didn't spend long afternoons curled in bed. "You don't want to become a daydreamer," Mutti had scolded.

And yet every morning Lacey left a cocoon that her mother was slowly spinning of her old European things: German landscape paintings in heavy frames, the gold-plated tea set, even the maroon brocade curtains unrolled, shaken out, hung over the new view of a park and a street corner crowded with fruit and flower vendors. Inside the apartment, the days were still *kalt* or *schön*, supper was still *Abendessen*, bread was *Brot*, and milk *Milch*. Outside, the sounds changed, flatter and more open, and with them Lacey changed, growing into a bolder child, a bestower of compliments and friendships, a mimic of her father. By the end of her first week at school, she knew that she was one of the prettiest two girls, and second place only because she wasn't blond. Furthermore, the prettiest girl was shy, so the stage was Lacey's to claim.

It took Lacey most of a year, but as soon as her full English sentences came, so did her popularity. It helped that Lacey was almost eight and the other girls in her grade almost seven, but she didn't credit her canniness to her age then. She simply thought she was quicker than the rest of them, and richer, though that wasn't true, either. Some girls' parents were very rich, with mansions and servants, and second mansions upstate and on the northern coast, but most families possessed a Puritan aversion to displays of flashiness and wealth. They spoke of their vacations in a code: place names, brand names, clubs. They chose clothes that looked expensive but plain. Lacey's sleeves of green velvet bows were a source of much envy, and some scorn, but she ignored the other girls' haughtiness because it did not frighten her. She knew it was only a matter of time before she was adored; she had her father's example to follow.

Her mother, in contrast, did not like the other school mothers, who had a slow, cold way of approving of people and struggled to understand Mutti's broken English. Her mother did not like the American churches, either. In Prague, they had always gone to Mass on holidays and special Sundays at the medieval cathedral. Lacey had been baptized under the grand old dome and floated through First Communion in a froth of lace, delighting her father's German Catholic family, who watched from the pews. That day, her mother had smiled, too, and pronounced her lovely, but she'd stood alone in her fur-hemmed dress, her own relatives uninvited or unmoved to come. Lacey had not thought this painful then, as who wouldn't choose Papi over anything and anyone? But her mother's agreeable attitude toward her husband's religion would not cross the ocean. Mutti found the American stained-glass windows too simple, the altar crude. The priests prayed too fast, as if they were on a stopwatch to finish their sacraments.

For three years, Mutti, Papi, and Lacey cultivated their own separate worlds. Mutti had the apartment, Papi the hotel, and Lacey her school. Some weekends they took train trips to the country and stayed at inns, where Mutti and Lacey lounged on terraces and drank egg creams, and Papi spied on the furniture and the menus and the entertainment. Though Papi always said the country inns had the best innovations, he never explained what these innovations were. Nevertheless, the vacations made them happy and close. At home, they parted ways and became polite strangers again. To Lacey, Mutti talked often, and wistfully, of Prague. She didn't like American soap ("like washing with clay"), music (swing was "for kids," and ragtime was "jolting"), apple pie ("so soggy, and the *sugar*, why ruin good fruit with so much sugar?"), English ("bleh, bleh, bleh, like their throats are asleep"), streets ("loud"), or shopkeepers ("rude"). Lacey, who was forgetting Prague, struggled to conjure the city in her mind's eye, but all she saw was a dark river, shrouds of old buildings, and a delicious slice of cream torte she'd eaten once at her aunt's tea table.

One day, a distant cousin of Mutti's, now in Brooklyn, got in touch, and a change came over Mutti. She pulled a small black prayer book from one of the Prague suitcases and began paging through it. She put on her apron and started planning menus. Inside the apartment, gatherings bloomed with other expatriate families, mostly Jews, and for celebrations and holidays that were new to Lacey. Passover. Rosh Hashanah. The first time Lacey heard Hebrew from her mother's mouth was at one such party, the table spread with spiral pastries procured from a Hungarian bakery, and little dice called dreidels in the children's hands. Lacey stared at the woman who raised her, unable to match Mutti's yellow curls and rosy cheeks with the emphatic, unfamiliar sounds. It was like learning at ten that your parent could play the saxophone, beautifully, and without hesitation. Mutti was saying a prayer, and other voices joined her. When they were all in unison, Lacey's mother glowed with a fierce fire, and Lacey had never seen her so lovely. Mutti was a small woman, dainty and pretty, but with the prayer inside her, she loomed. She took Lacey's breath away.

Papi wasn't in the room to see the transformation. Those days, he worked constantly, leaving early, returning late, even on weekends. Papi's hotel, which catered to wealthy Europeans, had not been as hard hit as other hotels by the stock market crash, but everyone was grasping for the remaining spenders. Papi had to fight to keep his clientele. He didn't comment on Mutti's parties, except to say once that Lacey already had a faith, and they shouldn't confuse her or put her spot at school in jeopardy. To this Mutti did not reply, but her cheeks went pink, and before the next occasion, she told Lacey she could choose to stay in her room or make some new friends. Mutti knew the right thing to say. While the adults gabbed, Lacey charmed three sisters into a giggling, candlelit séance under her bedspread and nearly set the apartment on fire. The sisters were bright and outspoken, and she liked them. But when the prayers came, Lacey sang Latin hymns inside her head to drown out the Hebrew. She would not betray her father.

Soon after Lacey's eleventh birthday, Mutti became pregnant again, growing round and slow. The parties stopped for a while, and the apartment returned to being the quiet cave of the past. Papi stayed home more, too, especially in the mornings when Mutti was unwell. He walked Lacey to school and asked her questions about her friends and studies, as if he took her opinions seriously. A new closeness bloomed between them on those strolls. They stopped holding hands, but Lacey caught Papi looking down at her with surprised pride. They talked about Mutti in a protective way, as if Lacey's mother had suddenly become the child in the family. "She'll be happier with a baby," he said. "She loved when you needed her most." Lacey nodded, as if she already knew this. "She loves babies," she agreed.

Mutti made Papi promise he would take a break, two weeks off, when the new child came. "Real weeks," she said. "Not just mornings." Papi removed his reading glasses and rubbed the red welts on either side of his nose. "I promise," he said.

When his son was born dead, he kept his word. Lacey had never seen her parents so tied to each other or felt so far from them herself. Two weeks they orbited one another, two parents and their remaining child, Mutti and Papi weeping, Lacey silenced and gouged by their grief. One morning Lacey woke up with her father sprawled, asleep, on the oak floor beside her bed. He didn't seem to know how he had gotten there. He was not drunk or hungover. He complained of chest pain and dizziness and went to the doctor, but if he was ill, Lacey was not informed. Instead, he lay in bed for two days while Mutti tended him. Then he returned to work, and Mutti bought a solo ticket on the ocean liner back to Amsterdam, then Prague.

"You can't go with me this time," said Mutti when Lacey cried and railed over her departure. "But I will think of you every minute of every hour."

"Why do *you* have to go?" Lacey raged.

Her mother bit her lip and would not look at her. "You'll understand one day," she said. It was all she'd say. Whenever Lacey brought up Mutti staying in New York instead, Mutti grew stern and told Lacey the conversation was over. But on the afternoon of Mutti's departure, Mutti hugged her goodbye for a long time. Her spine felt knobby under Lacey's palms, and she smelled faintly of drying blood. "You know how much I love you," she said. "More than my life." Lacey and Papi watched from the pier until the ship's immense shape disappeared into low-hanging clouds.

* * *

On their first morning alone, Papi set out the rolls, cheese, cold butter, and jam, but he forgot to slice the cheese for Lacey. Nor did he eat anything himself. He took three sips of coffee and dumped it out, washing his cup. When Lacey had finished her breakfast, he scooped her plate and mug immediately, scrubbed them, and wiped the table. Then he gave a little huff of breath and regarded the sink like it was an unwelcome guest. "You're old enough to come with me to the hotel after school now," he said to the wall. "If you don't like it, I can find you a governess. You shouldn't be here alone in the apartment all afternoon and evening."

Papi spoke in German, but he used the English word, *governess*, which sounded appallingly controlling and strict.

"The hotel," said Lacey. "I'll come to the hotel. Please."

Her father turned. There was a water stain on his trousers from washing the dishes. He didn't notice it until Lacey pointed.

"Mutti wears an apron," she said.

Papi did not answer. He plucked a towel and began dabbing the stain.

"I'll be seen and not heard, Papi," Lacey said, using her brisk, bright school persona. She mimicked stitching her lips, but Papi didn't catch it. He was still frowning at his pants. His hair was thinning at the crown.

"I know I'll like it," she added. "I'll be with you."

Papi smiled at her now, his eyes watering. New lines carved the corners of his face. For a moment, she thought he would break open, he seemed so full of emotion. But then he choked it down and patted her arm. "I'll have Bruno fetch you after school."

4.

FROM THEN ON, LACEY KEPT HER FATHER'S HOURS, working long, sleeping little, practically living at the hotel. Papi's world: seven stories of sandstone and brick, stately silence, and the cloying smell of cigars. The hotel was not large enough or expensive enough to be famous, but it drew a regular crowd of European business travelers who wanted familiar comforts: Turkish baths, a gentleman's club, concierges from their home countries who spoke multiple languages. In its quiet way, Papi's hotel delivered the eternal, a place of grace and courtesies, a refuge. While bankrupted Manhattan fathers shot themselves, Papi directed his stream of guests to taste his chef's lobster Louis. While dust storms drowned families in the Midwest, Papi reorganized his room assignments to make space for an earl's nephew in an entirely booked summer. The disastrous headlines did not correspond with hotel life; they could not. The news delivered doom after doom. The hotel delivered the same bright day.

Papi spoke seven languages himself and installed a French-style brigade kitchen, with a saucier and a pastry maker and a roasting station, but staff that could switch from osso buco one day to confit de canard the next. Papi specialized in adaptation, too. He cocked his dark head back whenever someone new arrived in his atrium, measuring the cut of their suit, the squeak or silence of their shoes, their clean-shaven cheeks or lush beard, and he often reassigned rooms on the fly. He liked to introduce guests to each other, but only if it served the purpose of impressing them. He kept discreet a certain city leader's affair with an Italian opera singer, booking them the same corner room and delivering the keys himself so they could bypass the front desk.

Papi was all charm and quick perceptiveness in person, but he liked his hotel to project dependability, solidity, and unchanging good taste. Heavy mahogany furniture filled his bedrooms. The atrium's grand piano was rumored to have been played by Liszt. A slim blond man sat on its bench on weekend nights, fingering out études and sonatas, instead of the jazz that was so popular. Papi's hotel was a place for affluent, aging men to retreat and hold meetings. Not a party spot. The dining room was a den of dark wood, lit by candles and lamps. The gentlemen's club had paneled walls, too, and one of them slid open to a smaller room, where liquor was poured. Lacey had never seen it, but she knew it existed, just as she knew that, if she had been a boy, she could have explored every corner of the hotel and wandered the streets around it. As she was a girl, Papi insisted she stay in his sight or go home.

So Lacey found her permanent perch in the little office behind the front desk, where the clerks sorted mail for the long-term guests and took their meal breaks. They were all ten years older than her, full-grown men, glad for their steady jobs, for Papi's fairness and respect. They treated Lacey like a little princess, except Bruno, who was a teenager still, and moodier, self-absorbed. Bruno didn't seem to think Lacey was any age or rank at all, just another fixture of the business. Bruno had a way of standing with his hands in his pockets, his dark blond hair falling in his face, and brooding, as if entirely unaware of others in the room. He appeared especially unaware of his boss's little minx daughter in her red ermine-lined cloak and

patent-leather shoes. Naturally, Bruno's reticence made him a so-
cial conquest for Lacey, and whenever he came into the office, she
barraged him with questions that were not-so-secretly designed to
prove her own sophistication. "What novels do you read? What opera do you like? Do you ever drink coffee without cream? Do you
have a cigarette for me?"

Bruno responded with exasperated obedience and, sometimes,
surprising confidences as they puffed together in the alley behind the
building, hiding from Papi, who didn't want Lacey to smoke so young.
Bruno didn't wish to work in a hotel like his father. He longed to be a
merchant marine. He said the words *merchant marine* like he had heard
them ringing in the air, and not like he knew what the career actually was. He boasted about going to the port one day and signing up,
sailing off to the West Indies. He said *West Indies* the same romantic way, like they were freedom itself instead of some sweltering little
islands across the sea. Lacey was sure the shipmen's hiring process
was far more complicated and competitive, and that, in the end, Bruno
wouldn't be able to bear deserting his strict father. But she never questioned him, honored and pleased by the intimacy. In turn, she told
Bruno that sometimes she was glad her mother had left. It was more
peaceful with just Papi. It was also divine to witness the men's world
of the hotel, to see the smart ladies they brought to dine. She drew
the women's outfits in a little notebook: the brimless hats, the column
dresses cinched at the hip, the skirt lengths that rose from ankle to
mid-calf, and imagined herself dancing the shag all night to a rollick-
ing brass band. She had become the daydreamer her mother warned
against, and she had fallen in love with America.

Lacey's hours at the hotel put her behind at school, but with her
easy sociability and aptitude, the teachers cut her breaks, and she soon
became expert at cramming for exams at the last minute. Besides, she
didn't see the purpose of too much learning anyway. One day, she

would work for Papi's hotel and meet a rich businessman and become a wife and mother. She wanted to have passels of children, she told Bruno, making him flinch. "No only children for me," she declared. "I want seven." She pictured them filling an uptown brownstone with their small bodies and bright voices.

In Lacey's thirteenth winter, just as her breasts came in, illness struck her. Between the many cigarettes, the late nights, and the steadily neglected and dirty apartment at home, Lacey developed a cough she could not shake. Weeks passed while she quaked alone on the couch, watching her mother's maroon brocade curtains, which had faded in the folds from never being changed. Her chest hurt and she felt old and frail, and truly missed Mutti for the first time. Papi was a terrible nurse. He hated to sit still, to wait. He bounced restlessly in the chair beside her bed or read aloud from the newspaper in a booming voice. He asked her anxiously if she was getting better. One morning, to please him, Lacey lied and said yes. She dressed for school. She arrived at her classroom, greeted her classmates, and burst into a coughing fit that lasted minutes. The headmistress ordered a cab to bring her home.

When Papi returned that evening, bearing parcels of dinner from the hotel, he looked crushed to hear of Lacey's failure. "Can't you just swallow the cough while you're at school?" he said. She blinked at him. He shook his head. "Never mind," he said. "Have a lamb chop."

The headmistress sent Lacey her books, and in the mornings Lacey took to reading in the living room on her mother's couch by the radiator. She ate a cold lunch alone, returned to the couch, and read some more, but by four o'clock she was only gazing into space and waiting for Papi. She memorized the detail on the cast-iron radiator, the vines and leaves pounded into the silver. She counted and recounted the thirteen panels of cherry wainscoting that ran around the wall. Freezing rain slashed the windows, and wind rattled the panes, but inside the apartment a deep hush reigned. Her cough, the only noise, sounded raw and animal.

In February, one long, lonely afternoon stretched into evening, then night, then midnight, then almost dawn before Papi came home. Lacey woke from a doze to see him hovering over her, his breath sour, the expression in his brown gaze one of startled discovery and regret. He had forgotten her, his only daughter, or he had deliberately tried. She was too much for him. A burden. Lacey closed her eyes, too tired to cry over this. The hand that touched her shoulder was leaden, and Papi turned away wordlessly. Yet in the morning, he was awake before her, her breakfast already on the table when she stumbled out, coughing, and his smile was warm as ever. If he remembered his betrayal, he gave no sign of it. Only when Papi left the apartment that day did Lacey burst into tears. She added her parents' wrongs together: all the abandonments and the selfish choices. Together they swelled into a larger hurt, like wasp stings that land close together. Then she pushed them down. She had to keep Papi. Papi was all she had.

Her cough persisted even as the winter broke. Her father brought in new physicians to examine her. They listened to Lacey's lungs with their cold instruments. Most said it was pneumonia, but their bitter balsams and syrups did not help. Lacey grew so weak, her legs felt like stilts and the walk to the washroom made her out of breath. Finally, a white-bearded doctor told Papi to crack the windows and gave him a series of onion compresses to heat and place on Lacey's chest. After two days, the tightness began to loosen. "Mother's formula," the doctor said, his beard wagging. "Scorned by my colleagues, who never recommend a simple solution when something complicated and expensive will do." After a week, he listened to her lungs again and nodded. "Improved," he pronounced. He advised that Lacey leave the city in the summer and get some country air. He knew of a girls' camp in the north that would give her rest, healthy food, and wholesome exercise. He gazed around Papi's dusty, stained countertops, the piles of unwashed shirts and trousers, and also suggested a maid.

* * *

In June, with a trunk filled with two sets of her camp uniform, two bathing suits, two pairs of sturdy shoes, a rain poncho, Papi's gift of several new British novels, and a pack of cigarettes reluctantly procured by Bruno and hidden in her socks, Lacey and Papi waited for her train to the northern town where an emissary from the camp would come to fetch her. The station was crowded, but it felt like they were the only people there, two figures against a blurred backdrop. Lacey sensed the fragility of her limbs, the way her traveling dress flapped over her bony ribs. The thought of leaving Papi made her throat go dry.

It was already summer. The sun glared, and a hot wind washed across both of them. Papi sweated in a gray gabardine suit, the jacket slung over his arm, a dashing swoop to his hairline. He looked posed for a brave goodbye as she faced him. But then his eyes slid down her newly expanded figure and he glanced off into the wavering distance. "Your mother will be back this summer," he said in a strained voice. "When you come home, she'll be here to see you."

Lacey's stomach dropped. It had been two years since Mutti left. She was a photograph on the mantel, a petite woman in a white satin dress, her veil falling to her feet.

"Is she staying?" said Lacey.

Papi kept scanning the horizon. "She wants to take you back to Prague. To live with her," he said.

"No," Lacey countered immediately.

"A girl your age needs a mother."

"I don't even want to go to camp."

Papi shook out his handkerchief and wiped his shining brow. "You have to get well," he said. There was something wounded in his voice.

"I'll be out in some bug-infested swamp for months, away from you and everything I love," said Lacey, entering a familiar argument. "How am I supposed to be well?"

Papi tucked the handkerchief back, but he was still sweating. "It's better for you. The fresh air. The company of girls, instead of Bruno."

"And then you'll send me off with *her*?" Her voice rose. "Why are you telling me now?"

Her father bowed his head.

"You've never even seen a forest," he said to the train platform. "You've never climbed a tree."

"I don't want to climb trees."

"You're an American," he said. "American girls climb trees. You'll love it."

Papi sounded somber and dull when he said this, as if he were quoting someone he didn't believe. This train station had no large white clock, but Lacey felt the echo of another moment: the caramel walls, the arches and platforms. Papi in his furs and homburg hat, staring hopelessly into the crowds for her mother.

The camp must have been a bargain he'd struck with Mutti. Camp first, then the decision about their precious daughter. Mutti and Papi viewed the camp in different ways, however. It was the mystery element in two entirely different futures. If Lacey got well at camp, then surely she could make the journey back to Europe. But if Lacey became too American, Mutti would have to let Lacey go. Papi was banking on Lacey changing, becoming unrecognizable. Five weeks in a wilderness, with canoeing and tennis and campfires. Shorts and swimsuits. *American girls climb trees.* Mutti couldn't take a wild, outspoken American girl back to her tearooms and salons. She would agree that Lacey needed to stay.

"I'll try to love it, Papi," she promised, her voice breaking. He nodded and opened his arms, but when he hugged her, it was carefully, as if he didn't want to hurt her or touch her too close. And when she leaned out the departing train to shout her farewell, he raised only one cupped hand, as if catching her praise, her adoration, unable to return it.

For the first week at camp, Lacey dreamed of losing Papi. One night, she dreamed of him walking into a dilapidated, unlit house, a silent silhouette, ignoring her calls to him. Another night, she dreamed that he had fallen into the green harbor. Although she reached out to him, though she plunged her arm deep, he did not take her hand and sank alone beneath the murky surface. All week she woke weeping, staring at the reddish-blond head in the next bunk, a quiet, sturdy girl named Edith. One cool morning, Edith was turned her way when Lacey sobbed herself awake, and her green eyes widened with sympathy, and she asked what was wrong.

5.

SOMEONE HAD PUT A POTTED PLANT ON THE PEDES-
tal of the lobby fountain. An unkempt, cascading shrub. Edith
eyed it with surprise, wondering when Lacey had last descended to her hotel's first floor. The plant was lopsided and a little
dusty, a poor replacement for the slim dark vases that rotated through
their youth. Its shape broke the fountain's symmetry: two terra-cotta
angels, two garlands of fruit, two whales, and two sentinels, half-
dressed and Grecian, guarding the shallow pool. Yet despite the invad-
ing greenery, the wall fountain had survived the intervening decades
without the slightest marks of time passing. It rose, floor to ceiling, the
peach hue of sand at sunset, with its alcoves of stone drapery and posed
figures. The angels' potbellies had not sagged. The whales' teeth had
not rotted. The sentinels' eyes had not clouded, and the lion at their
center, singular and spilling water from his mouth, had the same wise,
amused look, as if he had seen it all, all the decades in their satins and
furs and uniforms, the soldiers, the actors, the lovers.

Edith wondered if someone still raked the fountain's pennies every
day. Lacey's father disliked the sight of copper and silver coins pock-
ing the marble bottom. He discouraged the practice of penny-wishing
with a small sign, but people wished anyway. Raking had been Bruno's

job. Knowing Bruno's painful loyalty, Edith supposed the young man
had taken it on himself and hurried to finish each morning before Papi
arrived, to make everything perfect. Bruno had fashioned his own in-
strument from a guest's forgotten cane and used it daily to skim the
pool. In his dark suit, his chin dropped and long arms reaching his
baton across the water, he had the air of a conductor concentrating on a
particularly hard stretch of music. And maybe it was a difficult compo-
sition, daily, being Bruno, the surrogate son who stayed a servant. He
dredged every single cent. Edith teased him about it once, implying
he was cashing in, and Bruno exploded on her, shaking the hotel till
where he deposited the fistfuls of change.

Bruno hadn't liked Edith much at first, being intolerant of anyone
who might take advantage of Lacey's trusting nature, or influence it
for the worse. They were living through the years when selfish women
dominated the movies—the belle who insisted on wearing her gar-
ish red dress to the debutante ball, the other belle who married three
times and survived a bloody civil war without truly loving anyone. No
matter how their plotlines eventually punished them, the ladies started
out as beautiful and rich as Lacey was. A darling. Her evening gowns,
nipped at the waist, cascading to her feet, were subdued updates of
theirs; her voice had the same almost galling sweetness. Lacey could
flirt without meaning to drive men mad and dance close without acting
the whore. She only had to stop wanting to please, and she, like greedy
Scarlett, like jezebel Julie, could be gaily destroying reputations and
the rest of her privileged life.

Things must be pretty bad with Lacey now, Edith thought, for
Bruno to sound so relieved and glad to hear her voice. He was posi-
tively chummy on the phone, sharing bits about his sons and his recent
stroke, but he refused to say much about their oldest friend. Maybe
Lacey couldn't walk anymore. Maybe she had grown enormously fat.
Maybe her memory was gone and she'd become a wrinkled shell of

her old buoyant self. What could Lacey be doing up there, delaying for another long hour while Edith fossilized in her overstuffed chair? Maybe Lacey was addicted to the soap operas. She was the type to secretly adore their shameless glitz. Or maybe she was as lovely as ever, and it still took her forever to get her lustrous black hair and moonlight skin just right.

Edith's tongue was so dry now, she couldn't imagine croaking out a single hello. She contemplated getting a drink at the bar, but all she wanted was water with no ice, and ordering water at a bar looked cheap. Besides, the lobby was too crowded. If she crossed it again, she would have to lose her chair, and then where would she be, forced to stand, a prisoner of Lacey's infernal pride? Could she flag a desk clerk and ask for a glass? They had already humored her phone call to Bruno, and now she was asking for another special service? And what about the inevitable need for a restroom five seconds after her first sip? That would mean hauling the suitcase and finding the right door. The first floor was a maze of ballrooms and gilded halls. What if she tripped? Her elderly friends at home were breaking bones left and right. Hips and wrists, snapped like peppermint sticks. But she could not sit here much longer, either. Her knees had locked, and her bum was going numb.

After counting the wooden octagons in the ceiling—still twenty-four, they had outlasted the Berlin Wall and Greta Garbo, both fallen months ago—Edith checked the front zipper of the valise again. The envelope was still inside. She shoved herself to standing. Pins and needles erupted in both feet, but she bent slowly, grabbed the suitcase handle, and carried it over to the fountain. She limped past the bouquets of calla lilies that had replaced the old jade ashtrays. Past the reception desk, the mural of a solarium behind it, dreamy with sunlight. In the old lobby, a wooden wall once hung with compartments for room keys. Bruno could grab the right one without even turning to look. He could make it seem like the key chose his hand. Like he didn't have anything to do with it. Like he was merely the conduit to your fate. Edith wondered what he'd said to Lacey on the phone. *Expected for dinner in one hour.* The message came not from Bruno, but through the prim manager. Another hour. The nerve of it. Edith took another step. Her toes stung and buzzed.

Yet the closer she got to the fountain, the more its coolness beckoned, its cascading music. It was as soothing as ever. Shimmering and tranquil. Tears rose and Edith blinked them back. She was not going to cry tonight, no matter what Lacey said, no matter if Lacey sent her away without a word between them. Edith had arrived. She had made it to this tiny oasis where hope always mingled with letting go. And there it was: the thread of water spilling from the lion's mouth, the knee-deep pool, heaped with coins. No Bruno to sweep them now. The wishes stayed where they fell. She bent and opened her suitcase's top pocket, pulled out her change purse. It took some rummaging— why was there a paper clip in there, and why two Canadian dimes?— but she found her three shiniest copper pennies. She gazed at them, freckling her open palm, then tossed them in. All at once. All three together. It might be. It might happen. The pennies dappled the surface and descended sideways to rest among the others. Edith knew that if she looked away, she could not find them again, so she stayed staring, holding their shapes with her gaze.

6.

BY THE END OF THEIR SECOND WEEK AT CAMP— the week Lacey confessed everything to Edith while they gagged over their soggy eggs in the mess hall, lost a three-legged race, and canoed to the pond's farthest island and inspected its pebbled beach—Lacey couldn't remember what friendship was like with any other person. She'd had Bruno, and her friends at school, and the quick, fun sisters from her mother's holiday parties, but they were pale pastels compared to the vibrant primaries of a day with Edith. Laughing until they snorted, running until they gasped, whispering late in the night. It consumed her, being friends with Edith, and she forgot how much she missed her father. For the first time, Papi became an abstraction, an image in her mind's eye, a sadness that she'd once had instead of a heartache all day.

The two girls marveled at their differences. Edith was shorter and more muscular than Lacey, a stronger swimmer, and miraculous at crafts but unfastidious about her bunk or clothes, and always getting in trouble with the counselors for her mess. She was rarely the first to speak, but she had a husky, infectious laugh and was liked by many. Lacey on the other hand—tall, prim, helpless, and pretty—found her-self strangely nonplussed by camp life, where her sophistication held no sway, and she was often at a loss for what to say. She had never slapped a mosquito; she could not identify poison ivy. Her swimming was slow and jerky because she did not love wetting her head. About steering a boat, she knew nothing. The lyrics she knew by heart were all in Czech or German, and she mouthed the camp's folk songs and joke songs while the others belted them. Many of the girls had been coming to the camp for years, and they owned an easy familiarity with the cabins, the moths and june bugs, the smelly latrines, and one another. Nicknames and traditions abounded: Nan and Muffy and Lou-Lou, and short-sheeting and ghost stories and candles on the pond.

Falling into friendship with Edith was also, for Lacey, inextricable with falling in love with the northern summer. Never had she woken to birdsong, or plunged headfirst into cool water on a blazing day, or listened to the whispers of the oaks as a thunderstorm swept in. Never had the sun felt so warm and golden, or rain soaked her so completely. The shrill of crickets, alarming at first, began to soothe her to sleep at night. A toad hunched by a log was so intensely ugly she cried out in shock, while a fox slipping through the pines looked like the tip of a paintbrush dipped in orange. Her hands and legs became tan and useful. She could tie three kinds of sailor knots, and she could kick her way up a river current. Her face in the spotty cabin mirror was freckled; it also looked rounder and fuller. She was gaining weight back, and when one night Edith observed, "You're not coughing anymore," Lacey realized it was true.

Lacey also realized by then that Edith was not like the other campers. One morning, at the beginning of their third week, a storm swept in, lashing the cabin and ripping a screen door from its hinges. The door wagged there as the rain passed and the girls emerged and ran toward the beach for their swim lesson, the lawn cold and slippery under the soles of their feet. Lacey had chosen her navy suit with the drawstring belt; the white one she saved for boating days. Edith followed more slowly, wearing her lone floppy black suit, glancing back at the broken door. "What?" said Lacey. "Won't someone come to fix it?"

Indeed, someone did. When the campers returned from their swim, drenched and shivering, a tall figure in greasy clothes was hammering out the pins in the door's hinge. His bare arms were corded with muscle, and his hair was a wavy brown, but his face, handsome, broad, and unshaven, looked prematurely old. It was a face that spent too much time outdoors. A face that did not wear hats and scarves, or take regular trips to the barber like the girls' fathers and uncles.

The campers fell into a hush as they filed past. The man did not acknowledge them, but his plummy odor reached Lacey's nose.

Inside, the oldest girls wrenched the cabin curtains shut and slammed the inner door.

"I'm not changing," said one. "Not till he's gone."

"He can't see," said another. "The curtains cover the windows."

"There's a crack."

There was an odd exhilaration in their voices. The man stirred something in them, with his size, his soured good looks.

Lacey looked to Edith for her opinion and was surprised to see that her friend was not beside her. She must have muttered Edith's name, because she felt a hand on her arm.

"You didn't know," said a girl named Vera. "That's her father."

Lacey stared blankly at her.

"Mr. Holle. She gets a free bunk at camp because he's the caretaker. He lives nearby and they send for him for repairs." Vera wore a stern, pitying look. "She's ever so embarrassed when he comes."

Just then, the hammering stopped, and voices murmured on the porch. There was a chinking sound, following by footsteps. The girl at the window peeked out. "He's gone."

"Good, because I'm dripping all over," said Vera, digging in her trunk.

Edith entered the cabin while everyone's backs were turned, changing into their dry clothes for mess hall, and began to strip her own suit. Under Lacey's scrutiny, she gave an odd little grin and muttered, "That was my pa."

Lacey nodded, unsure what to say. She pulled her shirt over her head. "I'd like to meet him sometime," she said finally.

Edith narrowed her eyes, but her gaze softened when she saw Lacey's sincerity. "You're too much, Lace," she added, shaking her head.

From then on, Lacey noticed how the other girls sidelined Edith. They liked Edith—it was impossible not to like her—but only just enough. They tempered their affection almost unconsciously, leaving Edith out of conversations about their winter ski trips and travels to Europe, and never sharing books or clothes or home-sent candies with her, though they spread things abundantly among themselves.

Bothered by their snobbery, Lacey loaned Edith a couple of her British novels, and when she saw Edith only pretending to read them, far too fast, she told Edith the plots on one of their group hikes. There wasn't enough time in the camp schedule to teach Edith to read better, not out of sight anyway, but Edith shouldn't feel lost in conversations about books. So Lacey related all the plots to all the novels she'd brought, and then the ones everyone loved, like *The Secret Garden* and *Little Women*. Edith was an insatiable listener and had a sharp memory. She hoarded the stories like the sugared jellies Lacey gave her, sent by Papi, and sometimes Edith talked about the characters as if she knew them personally. On rainy afternoons, Lacey fell deep into a trance, reading, and often looked up to find Edith, chin propped on her elbow over her own open book, watching Lacey, envious. She made a promise to herself to give Edith a few novels in August. Let her puzzle over them in winter; Edith would make progress.

Meanwhile, Lacey would have traded all her possessions for the summer to go on and on. She didn't want to face Mutti. She didn't want to leave America or Papi, to be stolen away to Prague.

"I could live here forever," Lacey breathed one day as they sprawled on a mossy rock, their suits damp with pond water.

"No, you couldn't," said Edith. "First week of September, there'll be ice on the pond."

"Do you come here in winter?"

"Of course."

"What's it like?" Lacey sat up on an elbow, tugging at the wet tangles in her long dark hair.

"Dead quiet," said Edith. "The windows frost up and the snow gets so high it covers the porches. You can walk out on the pond, and it feels like solid ground."

"Do you ever walk all the way to the island?" Lacey found the island unbearably romantic, with its little beach, its fragrant stunted pines. A continent in miniature.

"No," said Edith. "I'd like to."

"We should make a pact to come here one winter and walk to the island," said Lacey.

"Sure," said Edith. She didn't sound that enthused.

"There's really no one here, for all those months?" said Lacey. "I can't imagine it empty."

"Porcupines were living in cabin eight," said Edith. "Fitting, really."

Lacey giggled. The girls in cabin eight were the prickliest snobs in camp. "Do tell."

"Porcupines are smarter than you think," Edith said. "They don't stay where they're supposed to."

"Did you trap them?"

There was an uncomfortable pause. "I had to chase them out," Edith said finally.

"With what?"

"With a broom." Edith stood suddenly and peered down the shore to the boat launch, where several girls were pushing out a canoe. They were halfway through free time in the afternoon. "Hey, no fair. I didn't know we could take out the boats."

Lacey didn't like canoeing because she couldn't steer, so she shrugged. "Where do they go?"

"Who?"

"The porcupines. When you chase them out."

Edith hesitated again, and then said flatly, "Into the sights of my pa's gun. You can't just run the critters from the cabins. They go right back in, soon as you leave. You have to get rid of them."

Lacey knew about vermin from the hotel. "My father puts out rat traps all the time," she added, lying back on the stone. Though her eyes were closed, she felt the tension in Edith's body, still standing. "Poison, too."

Edith didn't answer.

"Does that shock you?" said Lacey. Sometimes she thought that Edith found her too naive.

"No." Her friend's voice was strained.

Lacey cracked one lid and saw Edith finger a tiny sickle scar at the back of her thigh and drop her hand.

"Anyways," said Edith.

A dark unease spread through Lacey, imagining what the scar meant, but when she tried to speak, her mouth could not form the words. And then Edith was shouting and waving to a rowboat skimming nearby. "Pick us up, too!"

* * *

Edith never talked about the porcupines again, but there were other moments when another girl flickered beneath her cheerful calm. Once,

Edith ripped her shirtsleeve on a briar and a filthy curse exploded from her mouth. When Lacey winced, Edith hissed, "What? Never heard anyone cuss?" and rolled her eyes. Another time, after eating an enormous stack of hotcakes at breakfast, Edith disappeared. Lacey found her an hour later, staggering back from the pine woods. Her breath smelled like vomit. "Are you sick?" Lacey said, but Edith shook her head. That night, Edith did not eat, just pushed her food around, staring at it, like the hash and corn hid something dangerous. Edith whimpered in her sleep sometimes, too. "Please, please," she mumbled, but she never shared her dreams when she woke. "I can't remember what I dream," she insisted.

*   *   *

At the end of the camp's third week, the counselors announced that the ten cabins would be competing in Vaudeville Night for parents and relatives to watch: singing, dancing, theatrical excerpts, recitations, or historical tableaux. The word *wholesome* was uttered seven times, by four different counselors, twice in specific relation to hemlines, and twice to dancing. Each cabin could nominate a single performer or a group act. At the end of Vaudeville Night, a set of secret judges would pick one winner. All the girls in the winning cabin received a coveted gold bandanna and, as the crowning prize, their photograph would be taken and framed for the camp's history wall in the mess hall. *Vaudeville Night winners, 1933.*

To Lacey this announcement was news, but to everyone else, including Edith, it was a long-awaited chapter of camp life. The last hurrah before they all disbanded and went home. She and Edith returned that evening to find their cabinmates sitting on their bunks, a lamp burning, their eyes on Edith as soon as she crossed the threshold.

"Lights off," she said, a new authority in her voice. "We can't let on that we're already planning."

"Everyone's planning," said Vera, the freckled girl whose father owned six paper mills. But she turned the knob of her kerosene lamp and plunged them into darkness.

"It's already stacked against us," said a voice. "Cabin eight's got Norma. She knows real ballet. And their mummies will pay for the most divine costumes to be brought in."

"Norma's been limping, though," said another. "She strained her knee at lessons last winter. Besides, her papa wants her to stop dancing. Says its unseemly now that she's getting womanly."

"Change of plans this year," Edith said abruptly. "Dance act. Jitterbug."

"But cabin six did that last year and lost. It's not wholesome. The old crony judges vote it down."

"I was in cabin six and we should have won," protested another voice. "We got a standing ovation."

"Please. Cabin five was the best. We had Edith."

Lacey didn't know who said this, but everyone in the room seemed to approve.

"C'mon, Edith, you have to sing," said Vera. "You always do."

"She doesn't have to sing if she doesn't want to," countered someone else.

Lacey felt Edith sit down on her bed, beside her. "I'll sing," Edith said after a pause. In the dark, her tone sounded different. As if the emotion inside it had not quite settled into shape. It could have been defiance. It could have been greed.

* * *

At breakfast the next morning, Lacey looked at the wall of photographs in the mess hall. Every year, in every snapshot of the winning cabins, twined arm in arm with a changing group of girls, stood Edith, the only one unsmiling. Lacey watched her friend grow younger, photo by photo, until she must have been ten, her hair long then, and worn in two braids that dangled down her flat, skinny chest. In the other faces shone hope and excitement, even brazenness and glee, but in Edith's, no emotion whatsoever. It was like her body was there, but her soul had flown.

"Do you want to sing?" Lacey asked her later, after they'd gone to the first-aid cabin for a cut on Lacey's knee. Bandages in hand, they took the narrow trail to the bathhouse to wash it clean. Tendrils of overgrown timothy and Queen Anne's lace brushed Lacey's bare shins, a sensation that used to bother her and now seemed like the caress of friends.

Edith shrugged. The day before, her father came by to fix a leaking roof and she had been quiet since.

"If you sing, we can win," Lacey said. She'd been told of Edith's performances, how soulfully she sang, how she always got a standing ovation.

"Of course we can." Edith's voice was caustic. "And won't they be delighted, your mutti and papi?" She mimicked the German sounds perfectly.

"Why are you talking to me like that?" Lacey's words trembled.

"You all win, but what do I win? Another gold bandanna?" Edith stopped walking. She scowled and licked her teeth. "This is my last summer here," she said to the sunny woods. "My sister's getting married, and I'll have to stay home to help with my brothers forever and ever."

There was horror in her gaze, and when Lacey touched her arm, Edith wrenched back, as if burned.

"I don't want to do anything, all right? Some days, I don't even want to be here at all." She wiped her sleeve across her eyes and spun away, stomping down a path. "Don't follow me," she shouted back.

Lacey started after her anyway.

"Don't," said Edith, fury in her voice.

She was almost to the woods, but Lacey could catch her.

"Don't," Edith warned. "Just leave me alone, goddamn it."

The words gouged Lacey. She froze. Edith wheeled and sprinted off, the green branches bobbing behind her.

In the bathhouse, the water ran slow and cold, pumped from a shallow well. Lacey trickled it over her cut, rubbing at the drying blood, her head buzzing, her eyes parched. Over the weeks, she had revealed everything to Edith: her parents' separation, the death of her infant brother, the hotel world, Bruno and the cigarettes. All, except her mother's faith. And Edith listened, absorbent and sage, sometimes taking her hand and holding it gently in her dry one.

About Edith's home life, however, Lacey knew little, only that Edith was the second of five children and that her father, Mr. Holle, worked as a handyman for several summer properties. Clearly, he didn't get paid enough. Edith's uniform was tight in the chest and slightly faded. She had one pair of cheap canvas shoes and went barefoot whenever possible. Sometimes, when they'd come in from a long adventure, she ate rapidly, shoveling it in, smacking her lips and making her chin glisten. And then there had been the day with the hotcakes, the vomiting afterward. It pained Lacey to guess that Edith's overeating was from chronic hunger. Whenever Lacey asked about Edith's family, Edith slithered out from the conversation, with comments that were cryptic but fond. "Oh, my brothers are a pack of trouble at school," or "My ma said that the best taste on earth is butterscotch candy."

The cut on Lacey's knee smarted from the cleaning, and she wrapped it too tight, the bandage straining against her skin. For the first time she could see the camp's end: the packing of trunks and the sweeping of cabins one last time. A valedictory feeling washed through her. All the songs and jokes and swims would be over. Gone the hush of the oaks, and the deeper silence of the pine ridge. Gone the tickle of an ant on her forearm, the bats wheeling in the dark. The landscapes would retreat behind her and become memory until next year. She had seen the cycle with the other girls, the way they talked about the place, and she could see herself living the same waiting months they did, grieving first, then forgetting, then anticipating again. And yet Edith, their friendship, into which Lacey had rooted and grown—she couldn't imagine leaving it behind. It would be like ripping out part of herself. Stricken by the thought, she hurried from the bathhouse and after her friend, but Edith wasn't at the cabin or by the shore, so Lacey wandered the trails in the woods, searching. They were supposed to report for lindy hop lessons at three o'clock, but Lacey kept looking long after the bell clanged and found herself alone in a little glade with a lichen-covered rock, surrounded by firs. A place she had never been before. A nest of sun. She pushed through the knee-high weeds and sat down on the warm, scratchy stone. She rubbed at her tear-streaked face, sore with missing Edith, wishing it didn't hurt.

In her reverie, Lacey didn't notice the fawn that drifted from the woods until its big twitching ears caught her eye. The fawn nipped a few leaves from a sapling, then chewed, its jaw working sideways. Its body was the color of browned butter, and it stood on absurdly dainty legs and hooves. Lacey's jerk upright made the creature stare and then bound off, white tail shining. In the moment, Lacey did not think of the fawn's beauty or silence, merely her astonishment at its presence, but after she endured the scolding of her counselor and finally found Edith, waiting on their cabin porch, the animal rose again in her mind. The fawn stared with its round liquid gaze as the girls fell into each other's arms, crying, and Lacey blurted out her plan. She would invite Edith to come live with her in the city. The apartment had a spare room. They could go to the same school and to Papi's hotel, and maybe Mutti would stay, but she couldn't take Lacey away. Not with Edith there, too, like the sister she never had. The next summer, they could come back to camp together. Papi would pay for it all. He had to.

"I'll ask him. He won't say no," Lacey insisted with Edith's soft cheek against her cheek and Edith's strong arms around her shoulders.

"He will," said Edith in a resigned whisper.

"He won't," insisted Lacey, and then she was weeping about Papi, too, because she would see him soon, and Mutti. She missed her parents, and how they were kind, and spoiled her, and wanted the best for her, while Edith's parents wouldn't, or couldn't, in their need.

"We must seal our sacred bond," Lacey whispered, pulling away, and ran inside to get her sewing needle. A few moments later, she was holding Edith's thumb, poking the silver tip into it. Edith flinched but did not cry out and when Lacey pricked hers, they pressed their thumbs solemnly together, smearing the red between them. "Friends forever," said Lacey. She breathed the dampness of Edith's breath.

"Friends forever," said Edith, and then she swayed a little, her eyelids fluttering. "Oh, kid. This shows how much I love you. I hate the sight of blood."

* * *

When Lacey woke the next morning with pink, itchy welts all over her legs, face, and arms, Edith had a few on her hands and inner arms, too, from the oil that had spread with their embrace, but it wasn't enough to let Edith remain in the cabin. The counselors relied on Edith for boating and crafts, because she was the best at both, and she could fix anything. And the Vaudeville Night practices had begun in earnest, with Edith starring again. The poison ivy swelled Lacey's face until her eyes half shut and she lay in the dim building alone, staring at the rows of empty bunks, trying not to scratch. The days reverberated with memories of her winter cough, when she'd waited, bedridden, for Papi to return, only here Lacey could hear the sounds of laughter and splashing, the camp thriving without her. She wept often, her tears seeping through a crust of itch and pain. Edith came often, too, always bearing something—a palmful of fresh blackberries or blue yarn for a cat's cradle—but soon she swept out again, summoned by the counselors. One afternoon, bored and self-pitying, Lacey fished her stale cigarettes from her trunk, lit one with the matches for the kerosene lamps, and smoked behind the cabin, her swollen face stinging. The taste made her yearn to go home, to be her old alert, butterfly self, but then twenty minutes later, Edith crashed in, out of breath, holding fistfuls of a leafy plant, dripping dirt from its roots. "This will help," she promised, squeezing juice from the floppy green stem and dabbing it on Lacey's welts. A blessed coolness spread. "Hold one of these leaves underwater, and it looks pure silver," Edith said. "Jewelweed. I finally found it by the creek. Been looking for days."

"What a heavenly gift," Lacey said, sighing. "Thank you." She took the other girl's hand and squeezed it. "I don't deserve a friend like you," she added.

Edith winced. "You're the only one—" She stopped. "The others—" Her voice grew thin, disbelieving. "I'm just the help, except for one night all summer."

Later, Lacey would not be able to recall what she'd said to comfort Edith, if she'd said the right thing or anything at all, but she remembered how it rained all night. In the morning, the ground was so wet that pools appeared, little silver pools on the lawns, and in the woods, dark, glimmering ones, drifted with old leaves. Some understandings could materialize like that and recede almost instantly, but you never forgot them.

7.

ALTHOUGH EVERYONE AT CAMP PREDICTED THAT Edith playing Oliver Twist would be her best performance yet, Lacey disliked the act. Sure, she admired her friend's soaring voice during their rehearsals, and the grace of her movements as she strolled past her seated campmates, their cupped hands. Edith had written the song herself, about the orphans' struggle to survive. *I ain't gonna make it, but I'm gonna make it miiiiine.* It made people laugh and cry. But it was also a lie. None of the girls sitting around Edith in their rag dresses, fashioned from old bedsheets, had gone hungry for a single day, and they overacted their distress, clutching their bellies, gaping their mouths, rolling their eyes. They pictured themselves as symbols of the sorrows of their country, the breadlines and the Hoovervilles. But their performance disgusted Lacey. How close it seemed to mockery.

Edith, to Lacey's amazement, didn't seem to notice them at all. When she sang she was inside the song, and when she finished she went blank and merely nodded, emotionless, to any conversation.

"Oh, they're just having fun," Edith had scoffed when Lacey expressed her irritation at the other girls. They were on kitchen cleanup duty together after breakfast, washing the gunky pots.

"You don't think they ham it up too much?"

"It's Vaudeville Night."

"But . . ." Lacey faltered. She didn't want to pry about Edith's family finances. How could they be good? Driving into the camp, Lacey had seen the slumped, peeling houses, the rusting plows and wagon wheels in the yards. "Are your parents coming?" she said finally.

"No," Edith said quickly. She shrugged. "Don't fit in." When she saw Lacey's frown, she added, "I don't care, all right?" As if to prove it, she plunged both arms into the soapy water and began to scrub. "My great-grandfather was rich," she muttered. "Lost it all in a mill fire. People don't know that about me."

"That's awful," said Lacey.

Edith turned the pot in the water. "Might have been his fault," she admitted. "But still, he lost everything." No one talked about it in her family, she added, but it was their hidden tragedy. They had been rich once and lost it all.

*　*　*

Camp tradition dictated that the girls' parents could not officially speak to their daughters until after the Vaudeville Night performance. The parents were to settle at a local inn, have dinner together, and then ride to the camp to take a brief tour and find their seats. They were to watch and clap. Afterward, the prize would be awarded to the winning cabin, and then the camp was semi-officially over. The next day, daughters were free to show their relatives around, or to leave the campus altogether, returning only to pick up their things and drive home. All week, Lacey found it hard to sleep, imagining the pleasure of introducing Mutti and Papi to the camp, but now that they'd arrived, she became nervous. How would she keep her promise to Edith to take her away; how would Edith slide into a slot they had not yet made for her?

"I can't wait for you to meet Papi," Lacey said. "And Mutti. I wish we could have a fancy dinner and do introductions properly."

Edith was staring out the cabin window.

"I'd order cream of asparagus soup, and veal cutlets with new potatoes, and black coffee," Lacey added dreamily. "And a bottle of Ayala champagne to toast our friendship. And Havana cigars." She mimed a great puff and giggled. "That's how it's done at Papi's hotel."

Outside the window, the maple limbs bobbed in the mounting wind.

"Edith?"

"I feel like I'll recognize your parents straightaway," Edith said with a worried smile. Then she grabbed Lacey's hand across the bunks and squeezed. "It's almost here," she said.

The rain held off on Vaudeville Night, but the wind was damp and gusty, whipping costumes and sending props spinning. The counselors had erected the stage outside the mess hall, with a courtyard of benches, surrounded by lanterns. The results were both magical and crude. A faerie court. The grown-ups in the audience wore gray overcoats and carried umbrellas, their faces expectant. And old. They looked so old. Lacey had forgotten how a face could sag into a perpetual grimace or a half smile, how hair could thin and dull, how eyebrows could arch too high, overplucked. All summer, she'd lived with the young; even the counselors were in their twenties, and only the proprietress and her husband had worn expressions like the ones that regarded her now, settled into immobility by time and wear.

Papi and Mutti looked old, too. They were both slightly fatter than she remembered, and Papi's forehead seemed broader, while Mutti's hair was short and curled too tight. Mutti. Her mother. It was a shock to see the real woman—no longer a flat image in a photograph, but a living body, sitting close to Papi, as if she'd never left. Her roundness and smallness made Papi look big and stoic. Her hand tucked in his hand still glittered with her wedding ring. Papi's wife. They settled in the middle of the grown-ups and whispered to each other but stared at Lacey, consuming her. Mutti's attention troubled Lacey, after such a long absence. Papi's attention chafed, after so many days of belonging and blending in. Her poison ivy welts had almost healed, but her skin was rough, as if she'd suffered a sunburn. She hated that they'd both see her so ugly. Instead, she hoped they'd focus on Edith, wandering among the other "orphans" as Oliver Twist, singing a song of their struggle to survive.

You'll meet my best friend Edith, Lacey had written to her parents. *Everyone says she sings like an angel, but she is clever, kind, and good, too. She took care of me when I had poison ivy. She brought me juice from a plant called jewelweed to soothe it. She knows everything about this place.* She did not write: *I want Edith to come live with us.* She did not write: *I think Edith would like the city.* She did not write: *I think Edith is afraid of her father and trapped by her mother. She needs to escape.* For all she knew, Mutti would want to correct Lacey's affection for someone lower class, and would use Edith as a reason to kidnap Lacey away to Europe. Edith would have to prove herself tonight, and now she was singing and she was funny and raunchy, the way she jiggled her shoulders and hips, and made everyone laugh through the first verse and the second verse. She did not sing like an angel at all.

But in the third verse, Edith got serious, as she always did, belting out the final chorus. Her turn could hook you, the grin still on your face, but tonight the tug was deeper. The "orphans" had heard Edith in practice. This was different. It was not a performance, not like before, but exactly who Edith was, how she saw the world, as a giant, exhausting, harrowing joke, and Lacey watched the other girls drop their heads and hands, uncertain. They could not moan and fake physical hunger when confronted with real hunger. In the face of real hunger, they sat still, and glanced from side to side, to see if others suffered the same concern. And Lacey, as Edith's best friend, felt suddenly so empty that she wanted to bolt from the stage and run to the beach and stare at the dark pond and breathe. She could not look at Mutti and Papi, could not bear for them to try to comprehend Edith, so she missed the visitor who joined the audience, standing at the back, until Edith's last note faded over the gathered parents, and they rose as one, clapping and cheering.

Lacey spotted him like a flash of light—the broad-shouldered, handsome man with the coarse skin and drooping clothes—and then he was gone, and Edith vanished, too, leaving the stage and her admirers and exiting into the night. Lacey scrambled after Edith but felt a clamp on her shoulder and smelled a familiar cigar smell and folded into her father's arms for a hug. Then Mutti squeezed her tight and long, and kept gripping, her eyes watering. "*Liebchen*," she said, her voice full of emotion. "You're so strong. And brown, *mein Gott*."

Mutti's familiarity came back in a rush: her smoky, floral scent, the comfort of her embrace. Mutti at bedtime, humming. Mutti ladling warm water on Lacey's back in the bath. Mutti at the stove, tending a pan of *Würstchen*. And yet the longer Lacey looked at her, the more this Mutti seemed like an impostor, her image and texture not quite right. As if parts of her real mother had been rubbed away with an eraser. She blurred.

Lacey took a breath. "The next act," she said. "You'll have to sit down."

"How can there be more after that?" Mutti said in an astonished voice, and Lacey remembered this about her: Mutti loved great singers.

"Sit with us," urged Papi. "We'll make room."

Lacey hesitated, regarding them: Mutti and Papi, back together, close again, eager to see her. In a few more minutes, Edith would be gone.

"We're not supposed to," Lacey said. "Campers need to stay with our cabins. I have to go." She twisted from Mutti's grip and ran into the dark, toward the lot where the cars were parked. Trees bent toward her, poking her with twigs. Leaves slashed her arms and cheeks. Her heart thumped, full of awe and fear for Edith, her friend but also the singer on the stage who'd touched them all. Edith's singing was *more*, it was—in Lacey's mind rose the image of the Prague cathedral, its mighty dome—*holy*, no, not holy, but *sublime*. Edith's final notes were sublime. The realization drove into Lacey. Her best friend was sublime.

The frogs sang in chirrups and croaks, and there was no glow except starlight. Lacey's footsteps thudded, then crackled loud on the pebbled, leaf-strewn drive. If the pair of figures hadn't been talking in low voices, she might have missed them altogether, but there was Edith's familiar shape and the large silhouette of the man. Lacey called her friend's name.

"I have to leave tonight," Edith said without looking at Lacey. "My brothers are sick."

"How sick?" said Lacey, crossing her arms.

Edith didn't answer. Between her and her father, an electricity coursed. It was hard to tell if Edith was afraid of him or fascinated by him.

"Edith," Lacey pleaded. "Talk to me."

Her friend stayed facing away from her. For the first time all summer, Lacey did not own Edith's steady gaze. It felt like a garment was being pulled off, forcefully, over her head. The man said something so quiet Lacey could not hear.

"You can't go yet," Lacey said. "You have to find out if you win."

"I don't care that much," Edith said. "You can write me how it goes."

"You have to meet Papi and Mutti," Lacey said.

Edith was silent, her eyes on her father. Mr. Holle didn't seem drunk this time. He wore a shirt with a collar. It didn't look starched, but it was clean. An effort had been made.

"She's my dearest friend in the world, and she has to meet them," Lacey said to him. "It would be rude to disappoint them now. They've been dying to make her acquaintance."

How ridiculous and spoiled the pronouncements sounded, when up until tonight they were all that mattered. To her surprise, the man shrugged. "Go on, then," he said, with a touch of impatience. His voice was more nasal than Lacey expected.

"We'll catch them between acts," she said, tugging her friend's sleeve. Edith staggered and turned.

Walking beside Lacey, back to the stage, Edith seemed like a different person in the same body. She looked sickly and unnerved, and not the brisk, laughing, capable girl of camp.

"What about your clothes and things? In the cabin?" Lacey asked.

"I'll get them later. We come back in a week and lock up everything."

"You can't go with him," said Lacey. "We can run away down the road. We can get to the inn and meet Papi and Mutti. I know where it is."

"I have to go," Edith said.

"Are they really sick?" said Lacey.

"Two of them. Scarlet fever. He waited as long as he could."

"But your mother will . . ." Lacey's voice trailed off. As she said it, an iciness spread through her gut. How had she ignored the obvious so long? The faded, too-tight uniform; Edith's pauses when she talked about home; the emptiness in Edith's face in the mess hall photographs. Edith had no mother to watch her win, again and again. "How long ago . . . ?" she managed to gasp out.

"When I was nine," said Edith.

"You never told me."

"You never asked," said Edith automatically, and then, "But you shouldn't have had to ask. I thought you knew, because everyone knows, and then I wasn't sure how to say it."

They'd both stopped on the path. In the dark, Lacey took her hand, and Edith gripped back. *No mother*, Lacey thought. A heartbeat of words. *No mother.*

"Just tell me not to cry," Edith said hoarsely. "I can't cry tonight."

"Don't cry."

"Harder," said Edith.

"Don't cry," Lacey ordered.

She returned the tight grip, and they walked, palms locked, fingers gripping painfully until they reached the edge of the clearing. Edith slumped through the singing quartet and did not clap when it ended. In the intermission, Lacey gestured to Papi and Mutti, and they rose and left their seats. In the dark at the rim of the circled benches, they shook hands with Edith, who held hers out formally and spoke of her admiration for Lacey. "She's everyone's darling. An utter favorite," said Edith, as if she were Lacey's counselor and not her friend.

"Hardly," said Lacey, and she laughed to hide her confusion and sorrow.

"And this is your dearest chum that you wrote about?" said Papi, eying Lacey intently.

"Yes," said Lacey, breathing in, ready for her next request.

"Then she's our friend, too," said Papi, looking back to the stage. "I think they're about to start again. You come visit us anytime, Edith."

Lacey opened her mouth, about to spring the question, but Mutti stepped forward, taking both girls by the elbows. "Best friends," she pronounced. "You will always have this summer." She looked them both up and down, still in their orphan rags. "You mustn't be upset now. You will go home tomorrow, but you will always have this summer," she repeated firmly. "No one can take that away from you."

After that, it was impossible for Lacey to ask. She squeezed Edith tight. "Come stay with us," she whispered.

"Sure, kid." Edith patted her back. "I'll drop in the next time I'm in the big city." She stepped back, giving a dry laugh, but her whole body was shaking.

8.

WITHIN THE SEVEN-HOUR CAR RIDE THE NEXT day, Lacey left behind Edith, their crowded cabin, her musty mattress, the pond, the green shade and the buzzing flies, and came to rest in a third-floor apartment with two parents, a clawfoot bathtub, and the honk of horns below. The contrast sickened Lacey; she couldn't remember how she had once lived in these rooms, familiar as they were. The windows were so heavy and thick. Her bathroom with its flush toilet so private. The eiderdown on her bed so fluffy and soft. And lonely. She knew she ought to be grateful, but when she collapsed across her bed, she stared into empty space instead of a neighboring bunk and a quiet, receptive face. Edith was gone, erased. Whenever Lacey tried to picture her, Edith was still at camp, not nursing two sick boys at her house. Lacey couldn't envision Edith anywhere but camp. She was a fixture there, in Lacey's mind, like the dock and the island. The girls had promised to write letters, and Lacey started her first one that evening. *I am ever so tired today, but I won't sleep for worrying about you,* she wrote. *I hope your brothers get well soon.* But that night Lacey drank a little glass of gentian with her parents to celebrate her return and fell into a dreamless sleep. Her mother woke her the next morning late, the sun streaming in. *My first dawn without hearing the bugle,* Lacey wrote Edith. *I have to admit, I miss it. But I am so glad to be skipping mess hall. My mutti makes a delicious breakfast.* She crossed the last sentence out. It was unfeeling to mention a mother. *No more rubbery eggs for a year.*

Mutti had returned for good, or so she promised. She was a different Mutti, less brittle, slower to speak, deliberately kind. Day by day, week by week, the new Mutti infiltrated Lacey's days, replacing Lacey's old home routines—quick morning coffee with Papi, the walk to school with Papi, afternoons and evenings at Papi's hotel—with a full breakfast, a drive to school steered by Mutti's gloved hands, afternoons shopping, nights at home listening to radio dramas. Where Mutti learned to drive Lacey did not know, and how Mutti had grown this new placid expression Lacey did not understand. The apartment filled with her purchases: an art deco radio, rose-point glassware, shimmering paneled curtains to replace the old brocade. For Lacey's fourteenth birthday, Mutti took her to the salon to get her hair marcelled, and had Lacey measured for her first evening gown, a diaphanous cream-colored garment strewn with embroidered pink blossoms. Meanwhile, the news from the Old World was worse than ever. Two weeks after they returned from camp (two letters from Edith already, and two back, from Lacey), the German president had died and all power had gone to his chancellor, Hitler, who had already imposed strict laws for Jews. The worse the news got, the more money Mutti spent.

Papi frowned at the bills, but the hotel had done so well, he was looking into buying a second property, and he commissioned Mutti to drive the three of them around the city to investigate lots. None seemed to satisfy, and with each corner Papi eyed, his plans became bigger. He wanted to make something grand and lasting, a destination for balls and big bands and weddings, not just a building full of rooms for the night.

I don't know why, but they both seem desperate, Lacey wrote Edith. *Like they're trying to be happy on a stage instead of inside.*

Maybe the performance is to protect you. They don't want you to see them fighting, Edith wrote back. Her brothers had recovered, but it was a daily battle to get them to school, and her father kept drinking up the family's grocery money. *Every day I think of running away.*

In their letters, the girls were closer and farther apart than ever, confessing their fears about lives so utterly different. Edith worried over getting enough firewood for winter, and Lacey over Mutti's constant criticism of her manners, her posture, her grades. Edith was scared she couldn't continue with school; she had been truant so often, scrapping together odd jobs to pay for food. Lacey was scared about Papi, who worked too hard and might have another one of his collapses. Sometimes, while writing, Lacey's pen paused as she wondered if her own small trials only magnified Edith's, but she felt Edith needed her to say more in return than *I'm sorry. That's dreadful.* Edith didn't want pity; she wanted friendship. And besides, Lacey needed the letters for her own private outpourings. She couldn't tell her school friends what she told Edith, because it would trickle through their parents back to Mutti and Papi as gossip. Papi wouldn't care what Lacey said about him, but he would say she was judging Mutti. And then Mutti would say, *See, she still doesn't want me to stay.* So onto thin blue paper Lacey's thoughts went, folded and stamped, to Edith, along with the hopes they would see each other the following summer. Winter came, and with it, the cough again, although Lacey rarely smoked now, trapped by her mother's vigilant eye. The infection set deep in her lungs, and she lay faint on her bed while Mutti tended her, endlessly patient.

Meanwhile, over the months since camp, Papi had become a mirage, someone Lacey once loved, who faded behind Mutti and Edith. Sometimes, over breakfast, Lacey felt him studying her with a perplexed and pained attention, but when she stared back, he always looked away or flashed a disarming grin. Though Lacey missed him, she didn't know how to cross the new gulf between them. Her illness drained her of the vivacious energy that Papi was so fond of. Mutti blocked their old intimacy with her busy management. Worst of all, Lacey was no longer Papi's little girl, his *Schnuckelchen*. She had a bosom now and was nearly as tall as he was.

One night, with Mutti glued to the radio in the living room, Papi sat down on Lacey's bed and patted the lump of her ankles under the blanket. "Miss you at the hotel," he said, his voice gravelly, as if from lack of use. "Bruno misses you. His father had a stroke last week and—" He paused, swallowed, and then the words tumbled fast. "I don't know if he's going to be able to walk again. Hold a job. I'll take care of them," he said with certainty. "But it's a hard time. A hard time replacing him."

"Oh, Papi." Lacey pushed herself up and flung her arms around his neck, the way she had as a child. He held her briefly. For the first time, she saw his graying temples, a new coarseness to the skin of his cheeks and nose.

"Get well, so you can come boss Bruno around, will you?" he said. "Mutti can let me have you once a week."

"I will," she promised.

"Fridays, then," he said, standing. "I've got a new piano player on Fridays."

* * *

When spring came and the cough was long gone, Lacey brought up camp as often she could. "I can't wait to find out what cabin I'm in," she'd say. Or, "I have some ideas for Vaudeville Night." Every time, she saw her parents' eyes meet and watched their mouths frame empty promises and excuses.

They knew Lacey pined to go. They knew about the letters from Edith. Lacey hid them deep in her room, with the letter pages arranged in the wrong order, so that if either parent tried to spy on her, she'd find out. Neither did. They asked rarely about her friend, and when they did the cordial inquiries implied their lack of interest. About camp, her parents were evasive. Finally, her mother said, "Why don't we just have Edith come visit us this fall instead? I have plans to take you to Prague. You're fourteen and you need to know the rest of your family." And Lacey realized, all along, *this* was the act, the desperate show: Her mother would pretend to love America and her father so that Lacey would trust her again and go home with her. Not forever, or maybe not. And Papi would pretend to agree to this bargain so that he could have Mutti back, for himself and for Lacey, even though he thought Europe was growing dangerous with Germany rearming, flouting the accords from the last war.

At night, Lacey heard them arguing.

"It isn't safe," Papi objected. "I won't let you take her away, unless you promise, on your life, you'll bring her home in August."

Mutti's reply was hard to hear, but Lacey caught the words *my life, my life*.

"Yes, your life," Papi said impatiently. "It's not what is given to you. It's what you make of it. That's a lesson you've never learned."

Lacey hoped her parents might compromise on allowing her to stay in the city. Much as she missed camp, she loved being back in Papi's world, with the new cold-drink machine and polished wooden phone booth near the reception. She felt useful doing the daily bookkeeping for her father and helping guests with local restaurant advice. Her old pals, the bellhops and floor concierges, grinned and popped their eyes at her curvy figure, but they treated her with their old, easy affection. And then there was Bruno, who worked full-time in his father's old job. Bruno, nineteen, was man-sized now, with stubble on his chin and a haggard sadness in his eyes. His father's stroke had unseated his self-interest. The old brooder and boaster about the merchant marines had been replaced by a somber doppelgänger. Bruno still wasn't fun to talk to, but he listened. And he didn't seem to mind Lacey anymore; he looked almost glad when she pestered him for cigarette breaks at their old spot in the alley.

"Mutti and Papi, they fight over me like I'm a prize pony," Lacey commented one day while they smoked. "Neither of them asks what I want."

"What do you want?" Bruno said.

"Do you remember anything about Prague?" she asked. Bruno had been twelve when their fathers first met.

"Some," he said. "I remember the ship better. Coming here and seeing Lady Liberty and the harbor."

"I don't remember Prague," said Lacey. "Is it really so beautiful?"

Bruno nodded, his eyes on her. He dropped his cigarette and stamped it out. "Most beautiful," he said.

"I want to go," she declared, though the thought had just occurred to her. "I want Mutti to see me seeing it, so the fantasy is over. Whatever she imagines. That I'll love it like her. Or that I'll understand her finally. I don't know." She felt tears spark and she puffed furiously. A bit of ash fell off the cigarette's tip and burned her hand. She cried out at the sting and shook it away.

Immediately Bruno held out a handkerchief, for the smudge of ash on her skin.

"It's all right," she said, touched. "I'm all right."

But suddenly the pair of them were standing close together, and without knowing why, Lacey lifted her face and kissed Bruno softly on his damp lips. It was the shortest of kisses, more an impulse than an act, but she had never felt the pressure of a man's mouth on hers, or the taste of his breath, the presence of his tongue. The combination of sensations made her head swim. She blushed. Bruno stared at her, cheeks flushed, and backed up a step.

"Bruno," she said, unsure what to say.

"I have to go inside," he said.

"I'm sorry," she said. "I didn't mean it."

"I know," he said as he walked away, his shoulders dipped, tucking his cigarettes back into his pocket.

* * *

For three days, Lacey mooned over Bruno. He loomed in her mind with his thick brows and severely combed blond hair, the prickle on his upper lip, which scratched when they kissed. She imagined their wedding one day, in a curiously blank setting, and their future lives, even blanker, in a set of nondescript rooms. Her daydream Bruno was gallant and ardent, but the living boy could not have been more opposite. He evaporated the moment she entered the hotel office, his stare fixed to the threshold. He left cigarettes in her purse so that she would not request them. He even rolled his eyes when he heard her laugh at a bellhop's joke. At first, Lacey was befuddled. Then hurt. Then outraged. And then, one afternoon at the hotel, when Bruno bolted, knocking over a chair, as soon as she arrived, she became strangely relieved. Bruno was too exasperating to love. That evening, she went with a spouted brass can to water the atrium's plants, and a handsome hotel guest flirted with her. By the time she returned to the little office, warmed by the man's bold compliments, Bruno had shrunk to his former size, an overgrown boy in her father's employ.

* * *

On the day Lacey and Mutti's ship departed, Bruno came with Papi to see them off, and stood in the stiff push of the ocean wind, his hands tucked in his suit pockets. He looked made of something harder and colder than flesh and belonging to no one but the earth. A statue. A titan. *I love him,* Lacey thought, reviewing the kiss again, testing her feelings, but she knew by then it wasn't true. The kiss had been an accident, a turn taken too early on the way to a destination. If it meant anything to Bruno, he refused to say. He was her father's surrogate son, not her beau. He would care for Papi while they were gone. That was what mattered. As Lacey gripped the rail with her mother and waved at the retreating figures of her father and friend, her eyes watered at the possibility of never seeing either again. *I thought "What if I never see either of them again?"* she wrote to Edith later. *It was just a thought, but what if thinking makes it true? I wish I was with you, at camp. I hate the sea already.*

But she didn't hate kissing. Not at all. The kiss with Bruno led to a kiss with Tomas to a kiss with Max to a kiss with Franz. All the boys blurred that summer of stuffy Prague sitting rooms and streets so close and old, you could smell the horse piss in the cobblestones and the mold grown for centuries behind the bakery, where they tossed the burned bread. Each of the streets led to a different old friend or cousin to judge and admire Lacey, including many she had never met before, who had tiny replicas of Torah scrolls nailed at their thresholds and gray aunts clutching Hebrew prayer books.

To her mother's pals and relatives (except for Mutti's parents, who still refused to see them), Lacey was Lucie again, a girl they'd known as a baby. Mutti's longed-for daughter, her only child. Her precious. Returned to the fold. Day after day, Lacey inhabited this role. Lucie Weber. It was like wearing an itchy dress with a tight collar, playing that obedient, German-speaking girl with her cultivated manners. A display of Mutti's fine parenting, as if Mutti had not deserted Lacey for years.

Lucie Weber. *Loo-tsee-yeh Vay-burr.* Lacey hated the confinement that descended with her birth name. It only lifted with kisses. At the brush of Franz or Tomas or Max's lips, Lacey became no one at all. She was a body aflame. She was loveliness itself. She could feel it in the tremble of the boys' mouths and the gentle pressure of their fingertips on her waist. Their longing buoyed her. Their gingerliness made her soar. People had always called Lacey pretty, had commented on her good looks with envy and admiration, but now she sensed her own radiance, felt it pulsing, from the inside out. Her mother was pretty; some of her cousins were pretty. Lacey was beautiful. Her black hair fell to her shoulders, and dark lashes fringed her violet-blue eyes. Her snowy skin glowed. Her frame had lengthened and thinned, curving at the hips and breasts. Her shadow darkened the wall, graceful, a nymph of old.

If some stranger had kissed Lacey first, stolen her first kiss instead of Lacey giving it freely, to a dear and trusted friend, she might have been more fearful. If she had known what sex was, she would have exercised more caution. But the kiss with Bruno had merely told Lacey that a new power was hers. She could wield it anytime, and never be bored or lonely again. So whenever her mother dimpled her way into a third glass of herby liqueur at another relative's house, and began to slur happily about her childhood days, Lacey found herself a new skinny, knee-bouncing, stuttering teenage victim, made an excuse for him to show her the balcony or the next room, and proceeded to interview him with shy looks and the right smiles until they got close enough to kiss. It was easy. Exhilarating, too. She got better at kissing, boy by boy, and marveled at how revealing kisses could be about personality—Max with his open, hungry mouth, Tomas with his tidy, pursing pecks. Franz was the best, a locksmith with his lips and tongue, but he kept his pale blue eyes open the whole time and they made her think of a fish globe.

Because Lacey and her prey had only small stretches of time unchaperoned, she parted from the boys before anyone's hands went where they shouldn't, and traipsed away, leading her boozy mother down the stone stairs, both of them humming with pleasure and appetite. The Prague summer hung lightly in the air, storks in the chimneys and church spires poking the sky. It was cooler and quieter than the New World because there were fewer people and automobiles, and at night you could see more stars. She could understand why her mother loved it here, why she found America too brash and exhausting, with its new skyscrapers always rising in the east, its hobos and tent cities in the west.

Lacey liked Prague, but she didn't love it. The Prague teenagers, boys and girls, hovered close to the radio in the afternoons. They could hum the famous songs in the operettas, and dance light-footed to the latest swing tunes. When they spoke of the coast, it was the Riviera and the Amalfi, and not Jersey and Far Rockaway. They, too, knew of fathers who'd survived the Great War, only to lose their fortunes in the crash. They, too, knew of grown-up desertions and suicides. The ethnic Germans among them—Tomas's family, Papi's relatives— suffered the taunts of Czech nationalists to get out of their country. The Jews among them—Franz's family, Max's family—endured a deeper, borderless hatred that branded them "degenerate," "dirty," and "Christ killers." The teenagers all talked of leaving Prague, though they could not agree on where to go, except into the past, into the peace of the old empire. A gallows humor marked everyone's banter, an amused dignity in the face of doom. The girls were glamorous, the boys refined. But none were capable like Edith. Lacey could not imagine one of them steering a canoe or lighting a campfire or sewing up a ripped sleeve, good as new. Max and Franz and Tomas had pale skin and soft palms. Lacey decided she wanted to marry an American man, bolder and stronger, a rider of stallions and striker of oil wells, a maker of factories and fortunes.

After three weeks of harmless seductions, Lacey grew so sure of herself and her magnetism that she sought out more challenging quarry. At a party at a country estate south of Prague, she let her eyes stray across the ballroom and land on a burly, handsome Czech army captain. The ballroom was enormous, with balconies and a frescoed ceiling, a blooming of space after the close quarters of the city. Lacey soaked in its grandeur, her spine vibrating with the strings of a full orchestra. She wanted something consequential to happen. She stared at the army captain until he looked back, and then she ran a slow finger down the neckline of her dress.

The captain had to be ten years older than her, the possessor of a luxuriant mustache and muscular shoulders. From across the room, he gave a nod, as if to say, *Yes, I am coming for you.* And he did, materializing at her side moments later, with a possessive air. Close up, his nose was rounder, and bristles of beard already shadowed his shaven chin, but his bulk surprised Lacey most. He was a man, not a boy, with a full-grown trunk instead of a sapling's slenderness. His German was thick and reluctant, launching a one-sided interrogation: who was she here with (Mutti), how did she like America (it was terribly backward), would she care to dance (yes). Their foxtrot was a whirl; he was as strong as Papi, as fast on his feet, but his breath in her ear was hot and almost angry. At one point, the captain's arms flexed, and he drew her closer, his thighs and groin against her thighs, and her breasts pressing his chest. Before Lacey could respond, he relaxed his grip, but his gaze flicked to hers, assessing. She closed her parted lips.

Lacey did not suggest a retreat to the balcony, but she followed when he towed her there. She looked back for her mother and could not see her. She knew no one else except poor Tomas, who sulked and wandered off when he saw her dancing with the captain. The balcony extended beyond the windows to an alcove of wall. The captain stopped them both in the curve of plaster, out of sight, his gaze heavy-lidded, not meeting her eyes. "So," he said. It was not a question. "So," Lacey said in a flirtatious tone.

The night air was cold and moonlit, the wall coarse against her bare arms. Lacey shivered, but the captain did not offer his jacket. Instead, without another word, he lifted her chin and kissed her, then pulled her tight to him and began, with massaging motions, to stroke her waist, her hips, to ride her skirt higher, to slip his hand beneath it. At first, she leaned into him, caught by the sensations, but then his hand reached her inner thigh, and his thumb gently rubbed between her legs. The touch was so intimate, she wrenched back, knocking her skull on the wall.

"No?" he said, something dark and mocking in his voice.

"No," gasped Lacey.

"Never?" he said, running a finger down the slope of her neck to her collarbone. He bent forward and kissed the crook of her throat, his lips probing, the mustache tickling.

"No," she repeated faintly, her knees weak. "No, please."

The kissing went on. One palm plunged and cupped her nipple. Another squeezed her bottom, kneading the flesh. Lacey's head hurt. Her arms hung at her sides. Finally, the captain lifted his head and regarded her.

"You are a child with a child's desire," he scolded. Then he took her by the elbow and marched her back inside, ditching her at the edge of the dance floor.

That night Lacey wept and wrote to Edith for the first time since arriving in Prague, declaring she had sworn off boys and men; they were all *incorrigible*. The word wasn't accurate, but she didn't say anything stronger for fear that it would intensify her revulsion at what had happened with the captain. She read the letter over in the morning, appreciating the sneering authority in her voice. When she closed her eyes, however, she remembered the kiss, and the warm, sick feeling that spread when the captain touched her beneath her clothes, and she wanted to cry again, not with humiliation, but with frustration and rage. Why was the kiss hers to give, but everything else his to take? It wasn't fair. It would never be fair.

Lacey kissed three other boys that summer, but she couldn't get her old confidence back. The boys didn't swoon over her and looked a little embarrassed when the wooden contact was over, as if it were practice for them, too, and not the real thing. In the mirror, she saw all the pieces of herself—her dark glossy hair, her arching brows, the milkiness of her skin and her blue eyes—but they no longer fit into a single picture. She began to scowl and bite her cuticles. She was through with being Lucie and wanted to go home.

One day, with a stern, instructive air, Mutti took Lacey on a walk to see where Mutti had gone to school, her neighborhood, her synagogue. In one winding alley by the river, Mutti pointed out a small window bordered with plum-colored panes, high on the third floor. "My old bedroom," she said. "They've never forgiven me for marrying a goy." Lacey watched the window, hoping to see movement. But the glass remained blank, and Mutti tugged her along. "Come on," she said gently, as if Lacey were the one injured by her grandparents' indifference. "That's all there is to see."

She bought Lacey a poppy seed pastry and led her to a walled garden park by the river to eat it. But Lacey wasn't hungry, thinking of the plum-colored panes and Mutti's sadness, and her own disappointing lessons about love. She took a couple of buttery bites and slid the pastry back in its paper wrapper.

"Don't you like it here?" her mother said. "Or would you rather be sleeping in a buggy cabin?"

"I like it," Lacey said, bright and blank, eager to avoid conflict. "Everyone is so nice."

"I promised Papi that you would choose your own life, as I chose mine," Mutti said, raising her eyes to the leafy trees. "But when I day-dream for you, I see you far away from all of this, in some sunny place by the sea. No more cold, damp winters," her mother went on. "You know, Papi has gone to California to look at a property. It's a grand hotel, he says, one of the finest on the West Coast, and he knows that the owner is in financial trouble and looking for a partner. If they strike a deal, we may move there, and I won't be able to make the long journey back here." Her mother sounded suddenly girlish, though her crow's-feet were thickening and her thin lips had cracks where the lip-stick stained. "Or, if I did, I might not be able to return."

Lacey leaned close, smelling her mother's jasmine perfume. "Don't go," she said, suddenly missing Papi, missing the three of them to-gether, and being small and loved, ensconced between her parents in their great fur coats. After a whole summer with Mutti, this was what she missed, not Mutti herself, who remained inscrutable and self-absorbed, a woman who never finished her meals but left the dregs of them in front of her: the *rohlíky* with one bite out of them, the steak in parsley sauce barely sliced. At every gathering, Mutti chatted and laughed, but sometimes her hand reached out, palm open, as if of its own will, and closed on air and fell back to her lap. Mutti with her blond ringlets and small chin. Mutti who had squinted when Lacey stood in the tailor's shop, noting that Lacey's measurements had changed again. "I was never that big at her age," she commented. "In America, they grow to fit their country." Mutti had bragged constantly about the hotel and invited everyone to visit, to see its glamour for themselves. But she never talked about Papi, not as a man, not as a husband who loved her, who kept letting her abandon her child to wallow in the past. Papi was a majestic building of red stone on a corner where the trolley clanged. He was an atrium with the most marvelous fresco of Roman gods.

"Well, you couldn't go to that camp again," her mother added. "Or see Edith."

"She isn't there this summer anyway," said Lacey. "She isn't going back."

"Isn't she," said her mother, keen. "Have you heard from her?"

The walls of the garden were so deep in ivy, it was hard to see the stone beneath them.

"How would I?" said Lacey. "I've been here."

Had her mother read her letters? Had she read the one about the night at the country estate? Did she know about the kisses, the captain escorting her out and back in again? She must have known. She should have known. How could she have taught her daughter so little about boys and men?

"Mutti," Lacey began, wanting to ask. To find out about wedding nights, and how babies were made.

"There's something about that Edith," said her mother, standing up, brushing her skirt. "She's not an open book."

The questions died on Lacey's lips.

"We should go," said Mutti. "I don't like the look of those thunderclouds."

How funny, so many years later, to remember that California was first a dream of Mutti's, uttered inside a hidden garden by an ancient river, and that Mutti had warned Lacey then about Edith, though she never said why or what she knew. As they left the park, the ducks flew onto the riverbank, their wings still wet from the Moldau, and set to pecking the crumbs and nuts people tossed beside it. Heavy white swans arrived behind, scattering the smaller birds. Out of water, the swans stood waist-high and sharp beaked, and Lacey and her mother crossed the street to avoid meeting their small, greedy, shining eyes.

* * *

When Lacey and Mutti got home to America, a parcel was waiting for Lacey. She had held on to her two letters to Edith. She'd been unsure

how to mail them from Europe, and worried about her debt in corre-
spondence. How many missives would be waiting for her back in New
York? But Edith hadn't written Lacey any letters, either. Instead, she'd
sent the single parcel, carefully wrapped in brown paper. Inside its layers nested a wooden box, and inside that box, a slim blue bottle with a
cork stopper, stuck with wax. A note read: *This is goldenseal elixir, for
your winter cough. I made it myself from the roots and flowers around camp.
It's strong. When you get the cough, take a few drops in your tea every day.
It ought to cure you. We missed you this summer. Our cabin won again,
though! Edith.*

"What is it?" said her mother, circling. Lacey showed her the bottle and the note.

"I wouldn't drink that. She's not a physician," said her mother,
reaching.

Lacey clutched the bottle and told Mutti about the jewelweed, a
story she had recounted before, but now she made it sound braver and
cleverer, what Edith did. The camp days were hotter, Lacey's welts
larger, the miles farther to the creek where the plant grew. In talking
about Edith, Lacey suddenly pictured her: Edith's chuckle and her devoted affection. Edith's strong grip on the oars, Edith's voice soaring at Vaudeville Night. The memories hurt. The bottle felt warm in
her hand. Mutti was right. Edith had returned to camp again, without
Lacey, made new friends. *We missed you . . . We won.* Well, that was
fine. Lacey had kissed six boys and one man, climbed medieval towers, and tasted chimney cake with cream. She lived the summer her
mother wanted, became the girl who could dance and make light conversation and sip and dab, instead of the girl who could beat the others
in tag or carve an arrow's tip with a pocketknife. She had left behind
that wild, free Lacey, and Edith, too, and here was her final souvenir.

"It's mine," she told Mutti, anger rising in her voice. She set it back
in the box, rewrapped the paper layers around it, and carried it all to

her room, leaving the box in plain sight but tucking the blue bottle deep in her winter boots in the back of her closet. No one would find it there. No one would take it from her. Winter was far away, but winter would come. Mutti had already hinted that Lacey might be old enough to attend some debutante balls next spring, if she passed further training in dance and etiquette. "You need more practice with your manners," Mutti had said, "and less necking with the nearest boy." At Lacey's startled glare, Mutti pressed her lips together to hide a small smile. "Oh yes, I see what I see. And I know what's best for you."

9.

THE HOTEL WINDOWS WERE BLACK WITH NIGHT now, the lights dim in the skyscrapers, revealing their tiny tableaux of office furniture, an occasional lawyer still slouching over his desk, or a cleaning woman flicking a feather duster across the shelves. There was rarely anything to watch out there, except the occasional sex affair, so high in the air that the lusty pair forgot anyone could see them. Unlike in the movies, sex between two unwitnessed, ordinary people looked clumsy and ridiculous, their hips bopping madly, their fat rolls showing. Lacey pulled the curtains closed. They were heavy maroon drapes, an echo of Mutti's, but with a stiff, shiny texture instead of the mildewed velvet. You didn't have to launder drapes like this anymore, or rotate them in the sun. They were made of something impermeable that never aged. Just a little shake for dust now and then, and good as new.

She straightened a book and pulled the doors to the bedroom closed, too, leaving only the outer chamber with the couch and the desk, which would soon be covered and set for dinner. Her suite was large for a hotel, high-ceilinged, with crown molding and paned windows, but it was not a royal receiving chamber. Not an entrance hall. She opened the bedroom door again. The king bed's emptiness yawned below its arch of gold-and-maroon drapes. The valance with the double-tassel fringe suddenly looked boudoir. She shut the door.

At the latch's click, a fear flickered in Lacey. What if the whole visit was a ruse? What if Edith had not come to the city? What if she and Bruno were snickering right now about how they'd duped Lacey, once again? *She's probably all dolled up,* Edith would say. *Trying to act the queen.* Cruel images floated in Lacey's mind: Edith in her plain gray suit, smirking, her young face warped with malice. Bruno in his old hotel uniform, arms folded, shaking his head. They hated her. They both hated her. The walls of the room throbbed.

Lacey staggered to the desk. Inside an otherwise empty drawer, she found a faded envelope, the address crossed out, *RETURN TO SENDER* written across the paper. She lifted it to the light, scrutinizing it. The envelope was thin, but it held two slips of paper. One was a letter, and one a check for a sizable amount. The envelope had never been unsealed. Lacey tucked it in the novel she'd been pretending to read and sat down so hard her spine jolted. She forced her pulse to quiet, remembering Bruno's warm affection on the phone, and the simple plea in Edith's message. *I'd like to see you.* They didn't loathe her. Her fear was a failure of nerve. She would not allow it to defeat her before the night even began.

The deliveries she phoned for came first, and the young man stared at her midnight-blue gown and coiffed hair, the sapphire pendants dangling from her ears. She teetered on her heels, walking to her purse for the tip, but kept her head high, her voice chilly, and he actually backed out of the room, still gaping, and let her shut the door in his face.

When the kitchen staff arrived to robe the desk with a white tablecloth and set out the wine, she went to the bedroom and closed herself in. She picked up her phone and dialed.

"What was she wearing?" she asked without preamble. "You didn't say."

"How could I know?" said Bruno. "I'm not there."

"They didn't say a lady in a tweed suit, or a lady in a baggy dress? They didn't describe her at all?"

"They said 'old friend.' An old friend asked for you. That was it."

"So she looks old."

"Probably she looks old enough," said Bruno. "She's seventy, like you."

"Seventy-one," corrected Lacey. "She's a year older."

"Not that you're counting," said Bruno.

"And she didn't ask how I was? What did you tell her?"

"She asked if you still lived in the hotel, and I said yes."

"That's it?"

"Maybe she also asked if you ever left, and I said not lately, but I am retired and no longer on duty, so I could not be sure of this."

"You know I don't go out. Why would you give her the idea that I did?"

Bruno didn't answer with words. He made that noise in his throat, like a creaking door, when he thought you should know the answer to your own question.

"You don't want her to pity me," said Lacey. "You should know after all these years that I pity her. I always have."

She felt Bruno wince at the spite in her voice.

"All right," he said.

"And not because of where she came from," added Lacey. "Because of who she is."

"Okay," he said. "I have my dinner out now."

"Out where?"

"Out of the microwave."

"What are you eating?"

"Hungry Man something," he said with a sigh. "You tell me yours so I can pretend."

"I have ordered the salade niçoise for two, followed by the lobster bisque, the osso buco with a saffron risotto for a main course, followed by wines and cheeses and fruits, and because Edith probably still has that horrid sweet tooth, there's a dessert platter, too. Cappuccinos. Three kinds of liqueur, if we get there. And a surprise."

"Oh no, Miss Lacey," he groaned.

"It's perfectly all right. I disabled the detector," she said triumphantly. "I had a boy find the battery and take it out. Do you like my menu?"

"It sounds very fine," he said, suddenly sincere. "A fine welcome."

"It is not a welcome," Lacey retorted.

"A fine feast," he said, his voice retreating again. He was going to make an excuse and hang up now. But he must also know how her heart was hammering in her chest, and how tightly she gripped the receiver, needing him. Five minutes to the appointed time.

"Do you remember your first impressions of me, Bruno?" she asked.

"Hm," he said. "How soon this potato turns to rubber and the gravy to glue."

"Do you?"

"Bossy. And the apple of your papi's eye," he said.

"What about Edith, your first impression of her?"

Lacey couldn't remember exactly when Bruno met Edith. But she did remember Bruno at the train station for their move to Los Angeles, sporting a new mustache, and a solemn promise to follow them west at the end of summer. "You can count on me, sir," he'd said to Papi in German.

Edith was with them that day. Her bruises could not have fully faded by then. They would have been purple and yellow, her eye a blackened slit. You couldn't hide that mutilation with a hat, though maybe Mutti had bought Edith sunglasses, expensive as they were.

It was something Mutti would have done. You couldn't hide Edith's hitching walk, either, the way she favored her right foot for weeks.

"I don't know," Bruno said slowly. "To me, it was like Miss Edith was always here. By your side, while your mother drove you around to auditions."

"I need to go now," Lacey said, her bowels suddenly constricting with last-minute dread, and she said goodbye and hung up. She made a mental note to get one of the receptionists to order Bruno some restaurant meals, at least a couple of times a week. He didn't need to be eating frozen junk. He ought to watch his salt. She went to the bathroom, her midsection aching, and turned on the fan. The loud blasting sound shocked her ears, and she focused on hating it, the blare-blast of modern life that her parents would not allow in their apartments, though decades had passed, half a century; their eras were over and done, and now Lacey and Edith, too, were seeing their own closing lives. She steadied herself and let the fan's abrasive noise enter her. It didn't matter what she and Edith said to each other today. They had said it with the years already, the long wait and the not knowing. After a few minutes, the cramping eased and she straightened, flicking off the fan. It was then she heard the knock on the door.

10.

L ACEY DID NOT ANTICIPATE HOW DIFFICULT IT would be to small-talk and stare at Edith at the same time, evaluating the effect of years, so after her regal "Come in," and their brief, clumsy embrace, some silent minutes might have passed, during which trickles of water ran down the outside of the silver ice bucket and dripped on the creamy tablecloth. And then, when the ice settled softly as it melted, Edith might have laughed to herself. It was hard to say. No noise came out, but she blinked and cocked her head back, as if something in Lacey's appearance took her by surprise.

"You must be thirsty," Lacey said, chin raised. Lacey had thought a chilled white wine rather wrong for the osso buco, which would partner better with a hearty red, but cold wine had been Edith's standby, so she offered both, and cocktails from the bar, too.

"I'm dying of thirst," said Edith. Her voice possessed a certain asperity now, as if she were used to giving orders. Edith had turned into an oblong, her waist gone and shoulders thicker, and she wore her skirt high, over the bulge of a menopausal belly, but her face, oh her face, it was scarcely lined and just as vital as ever, capped by a froth of white-gray hair. She had donned an outfit that looked vaguely nautical, a striped shirt, a blue skirt and blazer, and shoes that could not properly be described as boots or sneakers, but some puffy mongrel in between. Her breath on Lacey's cheek smelled rancid, and though she hadn't smiled once yet, it was clear that her front teeth were caps.

"Any requests?" Lacey said. "Would you care to see a menu?"

"I could have a look," said Edith. She glanced around the outer room, taking in the heavy curtains, the ice bucket, the bottles of red and white. "Or I can have wine. You've got vats of wine. But I'm thirsty."

Thirsty meant plain water, Lacey guessed. She had not envisioned them sitting there, after forty-plus years, sipping plain water from tumblers.

"I'll get the menu," said Lacey, realizing too late that the menu was in the other room. She would have to open the bedroom door. "Or, if you know what you'd prefer, I can just order it." The phone was also in the other room.

"Is my suitcase in the way?" said Edith, pointing at her little valise on the floor. "I should move it if we're getting room service."

"Naturally, we'll dine here," Lacey said with as much dignity as she could muster. "One moment, please."

Lacey poked across the plush carpet in her heels and entered the other room, letting the door fall halfway shut behind her. But that was opening enough for Edith, who followed her, nosing over to the bookshelves, perusing every title while Lacey held out the cocktail menu.

"You've read all these," said Edith in a neutral voice.

"Most of them," said Lacey. She wondered if Edith still recognized which ones had belonged to Cal. Lacey knew which. Reading Cal's books, even the ones he had obviously never cracked, had filled her with a vengeful satisfaction. Almost gone was the idle, pretty princess who loved him with abandon. One thousand pages, then ten thousand, then twenty thousand pages she traveled, and still each new inked landscape altered her a little more.

"Is that what you were doing all day?" said Edith. "Reading? You don't seem to have a TV."

"Yes. I read."

"All day? Every day?"

It wasn't the right moment for Lacey to admit that she rarely fell asleep before dawn. Most of her mornings were lost, and many afternoons.

"I have my thoughts, too," said Lacey, fetching and holding out the drinks menu. In profile, Edith's face did look seventy-one: her chin sloped to her neck and her age spots showed. But it was remarkable how the years also prettied her, made her flat cheeks taut and defined.

"Your thoughts," repeated Edith, still scanning the shelf, ignoring the proffered menu. Lacey's arm was starting to ache. As were her feet.

"What do you do?" Lacey countered. "With your days?" She hobbled back to the nightstand and slapped the menu down. This was how it would be, the bedroom wide open, and Edith scouring Lacey's private life for whatever she wanted to find, then apologizing or explaining and waiting to be forgiven. In a moment or two, she would notice the paintings and ask about Cal, or expect to be told. That was not Lacey's plan, and not what she'd waited four decades to watch unfold.

"Unusual," said Edith, touching a book.

"What's unusual?" snapped Lacey.

No answer. Lacey snatched up the phone and ordered two gin martinis, dirty, neat, one with two olives, and one with three.

"Never mind," she said afterward to Edith, as if her friend had actually bothered to reply. "You can tell me everything about your life once we get our drinks. You must be tired," she added, one arm pointing the way, the other one shooing. "There's a couch in the other room where we can sit."

"I really don't drink anymore," said Edith, padding out in her big white booties.

"I don't either," declared Lacey, though it wasn't exactly true.

"Except on warm summer nights." Edith gave one of her old chuckles. "They must remind me of the West." The West. The way she said it, it sounded like a mirage. "We put away a few sidecars in our time, didn't we?"

Lacey had the distinct memory of Edith disparaging the sidecar in favor of the martini, because she didn't like her drinks sweet. "I did," she said.

As they sat on the couch, Edith didn't seem nervous at all, or apologetic, or even dramatic, but she wouldn't meet Lacey's eyes for longer than an instant, and though her spine was straight, she seemed to be carrying herself with a deliberate stiffness. Maybe she had back trouble. Or she leaked. They were both at that age. But when the martinis came, Edith downed hers. Lacey ordered two more, yet only sipped. This was her night, her room, her castle, and her three olives, meaty and salty.

She asked Edith about her summers, if they were beautiful like the ones at the camp, and Edith said absolutely, but now she lived farther from the ocean, so she never got the great big rainstorms and snowstorms of the coast. The woods didn't grow as dense, and the people, too, were different, even more closed in, both protective and wary of their neighbors. "Old Harold down the road," Edith said, "he never says a word to me, but one time my car got stuck in a snowbank up the hill from his house, and, wouldn't you know, within ten minutes he was out there with his pickup and chains, pulling me out."

Edith hadn't lost her clear, proper way of speaking, but the faint northeastern burr was back, leveling her vowels, squeezing the ends of words. She hadn't mentioned a "we." Old Harold didn't sound like husband material.

"Is that where you've been all this time?" said Lacey. "Living alone up the road from old Harold?"

"Alone," said Edith. "I haven't been *alone*." She looked around as she stressed the last word, as if the hotel suite said *alone* more than anywhere she'd ever lived. Well, maybe it did, if you were blind. If you didn't know one iota about Lacey and her life. "And certainly not 'all that time.' Did you think the years were so hard for me?"

Lacey wasn't going to answer that. She merely watched her old friend, taking long blinks, sphinxlike. Edith seemed to sink deeper into the couch, her knees jutting up. She hadn't worn hose, and her blue veins bulged in her pale skin, but her calves still had their old sturdiness and definition. Edith was still a walker, Lacey guessed. Strong and capable. Yet how many miles had Edith walked in four decades? And all of them in circles.

11.

"ALL THAT TIME, AND NO TIME AT ALL. A SCHOOL
never changes," Edith said into the silence. "New students,
new teachers come and go, but as long as a certain spirit
abides, the academy is a timeless place. I didn't realize that at first, that
I had signed up for timelessness. And power. All I expected at twenty-six was a life with Stan, as Stan's wife, helping him with his scholarship, doing the occasional entertaining, waking to a house where he'd
already stoked the furnace, and climbing into a bed at night with him,
cozy and warm. In the end, that's why we lasted, though marriages
were collapsing all around us. Everyone was sleeping with everyone
else, even tucked away in our little corner of New England. But Stan
and I had an agreement about what fidelity was. It wasn't romance. We
guarded each other's solitudes, so we each could flourish."

"Sounds dreadful," said Lacey. "Who was Stan?"

"Stan Morgan. You met him," said Edith, examining her martini
glass. "Tall, skinny guy. Big ears. He came to one of your parties. You
wouldn't remember him because he didn't notice you. But we hit it off,
and we saw each other a few times here, just as friends. We liked the
same neglected poet, and Stan wanted to write his biography. Then
Stan went back east because he had a sick father and got a job at the

academy. The Little Academy in the Big Woods, he liked to call it. Stan's humor was corny, which made him seem old-fashioned by the time he was thirty, but the students liked him because he was kind. When I left here"—a small pause, a sip—"I asked him if I could come there. If a secretarial job might be available. He offered something else, and after some deliberating, I took it. He was a good listener, Stan was," said Edith, her voice going scratchy. "He had an ear for hearing what people really wanted."

"Or he was in love with you," said Lacey. "And he wanted to snap you up while he had the chance."

"He loved me," Edith said, and was silent for a moment.

"So this school, it became . . . your family?" Lacey took a gulp of her martini. The gin burned in her throat. She fought back a cough, but it came out anyway. A choke-gasp.

"Two hundred students a year," Edith said. "Boys only, at first. In the sixties, it became co-ed, and we had to reconfigure the dormitories. Then we built a new one. Two hundred fifty students after that. That made things more profitable. I helped out in the admissions office at first, and then I began to work for the headmaster. He was a warm and gallant man, and a wonderful speaker, but his little secret was that he couldn't write. He struggled with reading, too. These days, they'd diagnose him as dyslexic, but back then, he was simply a rich kid who paid other schoolboys to write his compositions, and later paid his secretaries, less than his old friends probably, to write his letters and speeches. He could dictate fairly well, but ask him to sit at a typewriter and he'd stare at it all day, crumpled papers beside him." She shook her head, a superior look on her face. "Like most men who have secrets, the headmaster was exceptionally kind to the people who kept his, but also deeply suspicious of them. Stan got every promotion possible. I stayed the headmaster's secretary for ages. He didn't want anyone to know." Edith tilted her glass and finished the last swallows. "These days, no woman would endure what I did to get where I got," she said. "I didn't even know I wanted to be the school's first headmistress until I became it. And then I served the longest term in history. Fifteen years." She darted a glance at Lacey. "We girls were so conditioned, weren't we?"

"I suppose," said Lacey. "Though I also suppose not knowing what you wanted has always been a problem for you."

Lacey had contemplated meeting in the restaurant instead of this room, so that when awkward pauses came, they would both have somewhere to look: at the attractive servers hurrying by, at the wood-beamed ceiling or the Corinthian columns with their leafy tops. This room was too dull to distract from the hurt that was sure to come. And yet it was quiet enough to hear everything they said. No clatter and fuss to cover up the truth. Lacey needed to hear the truth.

Edith shrugged off the comment, a little shoulder twitch that lacked conviction. But her voice was confident. "I wanted to come *here*," she said. "I flew across the country and sat for God knows how many hours in that lobby, waiting for you to receive me."

"I had to prepare all this," said Lacey, gesturing around. "It wasn't just a trip to the dime store to fetch a bag of cookies."

"You could have sent word down that you'd see me."

"Of course I'd see you," Lacey said. She smoothed the couch pillows. "You knew that. Anyway, you always liked that room."

"You did. It was the Music Room. Your father booked afternoon dances there, to please you," said Edith.

"You remember," said Lacey. Dear Papi. Years after his death, Lacey still could not think of him without a surge of tenderness. The way long white hairs pronged from his eyebrows in old age. His spindly legs. His broad, liver-spotted hands. His mouth that no longer smiled. His eyes that never stopped their shine and twinkle, not when he looked at her, his precious daughter.

"How long did he live?" Edith said.

"Into his eighties. He outlasted Mutti by almost a decade. I cared for them both to the end, and then I moved in here."

"But that's—"

"Over a decade ago," said Lacey. "And no, I don't leave this suite often. I'm a recluse. But you didn't lose what I lost, so you don't get to judge me. You didn't see how it was after you left. America had won the war. We were supposed to bask in our victory, raise our families, build the future. But instead my marriage crumbled and I moved into my parents' house and the horror of their grief. Mutti's parents, her aunts and cousins, all dead, murdered. Franz, one of my first kisses, gassed. Papi's uncles, beaten and crippled in the Czech expulsion; Papi's father, blind in one eye. You were gone by then. You didn't see my living mother tear out every hair on her head. No, I mean it. She had to wear wigs. The top and sides of her skull went completely bald. But she and Papi loved each other. They were so close; you couldn't have wedged a toothpick between them. Mutti knew that Papi had saved all three of us, and given us a grand life, that he was a good man in a world of terrible men. She clung to him, and Papi was . . . What was the word you used? He was gallant. He was kind and gentle to his angry, bald wife. Eventually, she emerged—not healed, but able to live. They start going to those moody Italian movies at the art-house on Western. They campaigned for Kennedy. Papi took Bruno to Vegas to see Sinatra. Mutti had her temple; she became their top fundraiser because most people were either enthralled or terrified by her. Those were better times." Lacey paused, wanting to linger on the time when Papi had still been strong, when her mother's memory had not failed, when Lacey still had her own humming outside life: good-looking admirers, lunch dates and dinner parties, trips down the coast to Ensenada. When she had been her parents' beloved child again, but not their warden. When she still could have remarried and had another future.

The gin fired through Lacey's veins, up and down her arms. "But in her late fifties, Mutti began forgetting things. First, where she was and who she was talking with, and then how to have a conversation at all. She couldn't finish a sentence, she of the sharp tongue. Caring for Mutti destroyed Papi's health," Lacey said. "She had to be moved into a home, and Papi got the cancer, and somebody had to take charge of them both, so I did. Their appointments, their nurses, their house and holdings. Twelve years of it. Until I had no life left of my own. I did it because I was theirs. Their lamb, in a world of wolves. You never understood what it meant to be their daughter. You just envied me because I was their darling."

If Edith was still listening, Lacey couldn't tell. Her eyes had gone to the paintings of the flower, scanning them, as if piecing the three into one picture. The speech had tired Lacey's voice, but not her heart and mind. She felt more awake than she had in years.

"You were telling me about being headmistress," Lacey said. "Did possessing so much power make things difficult with your husband?"

"He had passed by then," said Edith. "Stan died young. He had an aneurysm, and one day it burst." She grimaced. "I was a widow in my forties."

"Never remarried?"

"No."

"That must have been hard on you both," said Lacey.

Edith glanced to her suitcase. "It was hard," she said. Another silence fell, freighted with meaning.

"Do you remember the time we ordered king crab," said Edith, "and we didn't know how to eat it, so we invited Bruno and asked him to crack the shells for us? He was so mad that the juice got all over his suit." She laughed her infectious laugh. "He kept complaining he smelled like 'sea brine.'"

"He loved to be mad at us," Lacey said, relenting a little. "It was a hobby for him."

"He sounded lonely on the phone," said Edith. "Does he visit?"

"He has his sons," said Lacey. Bruno had married a shy, intense woman named Viv, who raised his two boys, and then divorced him for an airplane pilot and moved to Denver. But the boys remained in town.

"The older one is still a drummer," said Edith. "He's forty and on unemployment. Bruno is mortified."

Bruno hadn't told this to Lacey. It was becoming apparent that he and Edith had talked for more than a couple of minutes, and that they still talked easily, joking and gossiping. Lacey's stomach churned. She couldn't decide if she was hungry, finally, or needed to be sick again. She didn't like laughing with Edith, or feeling sorry for her, either. Their meal would be arriving soon.

"I don't see Bruno," said Lacey. "I rarely see anyone. I used to take visitors, old friends, but when they stopped coming, it was all people from charities, and all charities want, in the end, is your money. They'll send some bright young gal to visit, and she'll chat you up for a while and leave behind the paperwork."

Edith was examining the paintings again, her green eyes roving.

"What was unusual?" said Lacey.

"What do you mean?"

"You said my books were unusual."

"Your taste," said Edith. "Most people have a kind of book they like—they like mysteries set in abbeys, or romances with cowboys in them. Or classics and histories: they'll line their shelves with impressive titles and fat, intimidating books. As a collection grows, it says something about its owner. But you prefer a little of everything. Or at least that's what's on your shelves. Therefore, it's hard to know what you like and, by extension, who you are."

Lacey had never thought of herself as inscrutable, not like Mutti, with her silences and reveries, or Edith, with her duplicities. "Maybe I'm no one," she said, surprising herself with the statement. "I've always been no one."

Edith laughed again, but it was a bitter laugh. "I find that hard to believe," she said. "I find that very hard to believe."

There was a rapping noise. "Room service," said a young man's voice.

"Will you let them in?" said Lacey, moving the wine bottles aside.

Edith did a funny little detour to her suitcase en route to the door, pausing over it, then hurrying away. Lacey hoped she wouldn't try to pay for anything tonight. Edith should know that Lacey would never accept. *My treat*, she thought of saying now. Except that sounded too cheery and frivolous. *My turn* was more like it.

12.

THE DESK WAS NOT A TABLE. AS SUCH, IT CRE-
ated some difficulties for sitting formally, end to end, because
there was nowhere for their knees to go. Instead, Lacey had
to sit opposite Edith in the middle, a bit too close, with the meal spread
out around them. Awkward, such intimacy. But inevitable. Lacey had
thought this through, had pondered replacing the desk with a real table, but she didn't trust the staff to come up with good, solid furniture
that matched the room. Likely they would cart in something light and
flimsy, and snap it open and be done with it, and all through the meal
it would wobble, and splashes of wine and gravy would land on the
cloth. The desk was heavy and elegant, down to its last clawfoot detail.
She had ordered it from a German woodcarver who lived in Van Nuys,
as a gift for Cal's twenty-eighth birthday. In one of Lacey's most grat-
ifying memories, Cal's eyes widened at the sight, and he ran a freckled
hand over its mahogany surface, declaring himself the luckiest man
alive. Lacey was pregnant then, for the second time, and she remembered his palm on the wood and her own palm on her stomach, and the
promise they both felt in that moment. Dear Cal in his twenties. How
his face could light up, and his voice could declare. *Luckiest man alive.*

His brightness was why people wanted to be around him, to work for him, to realize his dreams.

The cloth was not sized for a desk, so Lacey had asked the staff to fold the linen in half, and it draped to a curl on one side. Her side, where the drawers were. Edith's lay flat, with room for her legs, and just enough view of the back to recognize the wood. But Edith didn't recognize it. She should have. She should have known it instantly. Edith sat down and regarded the food instead, the green salads on their plates, the soups to the side, the main course still under domes of silver.

"Looks good," she said.

"They still have some standards," Lacey said, hoping the night would get back on track now that the dining stage had arrived. A Vosne-Romanée cabernet in their glasses. A basket of parmesan-crusted rolls. Balls of butter. The white candles in Mutti's shabbat candlesticks, the only artifact saved from Mutti's past, brought to California after her final visit to Prague, alone, the summer that Edith and Lacey had lived in the hotel. The last summer before the war. All that June and July, the girls had eaten meals like this, simpler ones, ordered by Papi from the kitchen, but the food had seemed finer then. Fresher. The salads looked slightly wilted now, the lettuce darkened at the edges. "Some standards," she repeated. "No one wants to work in the kitchens anymore. They want the tips jobs, where they can make 'connections.'"

"You keep track of the business, then?" Edith said politely, and bit a roll.

Lacey didn't like talking about the business. A few years after Papi's death, the hotel had nearly bankrupted. First, the neighborhood declined, then bookings and revenues, and then upkeep had lapsed, leading to more vacancies. Then the library fire nearly destroyed their corner of the city. The smoke damage was the last straw. Lacey had

had to choose between cashing out on a big sale to convert the hotel to a convalescent home or selling her shares cheap to another investor, who promised to update the bedrooms and suites, then restore the historic ballrooms and galleria. It was these last alterations, new this year, that Lacey dreaded seeing. What if they made a hash of the old grandeur?

"No," said Lacey. "It's too much for me. But the old-timers tell me anyway. The few ones left. How do you like the place? Does it look the same?" She couldn't hide the hope in her voice.

"Much the same. Remarkably," said Edith. "I didn't recognize anything else in the whole downtown, except for the old library tower."

"The neighborhood changed forever ago," said Lacey. "They bulldozed the Victorian boardinghouses and raised the skyscrapers. And then, for decades, hardly anyone moved into them. Everyone hauled out to the valley and beaches except the shoeless people."

"You mean homeless." Edith looked up from dabbing her roll in her salad dressing.

"They don't have shoes, either," said Lacey. "I saw a man with feet so black they could have been a gorilla's."

Edith hitched backward, as if lightly struck. "You can't say those things anymore," she said.

"I can't?" said Lacey. "He was a white fellow with feet that looked like a gorilla's. His toes were as long as my fingers and a sooty, shiny black."

"You don't know what happened to him," said Edith. "What made him that way."

"Not wearing shoes, obviously," retorted Lacey. She spread her napkin on her lap. She hadn't taken a bite yet. Edith had finished half her salad and was scooping the bisque.

"They let people out of the state mental institutions, but without a plan for them," said Edith. "A lot ended up on Skid Row, which had cheap hotels, until the hotels had to get up to code or close. So then what? The hotels closed. The street was the only option. It's been in the news for a while." She shoved her hard-boiled egg to the side of her plate and hesitated over the tuna.

"You don't like salade niçoise anymore?"

"More of a Caesar person now." Edith's eyes flitted to Lacey again, then away. Still the reluctance to face her openly, head-on. "Or just a few drops of vinegar and oil. I like to taste my greens. I have a large garden."

Of course Edith did, and likely it was the most gorgeous, verdant one on her street. Her road. With Old Harold. Wherever she lived. It pained Lacey that she didn't know, couldn't picture Edith's home, just the slumping, battered houses outside their old summer camp.

"Mutti took me to an exquisite walled garden in Prague once," said Lacey. "It was like the city had whispered a secret in my ear." She recalled Mutti's warning about Edith that day and frowned.

"This city will survive," Edith told her consolingly. "All over the country, people have abandoned their downtowns to the punks and gangs. But it will change, and then everyone will say 'remember when.'"

"'Remember when' what?"

"There's a certain young energy." Edith waved her hand toward the window. "It paints the air here. I saw it riding in," she added as if she were an authority on urban lives, instead of someone who'd lived in a frigid backwater for decades.

"That's called smog," said Lacey. Some days the haze was so thick downtown, it blurred the next skyscraper, and she could taste the grit through the windows, while down below streamed cars, cars, and more cars, their chrome flashing.

"No," said Edith, sitting taller. "It's something else. Tattoos and spiking their hair and wearing eyeliner. Boys *and* girls. They like decay. Damage. Ripped things. They like noise more than music."

"I've heard that," Lacey said sagely. "On the delivery guy's earphones. Even with the volume low, it sounds like someone smashing up their garage."

"Headphones," said Edith.

When had Edith become so bossy and sure of herself? Was it the job at the academy? Was it having a job at all?

"You must feel like an expert on youth," said Lacey.

"And you on silence."

"It's never fully silent here," Lacey said. As if on cue, a truck engine rumbled.

"And Broadway, what happened to that?" said Edith.

"The world's most glorious theater row isn't in the news, too?" Lacey said. "It ought to be."

Edith looked about to say something, then shook her head.

"Swap meets and flea markets," said Lacey. "Ruins."

She wondered if they were both thinking of Cal, his first premiere at the Court Theatre, Lacey on his arm, Edith following with her date, up the grand central staircase to the second floor. The Court Theatre reminded Lacey of the inside of a kaleidoscope, so bedecked and geometric were its walls and ceiling. Hallways led off to their balcony seats, but the gathered crowd wouldn't let them pass, especially not Cal. He was swept from her embrace into a huddle of producers, all men, all several highballs in, and all ready to spend money. Three different casting directors approached Lacey and begged her to star for them. "You have the face of Persephone," said one. "Your eyes are as dreamy as twilight," said another. Though the men were using her to get to Cal, she smiled and pretended to accept their interest. She was still bleeding and cramping from her third miscarriage, but she had stuffed her girdle with cotton padding and wore a dress that didn't

hug her behind, and she clapped fiercely when Cal took the stage afterward, and she smoked all night to keep her head clear. Later, she
buried the crusted red wads deep in the trash so that Cal would not see
them. He never knew how long she bled. He let her alone for weeks
afterward and never asked. He did not like to see her weeping.

"Wouldn't it be Grand to Hope to pick a Flower on Figueroa?"
Edith said. "That's how we remembered the street names."

"Oh, I had the map in my head," said Lacey. "I was an excellent
driver."

There was a snag of quiet.

"Do you remember driving us to the Danube?" Edith said.

The Danube, the old vaudeville house off Broadway's main strip.
A dim den with gray cloth seats and ancient filigree sconces that had
once held gaslights. The smell of must, the sticky stains in the carpet. You'd come out of it into bright day, blinking and shaking off the
feeling that you'd stepped back in time. Lacey had not thought of the
name in ages.

"That rat trap? It's where they had some auditions, wasn't it?"

"It's where they had one audition," Edith said in a strange voice.

"It burned to the ground," said Lacey. "Probably someone collecting the insurance money."

Edith stood up abruptly and asked if she could use the restroom.

"By all means." Lacey gestured toward the bedroom, wondering if she had neatened her makeup bottles and tubes after the last
touch-up. Edith's own skin must feel naked, but maybe she was used to
it, as Lacey was used to talking and smiling through a sheen of cream
and powder, and blinking with sticky lashes. The gliding pop of the
mascara brush, the smooth click of the lipstick tube were a summons
to memory, to a mantra that never changed: To be in public was to
be painted. Lacey wore makeup whenever the cleaners came to tidy

and turn over her room, and sometimes even for her phone calls with Bruno, feeling the red lipstick in her voice as they reminisced about the film award banquets in the hotel's grand ballroom, and the actress who threw her gin rickey all over her groping date.

Thinking of Bruno made Lacey want a cigarette, and thinking of cigarettes made her realize she hadn't lit the candles. She'd placed them on the table between the plates, but she hadn't lit them. Mutti's shabbat candlesticks were a yellowy gold—not those pale, washed-out platinums that had become fashionable—but almost yolk-colored in their hue. The candlesticks, decorated with vine leaves and grape clusters, tapered twice, in a way that reminded Lacey of a woman's figure: a neck, a waist, a full skirt. The first time she saw them, she thought *shepherdess*, and since then, whenever she regarded the candlesticks, the word returned to mind. *Shepherdess*. A country girl. What Mutti had feared her daughter becoming: a country girl, an American with crude manners, a native cunning. An Edith.

The golden grapes and vines felt nubbly under Lacey's fingers. Mutti used to light the candles at sundown on Friday nights and say a prayer under her breath, naming the dead one by one. She lived for her memories, Mutti did, but after Edith left, Mutti erased the girl completely, never saying her name. Only once, when her mind was nearly gone, had Mutti wondered aloud where Edith was. "You're always together," she'd said to Lacey resentfully. "Joined at the hip."

Lacey was waiting with Cal's lighter when Edith returned, but she didn't open it, asking instead if Edith was finished with her first courses.

"I'm afraid it's self-serve for the main," she said. "Though they'll be coming with the chilled platters in half an hour."

"Chilled platters," said Edith.

"Cheeses and fruit," said Lacey. "I ordered a dessert tray, too."

"Goodness. I'll need to save some room."

Edith looked different, coming back from the restroom. Flushed. Maybe she'd pinched her cheeks and bitten her lips, the way she used to, convinced that the tiny bursts of blood would pinken her for more than half a minute. Edith had never cultivated her looks. Still, men had found her attractive. More than a few. You didn't have to be a beautiful woman to be desirable.

"Well, we're not done, are we? We've just begun," said Lacey, flicking the lighter and dipping the flame to the candles. She hated that her hand trembled, but when she snapped the top back, it was smooth, and the sound, the sound was pure Cal. Swish. Click. For a moment, he lingered there with her. His broad-beamed body and his grace, the way he cupped a box of air with his hands when he talked. He was the kind of man you could sense in a room even if you entered it blindfolded—more vital than good-looking—but in a city of slick dandies and wannabes, Cal's qualities stood out. His masculine air of command, his earthiness, his vision. *Luckiest man alive.*

"I've been sitting so long," said Edith, not taking her seat. Instead, she walked to the window, turning her back on the two lit wicks. "Eight hours on two planes, and then the taxi ride. The traffic is murderous."

She was obviously fishing for an apology for the long wait in the lobby. Too bad. Try waiting for forty-four years. Lacey didn't speak. She watched the flames twist and then steady, lengthening, orange-gold. The lighter was warm in her hand. She wanted a cigarette, and she wanted Cal. It was stupid and unfair that she still wanted Cal, the old bare-chested newlywed Cal, lying in bed, who'd watched her cross the room with such satisfied appraisal she threw a pillow at him to break the spell, and they both laughed. She lifted the tablecloth and opened the desk drawer, sliding out the pack.

"You're not going to smoke," said Edith, turning.

"Why not?"

"It'll ruin my appetite," said Edith.

Lacey paused in her unwrapping, the heavenly scent of tobacco already filling her nose.

"Never mind," said Edith. "I don't have much appetite."

"You can save what little you have left," Lacey said primly, putting the pack back in the drawer, her heart speeding at the denial of her craving. She shut the drawer with a heavy thump.

"That's Cal's old desk," said Edith from behind her.

"You noticed?" said Lacey.

There was a pause.

"You kept some of his things, then."

Lacey did not turn to face her. "I was his wife," she said to their half-eaten plates. "I never stopped being his wife."

The statement sank through the air.

"What happened, on the flight?"

"I'm sure it was in the news," said Lacey. "Didn't you read that in the news, too?"

"Stan found out about it, through a mutual friend who was still here, in the city," said Edith. "The friend said Cal flew out in the fog and hit a hillside, and it was over in an instant."

There was more of course. Cal was probably drunk and the girl with him too young, and her family had to be bought off so they didn't make a scandal. Papi and a lawyer had taken care of all the details, so Lacey didn't have to. She merely had to walk through the house they'd shared and decide what she wanted to keep, while the rest would be sold. She had to sign the papers to pay off his debts, and stand by his grave at the funeral, and take the fake condolences from all the movie people who knew that she and Cal had been a sham for years. It was her starring role, the grieving widow of the once-great man. She still had the black dress and veil she'd worn, deep in the closet, and she wondered about taking it out and showing it to Edith now. Would Edith like to see it and touch it? Would Edith like proof of how much it hurt Lacey, losing Cal?

"It was over in an instant," Lacey agreed. "A miscalculation of altitude. Though nobody really knows."

"But you don't think he intended it." Edith's voice was cautious, as if trying to hide her emotions. Lacey turned and looked at her, and this time, for the first time all evening, their eyes met. After decades, that unbearable green gaze. A Gorgon's gaze, so penetrating it could paralyze you from the inside out. Lacey refused to be paralyzed. She would not be trapped by Edith, and nor would Cal's memory.

"No," she said. "I am quite certain he wanted to live."

Edith turned away and went to the window. From the streets below, a piercing sound rose, a fire siren followed by the heavy honks of the vehicle's passage. A second and third siren followed. "They're heading toward the jewelry district," Edith said, staring down.

He wanted to live, Lacey repeated in her head.

"It's been a long time since I've heard sirens," said Edith. "I forgot how loud they are. Do they make it hard to sleep?"

"I wouldn't know," said Lacey. "I rarely sleep."

"You used to." There was the wariness again, the suppressed emotion.

"I used to," agreed Lacey. "Because I used to feel safe."

"You never remarried, either?" Edith blurted. "I expected . . . after all those suitors you had . . . And to a man, they adored you, just as much as Cal. I pictured a rich, handsome widower falling head over heels, and you raising his children."

"A stepmother," Lacey said.

"A wife with a family," said Edith.

Lacey had received several marriage offers in her thirties. She even began a tentative engagement with a medical doctor, whom she loved, only he insisted on serving for several years in Africa, and Lacey would not leave her parents. The truth was, she had money and could not have children, so why did she need a husband?

"And not even Bruno, eh," Edith added.

Lacey snorted, but she couldn't summon the right witty reply. There had been a moment with Bruno. After Papi's death, after the funeral, after everyone had gone, they'd stood alone in the kitchen of her parents' villa, with its fading wallpaper and outdated fixtures, in a light that suddenly seemed like old light, and Bruno had cupped her shoulders in his strong hands and leaned close. "You are okay tonight?" he had asked, his brown eyes searching hers. What he'd meant was, *Do you need me to stay?* In the hesitating pause that followed, Lacey saw what it would be to finally know Bruno as a man, and that they could have been happy together, or happy enough for a while. But then, from her memory, jolted Cal's mocking voice—*When I'm gone, you'll marry old moony Bruno*— and she must have flinched. Bruno's hands fell before she even answered, and what could she say then but *No, you go home, I'll be fine?*

"And I thought you would act or write, until you got famous," said Lacey. "I imagined you living in the heart of a big city. Single forever. You would go to bohemian parties, and all your friends and lovers would be artists and poets and singers."

Edith looked at her hands. "I never had that kind of talent," she muttered.

"You didn't know what you had," said Lacey.

Edith was still standing, still clinging to her view to the street. Lacey wondered if she would ever sit.

"I didn't mean that you needed a man to feel safe," said Edith. "I just thought you preferred being married."

"You're right," said Lacey.

She removed their salad plates and set the main courses, lifting the silver lids, the meaty steam wafting in her face. "Shall we taste the next course? The chef will be offended if we don't."

13.

A GOOD OSSO BUCO NEEDS A MARROW SPOON TO scoop the richness from the bone, and a gremolata of lemon, garlic, parsley, and anchovies to be sprinkled across the top. Skip the anchovies in the gremolata and you miss the meatiness of fish salt. A flavor foursome—salt, sour, bitter, and savory—mingles best with the sweet veal. Osso buco should be served with a saffron risotto and asparagus, the yellow and green setting off the brown of the meat. The meal can sit for a bit, but it will start to congeal if left too long and the veal will go from tender and flaky to slightly chewy. The rice will glop.

If Edith had not lingered so long at the window, entranced by her fire trucks and ambulances, the main course would have ridden the edge of perfection. As it was, Lacey decided after a few bites that she should have ordered it separately and they could have waited for it. She'd been trying to accommodate a guest she'd supposed was hungry after sitting so long in the lobby and riding airplanes. She'd been recalling the way Edith at camp had tucked right in.

Edith at camp. Edith striding upstairs at the Court Theatre. How easy it had been, that morning, to picture them both young in her mind's eye, with smooth skin and flowing hair, with legs that could sprint or dance at a moment's notice, and appetites that matched. Now, watching Edith struggle to poke her fork into the meat and hold it secure, watching her gnarled hands fumble for her napkin, Lacey couldn't imagine the former fluidity of their bodies, or how they would possibly stuff in three more courses.

"Let's have the wine," she decided aloud. She could feel herself getting sober again and a headache replacing the buzz. "Red or white?"

"Red, I think," said Edith, eyeing the meat. "Pairs better."

"You never used to like red," said Lacey. "You said it reminded you of blood. The way it stained some people's teeth."

"That was the cheap stuff," said Edith. "And I've grown up."

"What made you grow up?" said Lacey, standing to reach the wine, pouring it into glasses.

"The first time?" said Edith. "I think people grow up many times. Not just once."

"The first time, then," said Lacey.

"When I walked into the room where my mother was dead," Edith said automatically. "And my youngest brother was alive and bloody, and he was crying. My sister had gone after my father to send him for the doctor, and there was no one else to pick the baby up. So I did." She took the glass Lacey offered and sipped from it.

Lacey had not heard these details before. She tried to envision a shabby farmhouse with a dead woman and a red-streaked baby inside, but the images refused to coalesce. Instead she saw Edith's bruises later. Her swollen, purple, oozing eye. The mouth that dragged down from a gash on its right side.

"And you?" said Edith.

"When Mutti came back from Prague in 1938," said Lacey. "And I saw that she knew her mother and father would die. That they would not save themselves from the Nazis, even though she begged. They didn't believe Prague would be next; they insisted on staying to care for some elderly neighbors, who were too infirm to leave. Mutti had bought steamship tickets for them, and she threw the tickets at Papi and screamed, and he just let her. He let her beat him with her fists, and then they both wept. She never saw them alive again."

Once the borders closed, the information dried up. Once the information dried up, they lived in hope, until they didn't. Mutti's Brooklyn cousin got the news through acquaintances who had hidden and hiked their way free: every Jew in Mutti's neighborhood had been arrested and sent away by train. German officers had moved into Mutti's childhood home. Behind the little window with the plum-colored panes, soldiers smashed the furniture and stained the linens with their drinking and whoring. No pretense of the lawful owners returning, ever.

"She must have been torn apart," said Edith.

Lacey nodded but said nothing. She was remembering the feeling of receiving Edith's sympathy, how it had once comforted and buoyed her.

"The second time was leaving camp that night," said Edith. "Leaving you. I thought I'd never see you again. That you'd forget me." She sounded wistful.

"I couldn't," said Lacey. "I remember running after you in the dark. All those sticks and leaves whipping my face. You were sublime. I had to tell you."

"You never told me," said Edith.

Lacey was quite sure she had.

"And you did forget me," said Edith. "A little."

"You forgot me, too," protested Lacey. "You went back to camp without me."

"That wasn't forgetting."

"You didn't write for a whole summer," said Lacey. "You just sent me that one package."

"That was a test," Edith said.

"I never tried it. Your remedy," said Lacey. "I never got that bad cough again. But I kept the bottle and your note. I only lost it when we moved, and by then you were with us."

"That was the third time I grew up," said Edith.

"You must have been frightened, leaving home."

"Terrified," said Edith. "I walked twenty miles on country roads before I caught the train, and I only had enough money to reach the central station, not a dime more to buy a map or pay for a cab. But people saw my swollen face, and they tried to help. Especially one man. He said he would escort me to your place, but then his hand on my arm squeezed tighter and tighter and the streets grew darker. I realized he thought he could take advantage, and I had to escape him. I got away and hid for hours in an alley, hoping he wouldn't find me, and then stumbled around until, almost at dawn, I found your address. I was minutes away from fainting, I was so exhausted. I didn't think your mother and father would take me in. But they did."

Lacey had been asleep when Edith arrived. She remembered waking to the closed door of Mutti and Papi's bedroom, the crack of light beneath it. The guttural sound of Edith's sobs inside. Papi in the hallway, his finger to his lips. "You never said why you ran," said Lacey. "You told Mutti, but not me, and she made me promise never to ask you."

Edith looked suddenly tired. "Did she?" she said. "I always wondered why you never wanted to know."

"I wanted to know," said Lacey.

Edith picked at her sleeves, an old habit. Her face was hard to read. "My father didn't beat us little ones," she said. "He cherished us. But you grew old enough, and he got suspicious. He decided you were stealing from his liquor. Or lying to him. Or making a whore of yourself. You got old enough, and he saw you wanted to leave him and that's when he turned. I was his favorite." A flare of pride at the last word. "So I got it the best, and then I got it the worst. As soon as I started developing, he told me I should stop going to school. That I wasn't safe from boys. They would strip me bare, he said. Can you imagine your own father saying that? *Strip you bare*," she repeated in a sneering, nasal tone, a thick country accent, her eyes squeezed to slits. "But I wanted to go to school more than anything, so I slipped out and got beaten when I came back. Then I slipped out again. Then he locked me in the woodshed. Then my brother let me out. Then Pa locked us both in. Eventually, I promised to stay home so my brother could learn to read and write. I promised lots of things, but I wasn't a fool. I slept in a bed with my little brothers, one on either side, head to toe, and they kept me safe when he was blind drunk at night. When he was regular drunk by day, he hit me for not being his little girl anymore and not being my ma, either. One night I counted out how many years before my youngest brother, the baby I saved, could run away and make it on his own. It was ten more. I didn't think I'd live ten more. So I sneaked out at dawn. Pa caught me by the woodpile. That time, he hit me with a stick of firewood. I guess he thought if I was too bashed up, I'd be too ashamed to leave, but I wasn't. I wasn't ever going to be ashamed again."

"I wanted to know," Lacey said again. "I've always wanted to know."

Edith's expression didn't change. "Well, now you do."

The harsh sobs from her parents' bedroom. Lacey remembered grabbing the doorknob, longing to burst through, to fling her arms around Edith, but her father held her back.

"The fourth time you grew up," said Lacey.

"That wasn't growing up," Edith said. "That was just survival."

"I don't understand why Mutti forbade me to ask you," said Lacey, remembering Mutti's stern injunction afterward.

"She wanted to protect you," Edith said, "from the ugliness I came from."

The suppressed rage in her voice made Lacey briefly lose her place in the room, in the night, in her own anger. *As if I didn't know ugliness,* she wanted to say. *As if I wouldn't see my own family murdered and my mother torn to pieces.* But that was later.

"And because I hit him, too. With a rock," admitted Edith. "I didn't kill him," she added when she saw Lacey's flinch. "But if he had decided to find me and press charges, your mutti wouldn't have wanted you to be involved." She blew out a breath. "She picked out the splinters in my face with the gentlest fingers and ran a bath for me and tweezed the rest. I thought they'd send me home, your parents, but they said I should never go back."

"Papi bought you a ticket to go with us," Lacey said. "The very next day. Papi said we couldn't leave you behind to your fate. Those were the words he used."

"He was kind," said Edith.

"He knew how much I loved you."

"Your mother didn't trust me," said Edith.

Lacey was silent, remembering Mutti and her reservations. "She had an instinct for some things," she said. "Late in life, before she lost her memory, she used to say, *I knew how to save myself. That's the only thing I ever knew.* She hated being the one who survived, but I think she hated even more that she would have sought survival all over again."

"There are many ways to survive." Edith pushed away her plate. "You can't always blame yourself for the fates of others. She made a career of it."

It was impossible to see the young Edith in her now, not with that set, determined face. A judging face. A woman who knew her own power. Headmistress of the Little Academy in the Big Woods. Edith had always been the receptive one, her secret, yearning self buried deep. The calm girl whose feelings came out later. Exploded sometimes. Only onstage had Edith seemed to inhabit her own emotions, and then so fully that it hurt to watch. The Danube. Now Lacey remembered why Edith had mentioned the Danube. Of course. It was the beginning of Cal.

"Is that what you came to tell me?" said Lacey, her stomach twisting. "That I shouldn't blame you for what you did?"

"Is that why you think I'm here?" said Edith.

Now Lacey rose. Now she walked to the window. In the ballrooms below, the windows were mirrored, fake, shining the lights of the parties back at themselves. Up here, the night went on endlessly behind its fretwork of glass. Skyscrapers to freeways to suburbs to mountains. Distance was what she needed now. Lacey looked down at the darkened street, the spinning cars, steadying her mind. All the talk about camp, about their old faithfulness, about Edith's running from home, it shaped their story around Edith's pain. But Lacey had never hurt Edith the way Edith had hurt her.

"I've booked a room for you tonight at another hotel," Lacey said, "and a cab can be called anytime. You don't have to stay, and you don't have to worry about where you'll sleep. You've found out what happened to Cal now. He died on his own terms. You were not involved. So you can leave whenever you want. You don't have to listen to me. We don't have to talk for the rest of the night about the wrongs between us. But if you stay, you'll hear me out. You vanished without a word to me four decades ago, and since then I've listened to that silence. Now it's my turn to tell you what I think."

Edith glanced again at the paintings on the wall. "I'm not leaving," she said. "Are you sure you know all the wrongs?"

"I know what I have to say," said Lacey. And then she opened the drawer to the desk, grabbed the pack, shook out a cigarette, and lit it. Edith cranked her head, searching the ceiling.

"Disabled," said Lacey, flipping the lighter shut and taking her first long drag. "I learned about the sprinkler system the hard way. I quit after Papi died, but I had a couple of relapses." As the smoke filled her lungs, and the rush followed, she watched Edith ease out a cigarette, but Edith did not touch Cal's lighter, because it was still in Lacey's grip. Edith had to bend to the flame her friend offered, to hold the cigarette between her old, shriveled, unpainted lips. She had to breathe in to make it catch.

"Fine," said Edith, coughing a little, swiping the smoke with her hand. "Go on."

14.

"LET ME FIRST SAY THAT I KNOW YOU RECOGNIZE these rooms, though the furnishings are different, and by day, the light would be different, on account of our taller neighbors now," said Lacey. "Papi wanted the apartment to be bright and airy. It was, until that dreadful bank tower rose up the hill. But you know you've woken here beside me many times, don't you? Stepping into these chambers must have felt strange, like stepping back to the past. You loved the chintz sofa with the big roses; it sat over there by the window. I preferred the matching armchair; I liked to tuck my legs beneath me. Remember the fringe lamps that we did our homework by? And those horsehair mattresses. They were always too hot in summer." She wanted Edith to picture it again, every bit of their closeness. "We even used the same shampoo. 'Soft as rainwater,' it said on the bottle."

"I remember," said Edith faintly.

Lacey put out her cigarette and lit another. Edith watched her with hands folded. "What did you make of the hotel, when you first saw it?" said Lacey.

"Long ago, or now?"

"Your very first impression. Long ago."

"It was magical. I felt like Cinderella," Edith said. "Every night, I was waiting for the clock to toll and to send me home in rags."

"You had trouble sleeping back then," commented Lacey.

"I was afraid he would find me," said Edith. "By day I could persuade myself it was impossible, but when night came, I was sure I heard his step in the hall."

"Sometimes you cried in your sleep. I remember that," said Lacey, although she didn't recall it. If Edith had been fearful, she'd never shown it. Instead, Edith had embraced the warm, winterless days, throwing out her wool and wearing Lacey's cotton tea dresses, ordering from the kitchen on Lacey's father's tab, learning about veal scallopine and croque monsieur, and how to balance her fork in her fingertips instead of her fist. It was Edith who ultimately excelled in the school they attended; Edith who got the highest grades and acquired the most friends, almost as if she'd been making up for lost time. She never talked about her family or explained to Lacey the beating she'd received. *Do you ever think about them?* Lacey asked once, the night before their high school graduation, imagining Edith crossing the stage without any relatives to clap for her.

Sometimes I think about what season it is, said Edith after a moment. *It's spring now and the wild irises are out. I used to pick bouquets for my sister.* And then, fiercely, *She'd be glad for me now.*

What about your brothers?

Edith had made a noise, somewhere between a laugh and a sob, but she hadn't answered. She never mentioned her father, either. In the intervening years, Lacey wondered about Edith and Mr. Holle on Vaudeville Night, how they couldn't stop staring at each other. Edith hadn't seemed afraid of him then. More like infatuated. Desperate. It made Lacey's gut wrench to think of that Edith now. No wonder they'd both buried that girl. "Did you ever see him again?"

"No." Edith smoothed the napkin on her lap.

"You had to be within a few hundred miles of home."

Her friend didn't answer.

"So no one found you, not one of your brothers, no one from camp."

"I had a different name, first and last," said Edith. "My boss, the headmaster, called me Edie and it stuck."

"Edie," said Lacey, her heart sinking.

"One of the academy parents thought she recognized me once," Edith said. "Someone from cabin eight. But no one thought I could go from drunk Mr. Holle's daughter to where I arrived," she added. "Did you try to find me?"

"No," said Lacey. When Edith waited, dubious, she added, "Never."

Edith tamped out her cigarette. She looked like she wanted another. She was like that, always feigning a lack of appetite for the things she really craved. Lacey held out the pack to her.

"Cinderella's jealous stepsister," said Lacey.

"What?"

"So many fairy tales begin with one woman envious of another, secretly or openly," said Lacey. "One possesses it all, and the other covets it. Beauty, treasure, a man's love. If only the fortunate girl knew how to divide her riches, how to share equally, the other would not hate her. But fortunate girls don't know how to share, because they can't see the difference between what they are and what they possess. It takes hunger and ugliness to see that. It takes wanting and lusting and being denied. You'd hungered all your life. I hadn't. Did it ever occur to you that I never truly knew myself? That by taking from me, you were teaching me who I was? I suppose you've come here to apologize or explain or show me what I've missed, but when you abandoned me, you already told me everything I needed to know."

"Are you so sure I abandoned you?"

"I'm not afraid of anything you have to say now," Lacey replied. "Anything at all. Because I know myself, and I am old, and I have few choices left. One of them is to fear death. All my life I have feared it, that healthy fear everyone has: that death would steal something from me. My remaining years. My golden days. But I no longer need golden days. Tomorrow will be the same as this day and the day before that, and I could live them, or I could let them go. You see, it's quite extraordinary what happens to you when you live alone for a long time, with only your thoughts for company. A double self grows. A mirror self. The one who lives and the one who watches her live. And the second self begins to understand that the first is terribly ordinary, has always been, even if she was once beautiful and happy. The second self says, *Don't be afraid of death or the truth. They have been waiting for you all along.*"

She paused, gathering herself. She didn't like the frown on Edith's face.

"Everyone's afraid of death," Edith said after a moment. "As for the truth, what choices did you think I had?"

The thumps on the door startled them both. Lacey hastily extinguished her cigarette and invited them in: two young men in dark red suit coats, pushing a cart. They both had close-cropped hair and a discreet, deferential manner, and Lacey couldn't remember their names now, but she knew she had requested them personally. They didn't meet the women's eyes. They didn't comment on the tobacco haze. They swept away the old plates and set down a platter bejeweled with grapes, pineapple, melon, and strawberries, a plate of creamy cheeses, and a three-tiered presentation of cannoli, petit fours, and tiny pecan tarts. The coolness of refrigeration drifted from the food and Lacey fought back a shiver, but she was suddenly hungry. She wanted to nibble at things that were simple and geometric, not that thick meat they had picked at. She saw Edith's eyes widening, too. How they had once sampled every taste! Sneaking down at the end of Papi's banquets and picking puff pastries off the buffet tables, daring each other to bite. Edith had gotten almost fat that year, while Lacey, under her mother's watchful eye, learned the careful, invisible way to spit out into napkins. Then Edith started working and stopped eating, too, going all day on black coffee.

When the young men were about to leave, Lacey fished a couple of bills from her purse and offered them. The men bowed and left.

"One day, you must have decided that hurting yourself was the only way to get free," said Lacey. "You knew it would tear you apart to leave your brothers."

"Maybe it did," said Edith. "But that's not my question: What choices do you think I had?"

Lacey picked up a slice of cheese and a grape and ate them together. The cigarettes had dulled her taste buds but elevated her sense of texture: the crisp pop of the grape in her teeth, the melting softness of cheese.

"You keep asking the wrong question," she said after she swallowed. "I don't think the truth lies in what future you could have chosen, but in what past you decided to deny. You either had to deny who you were inside, or to deny my abiding friendship. You couldn't have both. You couldn't be both the heroine and the villain. That's the problem with the fairy tales. At the end, only one woman gets to become queen. The other is banished, beheaded, or rolled down the stairs in a barrel of nails. Hideous fates for hideous females. So the storyteller constructs the crime that would fit the villain's punishment. And then she sets about making the monstrous woman who would commit the crime."

She hadn't thought this all out before saying it, but she was pleased by how her metaphors slid into place. Edith had never thought her capable of such articulations. Nor had Cal. It was eerie how Cal was present anyway, in this whole conversation, almost as if his memory nourished them, like nutrients the roots of trees.

"How much did you tip them?" asked Edith. "Just curious."

"Twenty each," said Lacey.

"Forty dollars?" Edith sounded staggered. "I only paid the cab driver a couple bucks."

"Oh, darling," said Lacey. "And you think I've been locked away."

15.

"SO I'M THE MONSTER," SAID EDITH AS THEY MADE A second small meal of fruits and sweets. "In this scenario. And you're the queen."

"That depends on what the ending is," said Lacey. "Where the tale comes to its stop. Sometimes the tale stops when the bride gets married to the king, and sometimes it's when the true queen has her revenge."

"There are wrong queens, then."

"And wrong monsters. A kitchen maid wears the coats of fearsome beasts, her face smeared in soot and dirt, but then she is washed and dressed, and—voilà—she's the princess beneath, after all this time," said Lacey. "You said there's no rhyme or reason to my book collection, but that's because the same story can be told infinite ways. We love; we fail. We love again."

"You have a bright outlook for someone who has left the world for years," said Edith.

"Have I left it? Or have I just chosen my world, as you chose yours? Just because mine has more invented people in it than living ones does not mean it is any less real."

"Invention *is* easier," said Edith. "It's easier to spend time with characters who can be closed up and slid back on a shelf."

"I can't be closed up and slid back on a shelf. And when I am alone, I am with me," said Lacey. *I am with me,* she thought. My back that aches from years of sitting by Papi's bedside. My ears that listened to my mother forget my name. My womb that bled out eight pregnancies, one by one.

Finally, Edith took a second cigarette and lit it with the flame from one of the candles. She took a couple of drags and watched Lacey thoughtfully.

"In all honesty, I didn't expect the lecture," she said. "Not from you. You sound more like him than you know."

There Cal was again, in Lacey's mind's eye. This time, he was pacing a set in the studio, where the replica of a shack had been erected for a new Western. Three thin, rough wooden walls defined the building. An actress was standing in the window of one, looking out. Cal was directing her.

"Your man is coming," he told the actress. "Your man is riding back, and he's done good deeds and bad deeds in the name of his honor, but I want you to understand something: That honor is *yours.* He entrusted it to *you.* He has put you in his heart above all things, and if he rides up now, with all the things he's done, good and bad, and you accept him, then he is still the hero. If you adore him, he is still a prince of men. But if you deny him, he has lost it all." He put a hand on the actress's shoulder, his tone warm, confiding. "This scene coming up, you need to show the camera that you know that. And you choose him first in your heart. Whatever he's done."

"The Hotel San Marco. You are free to go at any time," said Lacey.

Edith stabbed out the cigarette, half-smoked, and gulped her wine. "No," she said. "Not yet."

Lacey waited for her to say more.

"Waiting for my barrel of nails," Edith said. Her voice was light, but her eyes were serious.

"It wasn't supposed to happen," said Lacey. "The coincidence of events that day. And sometimes I wonder—if it hadn't, if we erased just those mere twelve hours from our entire lives—where you and me and Cal would be now. If you had told me before I witnessed it, if you had decided before I knew. If I'd had the chance to speak with you before you ran away. But you didn't give me the chance. Not then, not ever."

"Perhaps there was a chance, and you didn't take it," Edith said in an unreadable voice. She was eyeing the laden table between them. It was hard to tell if she cared what Lacey was saying, if she was hearing it at all, or if her mind was far away.

"I'm still not sure if you tripped or fell deliberately that day, but I know that you didn't stop yourself," said Lacey. "I didn't see your hands fly out or your feet shift to find a better footing. Once you started falling, you just let it happen. It was like watching an empty dress drop from an upstairs window, seeing it tumble to the ground."

Across the table, Edith's fingers had been reaching for a red strawberry, but they halted. Her whole body halted and went still.

"You remember, don't you?" said Lacey. "You didn't think I was there, watching. I was supposed to be home, but I went to the set to surprise Cal with the news that *Life* magazine wanted to interview him."

"Is that why?" said Edith. "I never knew."

"It is," said Lacey. "It was a long way to Agoura, and I almost got lost twice, but eventually I found the dirt road that led to the turnout where the trucks parked. I recognized the name of the studio painted on their sides. I saw the tracks carved in the dust from dragging the equipment and water. It was a long walk, and the sweat was stinging my eyes by the time I got there. I was excited to see the set. Sound recording was so bad outdoors that they shot most of the film inside the studio, but they had one crucial river scene, and Cal insisted it be done outside with a real river. He was a midwestern kid; in his head, he carried big, flowing streams. But this was the California hills, and even in May, most creeks were trickles in a parched bed of rock. Hardly enough to drown a man. So Cal had a plan: they stopped up one end of a ravine and carted in extra barrels of water, and the instructions were to dump the barrels and do the scene fast, before it all seeped out. The actor would slip and knock his head on stone, and then float facedown. The end. The villain's bad end. Nature killing him. No dialogue to the scene, just shouts and yells, so you, Edith, didn't actually need to be there. You were the casting assistant. The *assistant*. I'd gotten you that job, by badgering Cal for months. I knew you needed money. I thought you worked the auditions, one of those people who listens to hundreds of hopefuls and rejects all but a handful. A good job, one suited to your quick judgment. When later I found the shooting script in Cal's desk with your handwriting all over it, I realized you were so much more. Cal had promoted you to his chief script stenographer. Your changes went to the typists. Your dialogue came out through the mouths of the actors. You shaped the film. Maybe even defined it. If you had stayed around for post-production, it might not have been such a flop."

At this, Edith's eyebrows raised. She grabbed the strawberry and settled backward into her chair, holding it, but not eating. She liked the last part about her talent, clearly, but she didn't quite believe it. Lacey went on.

"Anyone could see that Cal had the smarts and the charisma to get investors, but he lacked discernment. He never could decide what storyline to pursue and what to cut. He leaned on you there, and then he came to me to confirm your ideas. How often he lay back in bed after making love to me and said something like, 'You know the scene in the bar? I'm thinking that Turner actually *forgot* his gun, out in his horse's saddlebag. So he's sitting there drinking, and Santer comes storming in, and oops, holster's empty, so what does Turner do? His hand closes on the whiskey bottle and he stays there with his back to Santer until just the right moment and pegs it right at Santer's head. What do you

think? The scene used to say, 'Turner swivels and shoots.' Turner's a
great shot, though. And why would he forget his gun? He's not the
type to forget. Hard to say what audiences would like better.' And of
course I would tell him they'd like the version where the hero slips up
and then chucks the whiskey bottle, because people hate heroes who
don't make mistakes, but they love heroes who improvise and triumph
in the end. Naturally, I thought the whiskey bottle was Cal's idea, not
yours." Lacey knew she should stop, wait for the response, the recognition, but she galloped on. "Imagine what happened to my memories
of those nights when I later realized the same conversations happened
in your bed, after your bodies slid together and parted, that every time
Cal was touching me, he was carrying your touch with it, and every
time I listened to his words, they were your words, and every declaration of love to me was violated by him repeating the same to you."

She hadn't expected to utter it so soon. The accusation. She intended to go in the right methodical order, the order of discovery, and
to say only what she knew as she knew it, but the telling had carried her
away. The lurid words stained the air. Too late to take them back now.

Edith's eyes dropped to the strawberry in her hand. After a long
silence, she dug her thumbnail into the side and pulled it out, removing
a tiny red chunk. Then she set the pierced fruit down on her plate and
wiped her hand clean with her napkin. When she spoke, her voice was
clipped. "I went and saw that film," she said. "It had sixteen endings."

Lacey couldn't hide her emotion. "He couldn't decide which one
was right," she choked out. "I'm guessing. By then, I wasn't advising
him, either."

"It wasn't like you pictured," Edith said. The flush was coming
back to her cheeks. "Me and him." The fruit slumped on the plate, its
wedge of flesh shining. "Did he claim it was?"

"I'm not finished telling you about my day in Agoura," said Lacey,
the redness filling her eyes. "Three times on that walk, I almost turned

around. I had lost so much blood the week before. Another miscarriage. I was further along that time, fifteen weeks, when I started
spotting and the spotting turned to huge clots seeping out of me. Cal
wanted to take me to the hospital again, but what could they do? I told
him to refill my prescription and leave me alone. I wasn't kind to him.
In my mind, my sorrow and Cal had become intertwined. He was the
light of my life, and also the dasher of my deepest hopes. I could not
keep his children. They sparked inside me, and then they leaked away.
So I took my pills and drifted until the bleeding eased, and then I rose
to shake it off and start all over again. The rare times you came to visit,
you always insisted I drink cool, plain water, remember? You said I
had so many tears to cry, I needed to make a cloud inside. You were
a true comfort, just sitting there, letting me be sad. I know you didn't
approve of me doping myself, but you never asked me to pretend to
be happy like Mutti would. Mutti thought unhappiness was her real
estate alone, even though she'd been through the same kind of loss
with my brother, and others. But she belittled *my* suffering. It was just
a beginning, she said about the babies. A false start. You're young.
You can try again. Get up. Be the smiling wife on the arm of your
husband. He's getting traction now. His career is taking off. He needs
you. You charm the men, and befriend the women, that's all that's expected of you. A few nights, a few drinks, a few dances. The rest of the
days to yourself. He'll always remember how you helped him. He'll
be forever grateful, even if you can't give him an heir. He loves you to
death, *Liebling*. He'll do anything for you. You hide behind this now,
you sulk and weep, and some other woman will move in. Trust me. It
happened to your Papi. It can happen to Cal."

Edith blinked, looking into the candlelight.

"Maybe I could have forgiven one slip-up," said Lacey. "Maybe I
could have explained it, one night's lapse in judgment, and not admitted to myself that what you had with Cal went further and deeper than

I knew. But it was a hot day, the brightness burning in every shard of metal, every fleck of shimmering sand. I left the track and started walking through the chapparal so as to surprise my husband. He used to swell with delight when I came on set, and I hadn't appeared in a long time. However he loved you, it was because he needed you, but Cal loved me because he could not stop gazing at me. It was that simple. Even five years into our marriage, even with the heartache between us, I was so beautiful to him. 'You're like a present in a bright blue bow,' he said. Unlike for you, a man's admiration was enough for me. I could live inside its walls and be content. I loved being a wife. I was satisfied with it, too.

"Leaving the track was a bad idea from the first. The bushes ran thicker and tougher than I thought, and the branches scratched my calves. I thought I heard snakes slithering. Bees were dodging in my path. But then I found a little line of beaten earth, something a creature had made, and I followed it.

"The ravine on the set was deep, and boulders of sandstone rose on either side, blocking my view. Though I could hear the men shouting to each other, and the clanking of something, I couldn't see. I realized they must have been ready to dump the barrels. I hurried forward, anxious not to miss the scene. The boulders were in my way, though. I would have to climb them, or down the ridge to get a view. While I was deciding, I heard Cal call a name: 'Edie, Edie, what do you think? How's it look from up there?' And when I heard your voice reply, I realized that 'Edie' was you.

"Sandstone isn't like other rock. It sits in its place, it looks imposing, but the minute you set foot onto it, you can feel how fragile it is. Ready to crumble. Sandstone is what a drought country makes of its drifts, in the open air, and not the long burial that creates granite or marble. I didn't know this then, and when I scrambled up the boulder to get a view, my feet kept slipping on the graininess beneath me. First, I saw my husband below, standing, legs wide, in a white shirt I kept ironed for him, wearing the crown of blond hair I kept trimmed for him, his brown eyes assessing everything. Handsome as the day, Cal was, at the center of spokes of men, some holding the barrels, ready to tip, some holding cameras, ready to shoot, some holding battery lamps and shiny cards to bounce the light, and the villain standing in the creek, wearing dungarees and a ripped shirt, practicing his grimaces. Then I watched Cal's eyes rise to the boulders opposite me, across the ravine, to you, standing in a crack between them, holding both sides, and I saw you seeing me.

"You shook your head, but it was too late. Cal called 'Action!' The water poured down the narrow chute, roaring and splashing, and Cal and one cameraman had to dance out of its path, but the villain spun and smashed himself convincingly, and I didn't watch the rest because across the chasm, I saw you slip and fall. You did it soundlessly. I don't know why or how. Any other woman would have screamed. The pitch was steep, and the water was crashing its way, and only a few scrub trees blocked its path. One of the cameramen spotted you first, and he pulled Cal's arm and pointed while you went tumbling toward the creek."

Lacey paused to pour herself more wine, but when Edith shifted to speak, she held up her hand. "Hear me out. He ran for you. He could run fast for a big man on any day, but that afternoon he bolted. He was an elk, leaping the rocks. He reached you before you fully stopped falling and caught you. I saw you look into each other's eyes. I saw the pain and worry on his face. And then I saw your hand cup your belly and Cal's hand cover it. Protective. And possessive. The mound was still small enough to hide from the world, but large enough for me to see. You knew and he knew, and you had known for some time."

16.

"I SHOULD HAVE STAYED AND CONFRONTED YOU BOTH, but, before long, my legs had carried me halfway down the hill to my car, and the blood was coming again, some last residue or maybe just the monthly courses returning," said Lacey. "I could never tell. I bled so much in those years. I kept new pads and a change of outfit in my trunk, swapping them sometimes between a luncheon and a matinee. In my more naive moments, I told myself that our American soldiers did not weep, going into battle; they simply readied themselves and fought again to win the war. Mutti's constant scolding would mix with my own longing to be brave, and I would trade my bloodstained girdles for fresh, clean linens. But that day, my hands didn't work, I was shaking so hard. The wet mess between my legs smeared all over the seat, my clothes. When I finally got changed, my mind refused to review what I had seen. Instead, I wondered if the crew had gotten the villain's facedown shot before all the water ran out. Cal had been worrying about the timing all week. Even then, I fretted over Cal's ambition and not my own happiness. It took me ages to get my clothes straightened up, but no one came to find me, and I drove away alone.

"Instead of going home, I headed to the sea. I loved to drive my old LaSalle with its sunshine turret top, and the headlights so close they looked like tiger eyes. Back then, many women were still intimidated to take command of a car, but it came easily to me, the flow of the freeway and the shifting gears. In truth, it wasn't so different from being in bed with a man, more of an intuitive game than a thinking one. Am I making you blush? I hope so. I hope that thinking too much ruined your lovemaking with Cal. I suspect it did, or would have eventually. He was a creature of appetites. I was as well, and that's why I needed the sea. Smog was rare in those days, and a sparkling light followed me south from the hills, over the rim into the great bowl of the city, where I zoomed west, passing our dense neighborhood, and then the grand estates, then the rickety beach homes, the oil derricks, and finally reached the great roaring wall of the ocean. I went there because I didn't want to be followed. I went there because I was hungry, and nothing could fill me, because what I yearned for could not be had. I wanted to be gone from my own life. For the first time, I felt real compassion, instead of pity, for Mutti and the long marriage that had split her in two.

"What?" said Lacey because Edith had pushed her plate away, tossed her napkin down.

"Never mind," muttered Edith, studying the tablecloth. "If you hadn't left so fast."

Lacey stared at her. In her mind's eye, she blazed.

"Never mind," Edith said again.

Lacey nodded. "At the beach, I saw you, me, and Cal as the pieces of an equation that could not be solved. I could not forgive both you and Cal, nor could I let you both go. Nor could I blame one and accept the other back. Dimly I understood that the hurt you had given me was different from Cal's, and perhaps greater, but my rage could not pin itself to a single motivation or act. My outrage was like the water poured from the barrels into the ravine, cascading every which way. My mind played out various future scenarios, the one where Cal divorced me and married you. The one where you became his mistress and I stayed his wife. The one where you tearfully gave up the child and begged my forgiveness. The one where you lied to me and claimed the father was another man. Even the one where you asked me to raise the child and left us, me and Cal, to build a family together. It seemed inevitable that I would have to accept the first scenario. My divorce, your wedding. I had no child to offer Cal, and your child, once born, would be paramount, as I had been paramount in keeping my parents together. I had seen your hand and Cal's hand on the life between you. You wanted it. He wanted it. He wanted to keep it safe and his.

"It was dark when I drove back, still undecided between confronting Cal and confronting you, or running away entirely. You rented a little bungalow that I visited often; it was my favorite place in the city after the hotel and our own house. You liked your home cluttered, just like your bunk in our camp cabin. You had pots of red and orange marigolds all over your front step, and dozens of books inside. You had started collecting teacups, individual ones, none of them matching. I loved the thinnest one, painted with green vines and a single pink rose. I always chose it when I came for tea. But I didn't go to your bungalow that night. I came here, to the hotel, to a room that Papi kept reserved for me and Cal, should we ever go downtown for the evening and stay out late, and not want to drive back home. With all my miscarriages, I hadn't slept anywhere that year but my own bed, but that night the hotel, and the room, called to me. I couldn't tell my parents what had happened; they'd been away in Europe all winter and spring. But I could stay in Papi's hotel, my little nest inside it. A safe place where I could hide, like running into Papi's arms when I was a child.

"Bruno was working that night. When he saw me, his face lit up, but when I asked for the room key, mine and Cal's, he disappeared for a long time, claiming he wanted to make sure housekeeping had kept the room clean. It could have gotten dusty, he said. How Bruno knew about you and Cal, but Papi didn't, is easy. During the war, remember, Papi was so busy—he opened the second floor of the hotel for soldiers in transit to the Pacific. The men slept in rooms and cots all down the hallway, sailors and infantry, the pale, jumpy ones shipping out, the tan, hardened ones coming home. Some were perfect gentlemen, of course. Others got rowdy and disturbed the paying guests. Papi loved them, but he had his hands full keeping the peace.

"The GIs were still coming through, heading back to their Iowas after armistice, when Papi and Mutti left for the American zone in Germany, to try to find both sides of their families. Mutti's Jewish relatives had been taken by the Germans, and Papi's German relatives expelled by the Czechs after liberation in 1945. A tracing service had emerged to help Americans find their missing, but the going was slow and full of false leads.

"So Papi may never have spotted your affair. The hotel was crawling with servicemen, and you knew the less visible entrances, all the ways we used to sneak in, long past our curfew. You would have taught them to Cal. But earlier tonight you asked me why I don't see Bruno often. I have forgiven him, but I have not forgotten. In the end he chose me, but back then he chose you. He protected your secret. He remembered your bruises, you see. The bruises at the train station. They made a deep impression."

Lacey could hear her own voice unspooling the tale, so confident, so assured, when the night itself had felt broken and fragmentary, chips and shards. If she stopped to examine a single one, her energy would falter and dry up. She didn't wait for Edith to interrupt, but hurried on.

"I took the elevator to the room alone, the key cold in my hand," said Lacey. "Already I was sure I could not sleep that night, and might never sleep again. The wakefulness coursed through me like a wind, and it hasn't left since. The war was finally over, and with it, the turmoil that had forced us all to live in the present. Day by day. Now I could see time stretching behind and ahead of me. I knew my mother and father would be mostly unsuccessful in their search, and that our past was shattered. As for the future, I was doomed to be childless, a son or daughter the only thing I ever wanted after a life of being my parents' only, their precious.

"I, who longed to mother, had not been chosen—and you, who had run away from family, would bear my beloved's child. Papi and Mutti would never become doting grandparents. Cal would never cradle our son or daughter. I, who had adored being my husband's helpmeet, would be denied the one compensation I craved. For the rest of my life, I would live with this unfairness, and grow older and uglier, with nothing to show for it.

"There's an old-fashioned term for young couples. People used to say a girl and a boy had an 'understanding,' which meant that he knew he had to marry her, and she him. If they fooled around in a dark lane, if they were spotted arm in arm, they both knew what was coming. They were taken. Off the market. An 'understanding.' Naturally, misunderstanding the 'understanding' happened all the time, and deliberately so. The shelves in the other room are full of those stories.

"You wonder why I ramble here. I'll tell you why. All evening, perhaps all four and a half decades, I've pondered your and Cal's 'understanding.' Indeed, in order to wrap my mind around it, I had to change. I had no perspective back then. I was a loyal wife bleeding out her one great hope every month, and a loving daughter whose parents had disappeared on a fruitless rescue mission to the underworld. But I couldn't see myself in either of those roles. Not from the outside in. This was why I could never act onstage. Or on camera. It was impossible for me to inhabit another character, another woman, because I could not perceive of myself as a *circumstance* as well as a *being*. I had no inner narrator, the way you do, the way you always did. No examined life inside my life. In retrospect, I think that's why both you and Cal loved me so, and also how you two could betray me. Your relationship was a performance, a play, and not your essences. Another cigarette?" Lacey said, as Edith had been staring at the pack.

Edith shook her head, her mouth closed.

"More wine, then," Lacey said quickly, refilling the glasses. "The elevator took forever. Seven floors. My reflection shone in the brass doors, but dimly. A female outline. No face. The key's teeth bit into my palm, I was holding it so hard. On the fifth floor, the elevator stopped, and an old couple got on. They hesitated when they realized it was going up, but continued in anyway, to wait it out, the rise to my floor and then the descent to the lobby. They decided this together, with a glance and a shrug. No words passed between them. They were that intimate. A sob rose through me, and I tried to shove it down, but it came out like a gulping cough, and they both stared. In the man's eyes was pity; in the woman's eyes, something else, a weary sympathy, as in *Oh, honey, what did you expect?* When the doors opened, I fled. The corridors had never seemed so long and anonymous. I shoved the key in the door, opening and slamming it behind me.

"The room was dark. I flipped the switch. As a reminder, I had not entered this room in maybe five, six, months. I expected the same neutral chamber Cal and I always stayed in, the brass lamps on the bedside tables, the large bed with its Mission-style headboard. The landscapes on the walls in their thick gold frames. Papi and Mutti loved romantic pastoral scenes with the blind affection of lifetime city dwellers. They fantasized about the simpler country life. Hills and clouds and sunlight, and little people with their little sheep. Their taste had made the room a comforting place for me as well. It was just familiar enough to be mine, and just blank enough to feel like a break from my life.

"Imagine my surprise to find the bed shoved to the side and Cal's desk in the corner by the window. The desk that I'd given him, that he'd marveled at, calling himself the luckiest man alive. The desk beside which we now sit. My getaway bedroom looked like an office. A study. On the desk sat a typewriter beside stacks of papers, and on a shelf behind were piles of books. I walked over to it, my heart sick with dread, and read the pages stacked beside the typewriter. The scenes were from the movie Cal was filming—a movie about an old miner, forty-niner, who goes to the Sierra Madre to find the treasure that his friend buried twenty years ago, before the friend's lifelong rival, the villain, finds it first. Your handwriting covered the paper, crossing out exchanges, rewriting lines. When I opened a drawer, your hairbrush and makeup were inside it, along with a few packs of hose. In the wardrobe, spare dresses hung. Your dresses. Mostly. One of them was mine, a little gray peplum number I'd been missing since the day you moved out of my parents' house. On the bed pillow, I found one of your red-gold hairs."

"You gave that to me. The dress," said Edith.

"Did I?" said Lacey. She knew she hadn't, and that several other items—a couple of bracelets, a blouse, a pair of pearled dinner gloves—had gone missing over the years. "It must have fit you better." Her voice was casual, unalarmed. Truly, she had never minded. She never minded that.

Edith shot her a glance. "Did he show up there, too? At the room?"

"Eventually," said Lacey. "But I'm not finished with my side of this." She forced a gentle smile. It probably looked ghoulish, but she tried. "I knew that Cal was not a writer, in his heart of hearts, but the way he talked about his scripts, it was clear to me that he labored over them, that he mapped out the scenes and beats, and then a few people at the studio refined the dialogue, as they always do. Cal praised you now and then for speaking up on set, but you both talked about your casting job so much, I thought it was eating all your time. I could not imagine when you came here, to this hotel, to write for him, except at night, when Cal was home with me. How naive I was not to realize that some evenings while I slept, drugged deep to escape my suffering, he met you here and you wrote together, and did other things. That while I merely adorned Cal, you completed him. That Cal was crazy about me, but he could not live without you.

"So when you ran away without a word, taking his child and his future, and my best friend, the sister of my heart, maybe you thought you were saving us. Maybe you thought we could piece our marriage back together without you in the picture. But you were wrong. Our marriage failed, and Cal failed, and who knows, maybe he did or did not see that hill in the fog. His career was in ruins by then, and I had finally asked him for a divorce. Your sacrifice was not a sacrifice at all. It was a theft. You stole everything, and then you left, and I hated you for it. I still do. And that is what I have waited four decades to say."

17.

WITHOUT PAUSING FOR EDITH'S ANSWER, LACEY rose and went to her bedside phone, asking for their plates to be cleared, and canceled the order for the cappuccinos and liqueurs. They were beyond sampling and tasting. A single glass of cognac would be a better final course, a not-so-sweet one, with a little spice to last on the palate. She forced her voice not to slur as she spoke and repeated her order when the staff person hesitated. She could feel the drunkenness in her legs and kicked off her pumps and walked barefoot back to the table. It made her feel younger, being tipsy, with her feet naked on the rug. Edith had also risen, had gone to her bag, as if to take something from it, but instead she moved it farther to the side, away from obstructing the cart the men would come with.

They approached the desk at the same time, but when Edith did not sit Lacey remained standing, too. They faced each other, wary and erect, and though Lacey searched Edith's eyes, she could not predict her response.

"What happened with your parents?" said Edith finally. "What did they find in Europe?"

"After several months, the tracing service located only one surviving cousin at a displaced persons camp outside Bergen-Belsen," said Lacey. "She was frail, but she'd survived. Her whole family, still missing or dead. Mutti's mother and father, also missing or dead. The United States would not take the cousin, so eventually she went to Israel. She's still alive, a tiny thing. Her daughters care for her," she added. "As for Papi's side, his parents had been deported to Theresienstadt, the old Czech fortress the Germans used to house the Jews. Papi's father had been beaten so badly in the expulsion, he was mostly deaf and could no longer see from one eye. My grandmother had to lead him around. They also could not get visas to America. No sympathy for ethnic Germans here. So Papi set them up in the American zone, in a spa town called Hannesburg, where he knew a hotelier. They lived another ten years or so, comfortable but unhappy. They never got their bearings in Germany." Like Mutti's parents, Papi's family had loved Prague with all their hearts and never wanted to leave it. They'd clung to the city, their beloved hilly streets, their castle, and their statue-lined river bridge, and their loyalty had drowned them. "Mutti and Papi came home, inseparable for the rest of their lives. But they never laughed again."

"I'm sorry," said Edith. "They were kind people."

"After I told them what you did, your name did not cross their lips," said Lacey. "They completely wrote you out of their memories."

Edith did not reply to this, but her eyes shone and her face looked puffy and distorted by some suppressed emotion. She stalked to the bookshelves in the other room and began scanning the titles as if looking for something in particular. She was still there when the busboys came in to clear the plates. Lacey tipped them again and lit another cigarette.

"What are you looking for?" she said.

"I can't exactly say," said Edith.

Lacey sat down at the desk. "I met a girl from our camp cabin once, at a party in Hollywood. You weren't there. It was some occasion Mutti made me attend with her," said Lacey. She recalled a patio strung with Chinese lanterns, and a sudden grip on her arm ("Lacey Weber, is that you?"), a freckled face, a flash of recognition. Vera, whose father owned six paper mills. An intense conversation followed, full of *do-you-remembers*. "Vera said that no one else heard that your brothers were sick with scarlet fever. That it was probably a lie. That you always collapsed after Vaudeville Night. Performing cast you into a deep malaise. That the year before, you almost drowned yourself in the pond that same night. The counselors tried to persuade you out of performing again. When they didn't prevail, they asked your father to come retrieve you right after, to spare you. And the rest of us." Lacey couldn't see all of Edith in the other room, just the profile of her, standing still with her right hand resting on a shelf. "She also said the next summer, the summer I was in Prague, that you spent almost every day hacking through the woods, trying to find goldenseal for me. 'Oh, Lacey,' Vera said. 'She missed you terribly.' I asked about Vaudeville Night. Did you sing again? And she said yes, but you left early. Your last year, and you never said goodbye. To anyone."

"I never did," Edith said. "I suppose you see a pattern forming."

"The odd thing is, I accepted her news at the time. A whole summer, digging up dirty roots for me, who barely appreciated them. I was used to being adored. But now I can't understand why I carved such a place in your heart. I am a patently ordinary person. Stuffy, useless, and spoiled, too, if we're to be honest. Why did you love me so, and why did you feel you had to lie to me?"

Edith wiped her eyes with the inside of her wrist. "Ay, where do I begin," she mumbled. "I'm not sure you've ever understood me, Lace. That's the first problem. You think everyone makes mistakes the same way."

"Or maybe you didn't love me," said Lacey. "You loved what I possessed."

"I loved you," said Edith, her voice full.

"And Cal? Did you love him?"

Edith took a breath, then shrugged. "I couldn't."

"Because he was my husband."

"No," said Edith. "And I didn't hate Cal because he was a bastard, either. But both are true."

"You haven't asked what Cal said about you, to me," said Lacey. "You don't know how we often talked about you, but we did, a lot, especially before we married. I'd meet him on set, and we'd go to an Italian place with deep red booths, where he could put his arm around me and they made the most divine flaming coffees. Cal would tell me about which actor was driving him crazy, and I would tell him stories about Prague, and camp, and meeting you. I wanted you to be happy, you see. I didn't want you to feel abandoned when I fell in love, and I thought if Cal knew you and loved you, too, then we three could be a family. Looking back, I realize my condescending attitude in this. How cruel and self-absorbed I was to think that you wouldn't find your own happiness, your own heart. But I told Cal about your family and your beautiful voice and the bruises, and why you'd run away, and how I hadn't known true friendship until you taught it to me. He was jealous of us, you know. He had never trusted anyone as much as I trusted you, and sometimes after we three were together and you went home to your bungalow, he would slip his hands around mine and pull me to his chest and kiss me deeply, and make me say I loved him first, and most of all."

"Most of all," said Edith, her mouth twisting. "Funny thing for him to say."

Lacey squinted at her, head tilted back. It didn't hurt, the comment. Not after all these years. But in the candlelight, she could not tell if Edith looked more hideous or beautiful than ever. There was something mysterious about a face when sharp shadows carved it.

"I should leave," said Edith. "You've made your case. I accept it. But I want to say some things before I go." She did not close the distance between them, did not sit at the wreckage of their meal, did not grab her half-full glass. Instead, she stood by the shelves, one arm propped, leaning.

18.

"HAVE YOU EVER NOTICED HOW OFTEN, IN THE old fairy tales and fables, the teller is a servant or a slave?" said Edith. "Aesop. Scheherazade. Even the poor old tailor's wife who recounted her stories to the brothers Grimm. All of them powerless, downtrodden. Readers want to be dazzled by tales of fame and money, but everyone knows that wisdom, the true treasure, comes from a suffered life." Edith lingered on the last words, emphasizing them. "By that measure, it's hard to know which of us should be wiser and, by extension, which would give voice to the authentic truth tonight. Because my version of us is very different from yours. And in my mind, it's the right one.

"You start your story on the day I left you. My version starts on the day we met Cal for the first time. You were nineteen. I was twenty. Miraculously I had caught up on two years of missed school to get my high school diploma. None of it seemed real to me, but there I was, in a sunbaked city by the sea, with a family that loved me and asked nothing of me but that I be your friend. Although America was not yet at war, in your house the storms of loss and change already raged. Your mother returned from visiting her family in Prague for the last time, and we all moved out of the hotel, finally, and into the house in the hills that your father built. What splendor it was to wake to your tile bath, to your gleaming icebox, to the lemon trees in the yard. What a thrill to see your father's hotel thriving, to hear he might buy out his partner and own the whole thing. But what sorrow to watch your mother's mounting dread. All that year, she couldn't use a knife in the kitchen. She couldn't cut bread. She couldn't cut a peach. Her hands trembled too much. She threw herself into relief and refugee efforts. The victories were small. Countries like ours had buttoned up their borders.

"I don't know who suggested the auditions for you. Probably your papi. He believed in distractions. His whole career revolved around inventing a second, temporary life for people, a land of luxury and adventure. Step in for a weekend, and step out again, refreshed. These days, I could see him running one of those amusement park resorts, or a video game empire. You're frowning. You think your father had more class than that, with his hotels and racetracks. But he liked the big bucks, and class doesn't make the big bucks anymore. It's not the goal. Trust me. The minute I retired from my academy, the board hired a headmaster who devoted himself to firing long-term faculty and building a new athletic complex. *Champions* was his favorite word. Mine had been *prestige*.

"Your papi loved money and he had a nose for it. But he wasn't snobby. Not him. Remember how the high school wanted to place me in eighth-grade English at first, with my ignorance, and my reading skills so behind? But you and your father insisted no, I'd enroll with you, in your classes, and you'd catch me up personally. And you did. You sat with me that first year and listened to me read aloud and checked my spelling and grammar. I advanced quickly. I was like a wilted plant finally touched by rain. I became an honors student by the end. Our teachers encouraged us both to apply for college. But for college, there were two problems: your grades were average, and I had no one to pay my tuition. If we could have combined ourselves into one person, then we would have aced the applications. Remember how we joked about that? No? I expect you wouldn't. You forget anything that derails you from feeling superior to me. Your parents were not big believers in universities, anyway; they were smart, and they read novels and magazines, but intellectualism was cumbersome to them. It ruined a perfectly good time.

"Perhaps this is a digression, but bear with me: I have a distinct memory of you and your mother, side by side, reading the same German storybook on the train west. The southern window's light bathed you in gold. You were leaning into her; she was stroking your hair. You read much faster than your mother, and you waited for her, each time, to finish the page, lick her finger, and turn to the next. After a while, Mutti looked up and saw me watching you both.

"'Don't let her marry a fool,' she said. 'She'll choose once, and she'll never choose again.'

"I don't suppose you remember that, either. It was a prickly statement, one of Mutti's zingers, and you liked to put those out of your mind. But it was the first time your mother acknowledged the power of our friendship, mine and yours, and your worst vulnerability. Once you decide you love someone, you can't undo it. You've cast your lot and you won't go back.

"Neither of your parents raised the question of me moving out, but I was too proud to freeload. After graduation, I found a position as a secretary in an insurance office and began saving for my own apartment. There wasn't any need for you to work, so Mutti began taking you to auditions. Plays, movies. In the morning, I dressed in one of my two cheap gray suits and rode a bus downtown to type memos all day, and you lounged about and drank too much coffee and fixed yourself beautiful and walked into a dark theater or a bright studio room and fumbled through another attempt at fame. You didn't really want the parts; you just liked the process of being a new feast for new

eyes. The propositions and dates that followed! With so many young
men off to war in France and the Pacific, it was lean pickings for most
gals then. Not for you. You're right—you couldn't inhabit any role but
your own—but, as Lacey, you triumphed. I became your auxiliary,
your guide, and your guardian in a stream of evenings, my own dates
always slightly disappointed by me in the beginning but liking me immensely by the end. I knew how to put men at ease, to let them know
we could have a good time, but we didn't have to feign romance. When
your mother asked me for reports, she never asked about my progress;
she knew marriage would always be a sham for me. I dutifully told her
what I guessed: you were charmed, giddy, sometimes briefly smitten,
but you were not in love.

"Then a Saturday came with an audition notice for the Danube, an
old theater downtown. It was a student affair, run by one of the acting
schools, and not very promising. No budget to pay anyone. But that
day was also one of the rare rainy winter days, and you and I were
bored, so we decided to go. Alone. Without Mutti, who was off to one
of her Zionist fundraisers. And after we got drunk on Bloody Marys
at breakfast, you insisted that I should try out, too. Just for fun. A
dare. We painted me with your makeup, and I wore one of your loosest
dresses, a navy shift that actually looked quite good on me, and you
drove us, weaving, wipers flapping, through the low pastures of stucco
until it became a forest of brick and stone.

"It smelled of piss outside the Danube, and several of the bulbs on
the marquee lights had been smashed and not replaced, but there was
a throng of young bohemians smoking under the overhang outside.
No neat tea dresses and belted waists for them. Some women wore all
black and had their hair capped to chin length, while others had draped
themselves in colorful fabrics like wandering minstrels. 'Wait,' I said,
after you parked the car and I re-fixed us both as best I could, while
you watched me quizzically. You couldn't understand why anyone

would want to look young and shabby and angry at the disappointing world, but already I could sense the power, the vitality of new ideas, emanating from the gathering. It electrified me. This, this, was what I had been missing all my life.

"We were still drunk when we darted through the drizzle and the crowd to sign our names to a list. The musty cave of the Danube made my nose prickle and I had a little sneezing fit. When I recovered, I felt myself sobering enough to assess the power dynamics within. For all the people milling around, acting important, their focus was one table by the stage, with two young men and two young women, talking animatedly, clipboards heaped before them. These would be our judges, and, as I assessed them, my heart did a flip. The attractive young woman on the right—who had tight curly red hair and a witchy face, with the kind of mouth that always curled downward—saw my gaze and gave me a wink. It was so bold, so saucy, the wink. It said everything. My knees went weak. I could barely stand."

"I knew," Lacey interrupted fiercely. "You thought I didn't because we never discussed it. If that's what this story is about, you could have trusted me. I knew."

"That is not what this story is about," said Edith. She finally pulled a book from the shelves and sat down at the desk, but the book had no dust jacket, and her palm hid the title on the spine.

"Go on, then," said Lacey.

"Meanwhile, you had found a copy of the audition scene and we read it together. It was a love scene, choppily written, with a twist at the end. You would probably butcher it but look adorable enough to get some votes from the men. Still, I realized we both had to ace our auditions to stay in this place, this enticing new world, so I gave you some advice.

"'Listen,' I said to you. 'If you want to make a man think about kissing you, you gaze into his eyes, then at his lips, and then into his eyes again, just the tiniest flick, like you can't bear it anymore. Like it's almost too much, your lust. You do that, you make your fellow actually want you, and you might get the part.'"

"I remember you telling me that," Lacey interrupted again.

"Of course you do," said Edith. "Because it worked. You got called before me, and you stumbled through some lines, but you did the eye trick and the fellow looked like he wanted to fall on his knees and propose right then. Then I got called——"

"And that whole theater, all those snobby, self-interested people, went silent," said Lacey. "You could have heard a pin drop on a bale of cotton. It was a scene we'd already watched a dozen times, and we were hanging on every word anyway. I knew you were good, but that day I realized again you could be great."

"You remember, then," said Edith, and her hands fumbled as she pulled out a cigarette and lit it. "And the party afterward?"

"It was at some dingy apartment building with a big courtyard. The rain stopped, so we stayed outside, but the damp air wrecked my hair. A lot of the people there opposed the draft," said Lacey. "I remember that, because I'd never heard of Americans being too cowardly to fight Hitler. It shocked me."

"You wanted to leave," said Edith. "But you stayed because I begged."

Lacey didn't recall Edith asking her to stay, only that the night dragged on at first. All those people with their silly anger, fussing about a peace that couldn't exist. *My grandparents are missing, probably dead,* she'd wanted to shout at them. *Keep your plowshares. I'll take the sword.*

"We went inside for more gin," said Lacey, "and you disappeared, with *her,* I suppose."

"Yes, with her," said Edith, smiling faintly. "Sweet Marjorie."

"You'd never left me before," said Lacey. "Not among so many strangers."

"That's when you met Cal," said Edith. There was something careful in her voice, like a cat creeping up on a mouse. "Can I tell you what I think happened?"

"By all means," said Lacey. She raised her chin.

"He came looking for *me* to offer me a part, and you talked him out of it. Because after all those auditions, you had nothing to show, and I had done one, only one, and they wanted me immediately. What would you tell your mother? She would be so disappointed in you."

Lacey forced Mutti's frowning visage from her mind. "He did want to offer you the part," she declared. "But I'm not petty like that."

Wasn't she, though? Didn't she look into Cal's spellbound expression and tell him that Edith had only tried out as a lark, that she didn't want to be an actress, that neither of them could bother with a student production? Didn't she turn it into a joke, with her best carefree Lacey laugh: the shoddily written scene, the mildewed theater, the people with their pretentious outfits and vain ideas about pacifism? Didn't she say she was just practicing for her next studio audition, and didn't she look at Cal, his eyes, his lips, his eyes again, just a flicker, because there was something in his intensity that made her lust for him? Choose him. Above all the rest. As their flirtation grew too heated, she remembered the Czech army captain and found a way to duck out—then waited a very long time for Edith to come back, Edith's eyes fever-bright. *My stomach's all fizzy,* Lacey remembered saying. *Can we go home now, please?* Edith obliged reluctantly, lingering as people began reciting poems from memory. Didn't they both abandon the scene together, though? Only, Lacey left her phone number in Cal's pocket, and Edith left Marjorie nothing but the memory of the pressure of her lips.

"I didn't like those people," said Lacey. "They were attacking the president. His generals."

"But Cal was different?"

"He would have fought, and bravely, too," declared Lacey. "He tried to enlist three times and they turned him down because of his flat feet."

In any war conversation, Cal whipped out his enlistment story. It did not buy him admission to the brotherhood, but it excused him enough to be accepted as a patriot. And then a stroke of fortune arrived the day after Cal and Lacey got engaged: Cal received a letter from the FBI, signed by Hoover himself, inviting him to apply to the bureau to become an agent. He'd been elated, cracking the remaining bottle of champagne to celebrate. *I knew you were good luck, Lace,* he pronounced. But when the first interview exposed Cal's connections to Communists during his student days, his application was closed. Cal was demoralized, even with his new job at the studio. *I didn't believe their nonsense,* he'd said about the student crowd. *I just needed a cast and a stage.*

"He wanted to serve," Lacey insisted.

"You still haven't told me what you said to him that night," said Edith.

"I thought it would be too much for you," Lacey lied now, because after the long talk with Vera, the girl from their camp cabin, she had justified the night that way. "You were so exhausted and forlorn after acting. Those performances took something from you every time. And what if the night came when you didn't have anything left? I didn't want you to destroy yourself."

"To destroy myself?" Edith repeated.

"You found out on your own anyway. I remember," said Lacey. "You went off to your own auditions after that and got no callbacks. You could have stopped time with your talent, but you didn't have the figure they wanted," she said. "That made you mad at me, and that's when you moved out and got your bungalow."

"I moved out because I wanted my own life," said Edith.

"You just did it to us one day," said Lacey. "No note. All your things, gone. A couple of hairpins on the floor. Mutti and Papi were terribly hurt. I didn't show it, because I wanted to support you, but I was hurt, too."

"Your mother never gave me my own key." Edith's voice was cold. "Always scratching at the door like a stray cat. That wasn't me. That was never me."

"They offered you their home."

"They gave me a ticket, which is more than I can say . . . ," said Edith. Her mouth twisted like she had a bad taste. "Well, I knew you wouldn't see what you did."

What you did. Lacey felt her whole body buzz.

"All this time, I thought it was his fault entirely," she retorted. "The sex. That Cal forced you, because I couldn't imagine you enjoying it. You didn't like men that way. What did he offer you? A credit? A role? Or are you telling me now that letting Cal screw you was your colossal revenge against me for keeping you from some two-bit part in a penniless student play?"

"I liked men fine," said Edith. "The interesting ones."

"Did Cal seduce you, then?"

Edith's eyes narrowed, but she didn't say anything.

"Did he wrap his big hands around your hands and pull you to his chest and kiss you?" Lacey was torturing herself now.

"You know, I saw him with another woman that night," said Edith, "a little mousy thing, in the bedroom next to me and Marjorie. Cal had a type. He liked the ones with bruises. The affairs were a compulsion for him, a bad habit, quite separate from loving you, at which he excelled." Her voice deepened. "I tried to warn you. Your mutti did, too, but you never listened."

"Cal was a gentleman with me," Lacey said. Her breath would not stay steady, and she gasped at air. "Always."

"He was," said Edith. "You were his queen. He loved you all his life, and I have no doubt that you were the one who flashed in his mind's eye the moment before he crashed into that hill."

"Then why?" Lacey said. "I can't understand why, if you hated him, if you knew who he was—and if you knew I loved him and he loved me, why?"

Edith was silent. She set aside the book. She took the tube of Chap-Stick from her purse and ran it over her lips. When she finally spoke, her voice was low. "Why do you think I ran away and didn't come back? Because I don't have a good answer. I didn't have it then, and I still don't."

"He touched you first, I imagine," Lacey said, closing her eyes. Her head was spinning.

"Lacey, don't."

"He took off your clothes. Or did you take them off? Was it a wild, ripping sort of frenzy, or a slow seduction?"

"Lace."

"Only here, in the hotel? Or in your bungalow? You don't usually get pregnant from one time."

"Sometimes you do," said Edith sadly.

"I find it hard to believe anything you say."

"I don't blame you. I don't believe myself."

It was not an apology. It was not even a distant cousin to an apology.

"You said the suffering person would tell a different story, a wiser one," said Lacey. "I don't think a wise story ends with *I don't know what happened and then I ran away.*"

"Maybe that's not our ending, then," said Edith.

"I've sorted through dozens of interpretations myself. In my sillier narcissistic moments, I wondered if you had been in love with me," said Lacey, "and jealous of my affection for Cal."

Edith shook her head. An emphatic no.

"But you never tried to kiss me," said Lacey. "You would have

tried, if that were true. Besides, getting pregnant with Cal's baby
to make me finally notice you is simpleminded, and you were never
simpleminded. I'm the simpleminded one. So then, I wondered if you
were trying to expose who Cal truly was. To show me his horrify-
ing flaws. But why waste your own body on that enterprise? There
were other women, apparently. Briefly, I wondered, horrified, if he
had attacked you. But Cal admired you. So maybe you made a bet and
lost, or a bargain I could never understand." She cocked her head. "*We*
don't have an ending, though. There is no *we*. There hasn't been for
forty-four years."

She liked how her voice resounded, loud and clear, but Edith
seemed distracted by the desk.

"What did you do with the script? The one I was writing? I left it
on this desk," she said.

"About the miner?"

"No. The other one."

"I burned it."

"I thought as much." A hesitation. "Did you read it?"

"No. A few pages."

"It was about a friendship. Two girls, one rich, one poor, in a frontier city, facing life together." Edith sounded wistful.

"I know. I read the beginning." Lacey felt heavier than ever in her
life.

"It was a new kind of Western," Edith said. "No one would have
known what to do with it for a while, but after the studios broke up,
it's anyone's guess." Her hand swept the tablecloth, as if smoothing an
invisible page. "Things were changing. I could feel it in the air. Cal felt
it, too. But what made me exhilarated made Cal afraid. He liked the
limits of his profession. Of all the people at that party after the Danube, he was the most conventional."

"Except for me," said Lacey.

Edith smiled, a sad, close-lipped smile. "You're not conventional at
all. You're a true original, Lacey-Lucie Weber-Crane."

Lacey sat back and absorbed this. It was the kind of compliment
that used to please her, back when she believed it herself. Then she
said: "Why did you write that script? So many stories you could tell—
why write of our friendship?"

"Maybe it was the only story I had," said Edith. "Or wanted to
have."

Her voice went hoarse, and for a moment the young Edith shim-
mered in Lacey's memory, stepping behind her onto the train to the
West, her bruised face shining.

"And yet the stories about female friendship rarely end well," said
Lacey. "I've had years to read on this, and I've come to my own hum-
ble wisdom on the matter. Maybe it's not the wisdom of the powerless, but the wisdom of a prisoner. Maybe the two have some kinship.
Look how few tales there are. Of sisters, many. Of best friends, hardly
any. Athena and Pallas were best friends, girls together, god and titan,
training to fight in the wars of men. But all it took was one interfering
move by Athena's father and she accidentally stabbed Pallas dead. She
lost her friend forever. How many of us have done the same: stabbing
our friends by stealing their crushes, or by simply having more—a
better dress, a better house, children who excel—while they have less?

"No, I think you wrote the script because you knew that true, devoted friendship between women is a fantasy that life dismantles. No
matter how strong we are, how hard we love, life is stronger still. True
friendship could only exist in the dream world where you conjured
it." Lacey looked not at her friend, but at the bookshelves, lined with
volumes.

"How I wish it were not so!" she said. "But you only have to follow
our timelines to see the destruction play out, over and over. As girls,
we meet, we fall for each other, we see our futures wrapped as tightly

together as our girlhood life. For months, we live in our makeshift home. Our cabin in the woods. You lie on your bunk; I lie on mine, and we whisper to the moonlight about our hopes and fears. Our bodies are smooth, not fully blossomed and split by puberty. The pond waits outside to immerse us to the neck, its cool, buoying touch all that we know of being held.

"From the safety of the cabin, boys and men are ideals, or enemies. Shadows that cross the windows outside. We read about *them*, and their friendships and loyalties. *Their* stories are always about war and death. External fates. Achilles and Patroclus destroyed by the opposing army. Christ and his apostles torn apart by Pharisees. Their betrayals are about bravery and brotherhood, or the lack of it.

"But you and I can't live within our thin wooden walls forever, studying the fates of men. Only a summer. Or two, or three. Our bodies become women's bodies. And soon, everywhere, mothers begin eyeing us, weighing our chances for a good match. *We* are a good match, we two girls, best friends, blood sisters, but it is impossible to choose each other. Choosing each other is choosing the past. We need futures. Already the cabin seems smaller, flimsier—hardly the stout houses of the boulevards and avenues, the domains of our mothers and fathers. And inside, certain parts of us begin melting to puddles whenever certain boys, or girls, pass by. It's not long before we're being touched in the dark, by others. After dances, after dates, we go with them, our crushes, and we are pulled apart, to separate rooms. We whisper about this when we get back together, but the old conversational flow hits pauses and full stops. We giggle. We squirm. It's impossible to know if our bodies hum and yearn in the same way. We try to explain the sensations, but it makes us feel more alone.

"The longings turn to dates, to steadies, to weddings, and nights in the arms of others. Being a wife or a not-wife separates us further. No more whispers in the bunks, no more speculations about *who* and *when.* We have arrived at those distant destinations. Breakfast must be served, lunch and dinner must be planned, or our career outside the home summons and grinds. There is no cabin of dreams anymore. It has receded to memory.

"If we become mothers at the same time, a second sisterhood begins, but suddenly our affection pales in comparison to our love for our children. We know, for the first time, that we would choose our sons and daughters over anyone, over our husbands, over each other. Even over ourselves. Unlike the men, who fight soldiers and centurions, we women must fight our own hearts. Betray our own girlhood desires."

Lacey summoned a big breath and talked through the hitch in her voice. "We cannot love equally," she concluded. "We will never love equally. Our faithlessness begins in love. And that is why your story, your version, will always be a lie. It is why you cannot explain what you did to me, even now. Because you would have to admit to yourself that you wanted a child as badly as I did. You wanted it more than you loved me. And more than you loved Cal."

"Oh, Lacey," said Edith. "You would see it that way."

"Tell me another way to see it."

Edith raised an eyebrow. "Can't there exist a woman who desires never to marry or bear children?"

Lacey had prepared for this. "The witch in the forest," she said. "She is an exception. She lives outside the boundaries of convention, but she suffers the conventions as much as anyone. She can be a figure of power, a bestower of gifts—as long as she accepts her permanent exile." She shrugged. "Maybe you became her eventually."

"The witch is always old, in the stories," reflected Edith. "No one bothers to tell what she did when she was young."

"She ran away, obviously," Lacey said. "Or she stayed in the cabin of dreams until it became something else entirely. A magic place, unreachable, except by the occasional wanderer."

She waited for Edith to challenge her. Edith continued to look contemplative, unbothered.

"You assume that the witch never finds another witch," said Edith finally. "That she is doomed to be the only one. Or that the lady queen won't find another queen to pal around with."

Lacey was about to reply, but Edith went on. "In some parts of the world, it's clans of women who run things together," Edith mused. "And let's not get started on how poverty or segregation might affect your theories."

In their youth, Edith always liked changing the radio channel, searching for a better song, when a perfectly good one would come on if they only waited. She seemed to consider it an act of self-improvement, seeking the new, confusing herself with possibility.

"I'm not talking about clans or poverty or segregation," said Lacey. "I'm talking about the friendship of a lifetime. A great platonic love, young to old. Above all others." *Über alles.* The German came to her, not as the snatch of a horrible patriotic song, but in Mutti's dark, warning voice.

"There must be other outsiders than the witch, though," Edith said, head tipped back, scrutinizing the shelves. "There's clever what's-her-name."

"Clever what's-her-name who did I-don't-know-what-happened?" Lacey said sharply.

Edith winced, then turned from the books to regard Lacey. "I'm sorry about what happened to *you*, all the miscarriages," she said, earnest and frank. "It broke my heart to watch you suffer."

"It didn't break it enough," said Lacey. "I don't accept your sympathy. I won't."

"That's fair," said Edith. "I offer it anyway."

"One thing that casts my theory in doubt is how you fell that day," said Lacey. "As if all your bones had turned to dust inside your body.

You plummeted. You didn't try to stop yourself, not with your hands and feet. You didn't curl to protect the child. It was the most extraordinary sight. You looked at me, and then you dropped. Do you remember what you were thinking?"

"No," said Edith.

"But you saw me."

"I saw you."

"And seeing me made you fall?"

"No," said Edith. "I slipped. And all I know is that, when I stopped falling, I no longer wanted the child to die."

The last claim was clear and audible, but it wouldn't sink in. A clog of syllables, a bad translation. *I . . . wanted the child to die.* It contradicted Edith's hand on her belly in the canyon, the fingers curled, protective. Lacey grabbed at her wine. She had to take two swallows before she could formulate a reply. "Before then, you did? Want it to——?"

"I wanted it out of my body. From the instant I knew I was pregnant," Edith said, defiance in her voice, as if she stood accused of loving the child. Something in her expression contracted, folded itself smaller. "For a while, that desire felt like the same thing as wishing it dead."

"What changed?"

"I saw you. And it hurt, the fall. It shocked me how much it hurt," said Edith. "The pain made me realize I could no longer go on being numb and hopeless to my situation."

For years, Lacey's mind had replayed Edith's protective hand in the canyon. She had assumed her friend had always yearned for a child, despite the facts of her life. It never occurred to her that the fall was a turning point: Edith didn't want the baby; then, after she fell, she did. And yet the small swell contradicted Edith's statements. Their city was full of actresses who got in trouble and got out with their stomachs still flat as asphalt. Surely Edith could have found a doctor in time.

Lacey said so.

"I don't like doctors," Edith said. "I didn't trust what they would do to me."

"You always had your own remedies," said Lacey, remembering the cool juice of the jewelweed, the blue bottle of goldenseal.

"There was a botanica that sold the tea I needed, but the woman told me I could feel sick for days or weeks. And it might not succeed. I couldn't risk it, not with the production as it was."

The production. As if that wretched movie had mattered to anyone, then or now.

"They had to edit Cal's cry from the footage," said Lacey. "He cried out when you fell, while the actor was faking his own drowning. It makes an odd gap in the soundtrack."

"I saw that, in the film," said Edith.

Suddenly Cal was present with them again, the way he'd galloped through the stream, his trousers soaked to the hips. The fear and love in his face. Yes, it had been love.

"I cried out, too," said Lacey. "I remember. But the sound didn't get caught by the mics."

Edith shifted and stared at the book on the desk.

"I felt like I was bleeding to death that entire year," said Lacey. "Did you know that?"

Her friend shook her head. "Of course I did," she muttered. "I would have done anything to trade places with you."

The words hung in the air.

"I didn't mean that," said Edith.

Lacey almost smiled, a bitter smile, but instead she stuck another cigarette in her lips and lit it. She took several puffs.

"What's the book?" she said. "The one you picked."

"Oh," said Edith, holding up the spine. "*Little Women*. I remember us talking about it at camp. You said you were an Amy, and I was a Jo."

"That's because I wanted Laurie in the end. I loved him," said Lacey. "Jo was too complicated for me."

"Yes," said Edith. "She was a gambler, not a player."

Lacey frowned. "I don't remember Jo having vices," she said.

For a moment, Edith's head bent to the book. She appeared to be listening to some inner narrator, and then she nodded. Decisive. The headmistress.

"Two people sit down at a poker table," she said. "The player thinks he is playing a game. With a little luck, a little skill, he might win. The gambler knows that he is making a series of bargains. He sees each card, each decision, as a chance to go deeper or get out. There is no middle path for the gambler. No 'I'll just play for a little while and see what happens.'" She paused to regard Lacey. "You follow me so far?"

Lacey nodded, although somehow she knew that she didn't want to hear came next. "I don't think the March girls even played whist," she observed. "Nice girls like them."

"The gambler will either win it all or lose it all. No in-between," said Edith, ignoring her. She was getting into it now, her voice deepening, her eyes dark. "The problem is, most people are players. And they think the gambler is cruel when he takes everything, and degenerate when he loses all he has.

"I recognized Cal as a gambler from the first time I met him. After I left Marjorie that night, I saw him talking to you, and saw you escape him. I was the mousy girl who went into that room with Cal and let him kiss and fondle me, and then I grabbed him by the balls and told him to stay away from you. Brave move. Foolish move. I might as well have painted a sign over you, advertising 'Treasure Below.' Pure gold. Cal pursued you and fell in love with you instead. Deeply.

He wanted to make you a good life. That's all true. He wanted to be a brave soldier and a devoted husband and a brilliant director, but he also wanted it all, and all included me."

Edith sat rigid, her neck corded. She could have been made of stone. She didn't touch her face or blink or waver over her words like liars usually do. She was speaking lies, she had to be, but she looked like she was telling the truth. Lacey tried to shut her ears, but the voice went on, hard and bright.

"Meanwhile, I needed a chance," Edith said. "I saw what you got: daughter of a rich man, wife of a famous one. I saw what I got: insurance adjustor assistant secretary. Drab female in a drab office growing drabber until she dies. I took the casting job you arranged, even though I knew it put me in Cal's way, alone, without you. I made sure to date others in the studio. I even had an obvious fling with Sandra, that gorgeous gamine in the editing department, to show I was not interested in men. Not that that ever works. One night, after the auditions closed up, Cal cornered me and implied a trade. A promotion, a credit, in exchange for you-know-what. I told him no. I told him no for weeks, even though the production's script was wooden and predictable, and the actors hated it. I told him no until the evening I eavesdropped on the producers' wives in the restroom at a production dinner. They were mooning over Cal, his looks and his charm, and also lamenting that their husbands might fire him soon. That evening, I worked on the first thirty pages and left them on Cal's desk, with a note explaining what I'd overheard in the restroom. He saw the quality in my edits and begged me to do the rest. He was up to the hilt in debt already, buying your new house, filling it with your expensive taste in furniture. He needed me. You needed me. So I rewrote the whole script, trepidatious about Cal's bargain. And I misjudged Cal again. Because when the next meetings rolled around, and the producers praised him for the changes, Cal credited me. Me. Edie, from casting. At a meeting with all the writers, he named me chief script stenographer on this movie. He didn't let anyone bat an eye. And afterward he promised he would take my next script straight up the line. I was sure he'd waived my end of his deal, because I'd rescued him from a tight spot. And because I was good." The last words burst from her and she paused. "I was really good," she repeated softly, her eyes downcast.

Lacey resisted the urge to speak. She had to hear everything. It had taken her the whole afternoon and part of this evening to muster the courage to hear it all.

"Cal set me up in that room in your father's hotel," continued Edith, "and I worked all day on the production and wrote at night. Cal met me, and we went over the scenes to the new movie, my original story. The collaboration was magical. The loneliness and grief that always overtook me, that always rubbed me out after acting and singing, didn't come because the words were there, still on the page, and Cal was there, listening. He was a first-class enthusiast, remember? He could make you believe in yourself and summon the best you had. He poured the gin, he posed the twists. In his glow, I typed like crazy. We read the scenes aloud and revised them on the spot. I forgot the gamble and became a player, and that was my great error. Because Cal never stopped gambling. He played a long game. As the success of his production grew assured, as my new script unfolded with his help, he pressured me again. He declared he was mad for me. He said his lust was eating him alive." She paused, seeing Lacey's face. "I'm sorry. I know you don't want to believe any of this about him. I've never wanted to tell you."

Lacey felt a wetness in her eyelashes, but she kept her voice steady. "I have had plenty of time to accept it," she said.

"Eventually he wore me down. I gave in, one night when we were drunk." Edith shrugged, but her mouth scowled. "It meant nothing to me, being touched by him, except that I knew it would hurt you. But deep inside, I thought it might also solve the impasse in my position, that if Cal and I went to bed together, I could hold something over him. Someone he didn't want to lose. Me. Or you. And I was right. After that night, Cal left me alone, out of guilt or regret, I suppose. Maybe his curiosity died. I was unexpectedly careless, though. One clumsy groping with him, and I got pregnant. When I told Cal about it, expecting blame or denial, he said it was a sign. We were meant to create together. Of course, a woman like me would not want the child; he knew a doctor who would get rid of it, but couldn't I *see*? Our 'mistake' had been a mistake of the flesh, but not of the spirit. The conception *proved* there was something between us, some masterpiece to be made. Cal would climb to lasting fame, and I would be hitched to him, to Cal's career, as Cal's muse-wife, his handmaiden. The lust was over, but the true marriage of our minds could begin. I would become a second you. I can't tell you how the dream excited and yet disturbed me. You know how persuasive he could be. And for the first time in my life, I could see a real horizon. It was everything I wanted, and yet nothing I wanted. I didn't get rid of the child, because it was the one card I had left to play." She hesitated again, watching Lacey. "This story, it upsets you. It makes Cal's love for you seem like a lie from the beginning. From the Danube. But Cal would have pursued you to the ends of the earth. He worshipped you, body and soul, from the moment you met."

A blankness had descended through Lacey. "Luckiest man alive," she said thickly, "that he can't hear us now. He can't know how deeply we've both come to despise him and smear his memory." She was on a stage, in the spotlight. She was speaking to an audience, but her lines jumbled in her mouth.

Edith jerked back, her eyes wide.

"You still side with him," she said, "when he forced me into it."

Sides. As if there had been sides to that day, that night, instead of a formless shadow that had risen over the rest of her life.

"No," said Lacey. "I heard everything you said."

Edith considered this, then nodded warily, studying Lacey as if for the first time.

"You can borrow the book," said Lacey. "Have it for your trip home."

She didn't like how relieved Edith looked, as if they'd covered it all, and now it was time for good night.

19.

"YOU DIDN'T ASK WHAT HAPPENED BETWEEN CAL and me after," said Lacey. "Only how he died."

"I guess I thought you threw him out," said Edith. "For a while, anyway."

"I left a pile of ash on the desk," said Lacey. "Your script, or yours and his. Out of respect for Papi, I doused the embers with water so the room would not be damaged. And then I left. I saw Cal coming into the hotel as I was leaving, but I knew all the staff staircases and he never spotted me. Once Cal had gotten into the elevator, I found Bruno and made him swear on his life that he hadn't seen me enter, hadn't fetched the key for me. That no one was to reveal to Cal that I had been in the room. That way, he would think it was you.

"Then I went home, and stripped from my clothes, my blood-crusted pads, and got in the bath. I sank myself to the head and plunged under a few times. I wanted to die. I wanted to die so that you and Cal would feel regret. So that you would be ashamed. Forever marked, like Cain. I tried to drown. But my lungs would always force me to the surface, and I would sit up gasping. The water was pink and cool by the time Cal arrived. I heard him enter the bedroom and toss down his keys, but he didn't come in. When I finally emerged, shivering and wrapping myself in a robe, he was kneeling on the floor. He begged me to forgive him, and blamed you for bewitching him, and also claimed he was so lonely and melancholy, he hadn't felt right about touching me. Even when we had made love ever so gently, it had felt like a violation. One night, late, he'd given you a ride home and it happened. It *happened*, he said, just like you did, like two grown adults were not in control of their bodies and minds. He said you had always been besotted with him and he had had a moment of weakness.

"He was lying, of course. By then, I knew the only thing you cared about had been that pile of papers on the desk, and whatever you carried inside you that was yours alone. I had burned the first to ash. Over the second, I had no control. But I could keep my life, my station, as Cal's wife, his star rising by the day, and hold his arm at the parties and premieres. And I did. I would not forgive him, but we could stay married; I would spend his money and he could bed whomever he wanted. Your condition made it clear that the miscarriages were the fault of my body, and I lost all desire for lovemaking, linked as it was to my horror of bleeding, and seeing you fall, and your palm on your belly and his palm covering yours.

"I told Papi to close our room at the hotel, and to move the desk back to Cal's studio. He did what I asked. My parents were devastated from their trip to Europe, and they registered the change in the three of us—you gone, Cal and I estranged—but my pain was the ripple of a tossed pebble after a boulder had splashed. Their hopes had been dashed for Mutti's parents, and Papi's family was struggling with their health and relocation. My shattered marriage was something that could be fixed, with time. With patience. They knew. They had done it, too. 'You deserved better,' Papi said to me. His eyes were tender. 'You hold your little girl in your arms, and already you hate the man who would hurt her, the man who is probably still a boy, holding his mummy's hand. And you think, *If that little bastard comes within a mile of here, and I will fight him. I will tear him to pieces.* But you can't find that boy; your daughter is the one who will. She grows up, and she chooses that fellow over there, *him*, she needs him, that little bastard, and you cannot deny her what she wants. You loved Cal. You chose him. I'm sorry that he is such a fool.'

"'A thousand days,' Mutti told me one day, gripping my arm. 'That is what it will take you to forgive him. No less. But more? That is just you nursing the tit of your pain.'

"As usual, Papi was dear and Mutti was right, and after three or four years of me pretending to be Cal's loving wife, a certain cynical fondness returned to our relationship. Cal was a good dancer and conversationalist. He remembered holidays with lavish gifts. He was always proud to introduce me around. In turn, I flirted with the right studio men to keep us on the lists for the right parties. You could say we had an 'understanding.'

"But without you to mask Cal's flaws as a director, his wishy-washiness began to show. After two flops, he was assigned to a different position in the studio. He had a fancy title, but it was really a screening job. Eight hours at a desk, reading scripts, taking meetings. Ushering other people's ideas through the system. And then the studio system broke to pieces, and massive layoffs swept across the industry. Cal kept his head down and worked harder than ever, but someone dredged up his student connections, and one day they fired him for being a Red. Just like that. Here's a crate, pack your things, and the chap from security is waiting to escort you out of the building. Cal's film career was over. Forever. He was thirty-five years old.

"If Cal hadn't been married, he might have left the city, pursued another life, but he had me to support, and my comfortable life, so he got another job, making TV commercials. It was cheap, tedious work. All his pent-up anger and humiliation had nowhere to go. He started drinking, and spending nights away from home, obvious nights that embarrassed me. It became clear he had a gambling problem, too. You are right about that. Cal was always a sucker for a bet, and having nothing left of himself to play, he gambled our nest egg from Papi. I would have stayed Cal's faithful wife if he had remained well, but he became sick and addicted, and I couldn't watch him destroy himself. Cal would have to dry out or I'd divorce him. One day, I told him so in no uncertain terms."

Lacey did not let herself remember Cal's face that afternoon, how his mouth had caved inward with disbelief when she'd uttered the word *divorce*. She did not hear his shocked cry or note his abject silence, and ignored the bitter, suspicious Cal that emerged later, accusing her of cheating, of betraying him, of flinging herself at other men. She blocked out her own sobs, on her long nights alone, after he moved out. She blocked out her hollow dawns. She refused to recall how tenderly Cal had spoken to her on the phone two days before he died, promising he was finally on the mend, that he would do anything to deserve her again, and how she'd slowly, gently hung up on him.

Instead, she opened the novel she'd been reading earlier and pulled out the faded envelope. "After he died, I had his desk moved back to our house. I found this inside it. It's dated about a month before the plane crash, a few weeks after my ultimatum. You see—it's your address in his handwriting, and your reply in yours, *RETURN TO SENDER*. Cal must have hired someone to track you down, and then he mailed you this. You sent it back without opening it." Lacey smoothed the envelope with her hand. "It's thin," she said. "If you hold it to the light, you can see the check inside it. For a considerable amount of money. Especially for a man who was living beyond his means, whose debts would force his widow to sell their house and move back in with her parents. There must be some note with it," she said. "You didn't read it."

"You didn't, either," said Edith.

"Would you like to read it now?" said Lacey, her tone light. She held up the envelope. "You were never curious about whether he still had feelings for you, whether he wanted to see his child?"

"*His* child," said Edith. "Why not *mine?*"

Lacey refused to be detoured. "He was the father, was he not?"

"Yes," said Edith.

"And you were too far along, I think, for any procedures."

"That's true."

"So either you kept it, or you gave it up."

"What do you think I did?" There was a note of challenge in Edith's voice.

Lacey met her eyes. "In the end, I think you gave it up," she said finally. "But when you left you weren't sure what you'd do. Still, why would Cal send you money? To buy you off? You were already gone. You hadn't demanded anything. For the child, then. You knew where it was."

"He," said Edith. "His name is Daniel."

Daniel. All these years, Lacey had been sure that the child was the reason that Edith never came back. But the way Edith said his name now, her tone regretful and distant, it wrote the air with a different finality. She must have let them all go, every trace of Cal, of Lacey, of her own baby. It was hard to believe.

"I know that much about him," added Edith. Her shoulders hunched. "A name."

"Nothing else?"

Edith reached out and slowly spun the three-tiered dessert tray, but she didn't take anything from it. She just stared at the remaining array of tarts and cakes, and then abruptly leaned back in her chair.

"When I flew into New York, Stan met me," she said. "Stan had his own agenda. He had made the mistake of flirting with a former student, and had fallen under suspicion for being gay, which indeed he was. Stan was worried he might lose his position at the school, so he proposed marriage, the best of friendships, and a good job for me. But there was a condition. We would not be parents. The child would be adopted by others." Her voice sank on the last word, as if *others* were a euphemism for what she really wanted to say. Kidnappers. Abductors.

"Stan had been abused as a boy," continued Edith. "He knew that I had been beaten by my father, too. He saw parenthood as a prison for us, in which we could constantly relive the suffering of our young years. Stan also worried that we were twisted inside, and we might inflict our pain on the next generation. 'It should stop with us,' he said, one of the only times he ever raised his voice to me. In retrospect, I resist him shaming us that way. It was brainwashing. But back then, I accepted it. I was so exhausted and hurt, by my mistake with Cal, by abandoning you and your parents. I just wanted to see a simple, clean future, but also one where I could read and think and be part of a real dialogue. Marry Stan, and this future was mine. Keep the child, and I faced lifetime bondage. I would have to get some low-paying secretarial job, and never see the kid and barely support us both. Or I would have to marry a different husband, just to provide for us, and be doomed to more pregnancies." She paused. "It seemed an easy choice, but still I balked. I waited. I grew heavier. I was running out of money.

"Then, through the school, Stan found out about a couple who were desperate to adopt. At his urging, I met them. We had dinner together in some subterranean tavern on the upper East Side. The mother was Jewish, like your mother, and like you, she couldn't carry children to term. The father was an immigration lawyer, working to get European refugees visas to the United States. They were kind and warm, and they genuinely appeared to cherish each other, like your parents. We only gleaned one another's first names; we all felt it best that the adoption remained anonymous. Forever. They had one condition for me: the child would never find out he was not their natural-born son. When I left their company, I told them I needed a week to think about it, but I already knew. They were perfect. They yearned for a baby, while I did not. They would give him a proper home, while I could not. They would pay for a safe birth and a tidy sum for me to set up a new life afterward. In return, I would never expose myself as his mother. 'If it's a girl, she will be Daniela, after my father,' said the mother. 'A boy will be Daniel.' That's all I'd know.

"As part of our agreement, they booked me a room in a home for unwed mothers, where two sisters watched closely over us and locked our rooms at night. It was a long winter, bitterly cold. I remember my hands aching deep in the knuckles and my wet hair freezing against my pillow. The other unwed mothers were all teenagers. One child was only twelve. They formed their little bands, had their little spats. Their innocence was cloying; the only thing they wanted was to resume being girls, to go back next summer to their bonfires and dances. They didn't know they could not be girls again. Once their baby was born, they would forever carry another burden, curled inside them: the fear they had done the wrong thing, giving their child away to strangers. No, they would never be girls again. Most of them scorned me, a woman of marrying age, whom nobody wanted, but one became my friend for life after stopping me from chugging a bottle of floor cleaner and ending it all. She saw that sometimes my head was clear, and sometimes it clouded as the changes overcame my body, as my breasts throbbed and my belly grew like a beast's. 'Watch over me,' I begged her, and she did, until my labor came.

She was the only one who learned my real name. I went by another during that time because I needed to be someone who stayed and bore it, instead of the one who always ran away. Later, the girl found me at the academy. I gave her a job and she nearly ruined me. She'd become

a drinker and loose-lipped. But with enough cash, she vanished will-
ingly again. We still keep in touch." Edith's mouth quirked. "I suspect
I will always 'owe' her."

She spun the dessert tray again. The cakes twisted around their
axis.

"The birth was long. My body did not want to surrender the baby,
because my mind quailed at seeing the child alive, seeing its helplessness, so like my youngest brother's, whom I'd abandoned. I screamed,
I threw up, I felt my insides squeezing me to pieces, but I could not
dilate more than a couple of inches. Finally, the doctors gave me a
sedative and I went into a twilight sleep. When I woke, the child was
born and gone. A nurse told me I had delivered a healthy boy. Daniel,
then. It took three weeks for my ravaged body to heal. I felt like a sack
that had been ripped for its grain to dump loose. The doctors had torn
me and stitched me up. My belly bulged and sagged. As soon as I could
walk, I paced my freezing little room in the sisters' house, working off
the pounds.

"One day, Stan came with a bouquet of yellow rosebuds and an
envelope of cash from the adoptive parents, and he asked if I was sure
I wanted to marry him. Even when I said yes, Stan made me sleep on
it. In the morning, after I had counted the money and the roses had
opened, I said yes again. I could have chosen otherwise; the money
was enough. I could have returned here, or gone overseas, but any
other future left me vulnerable again. Stan's stability and kindness,
and his childless house, were secure destinations. A home, not far
from the beloved forests of my childhood. We went to the town hall
near the academy and tied the knot. On our wedding night, we talked
and talked and held each other, but Stan never touched me naked. He
told me that he had trouble loving men, but that he could not desire
women. I told him I loved both women and men, and that I needed to
be free from conventional ideas of fidelity. We agreed that we could

both have private, discreet affairs but that our marriage would be our lifelong companionship and our public identity. Over the years, nothing altered the pledge we made to each other in that dusty town hall. Stan was my dearest friend, and I was his. We treasured each other. I don't expect anyone now to understand this, least of all Daniel, wherever he is now." Her voice trembled.

Lacey fingered the stem of her wineglass, struggling to suppress the vision of a young, big-bellied Edith raising a bottle of floor cleaner to her mouth. Or the vision of Edith lying bloody and deflated on a narrow bed, her baby taken away. Pitying Edith for her hardships couldn't explain anything; it just paved over Lacey's anger with sadness, like tar over gravel.

"But why would Cal send you money?" said Lacey. "If he went through the trouble to find you, he could just as easily have found out that you were not raising the child."

"I don't know," said Edith. "He must have thought I could pass it on."

"Perhaps the money was for something else," said Lacey. "He thought you might work for him again. His muse-wife. He could have been clutching at straws after his career tanked."

"Maybe," said Edith.

"Why deny it when it's true?" Lacey said.

"I never opened the letter," protested Edith. "You can see that for yourself."

"But there was something else in the desk," said Lacey. "A package with a copy of a full screenplay, no return address, but the postmark from New England. *You* had written him first; you had sent him that story again, the movie script from my hotel room. The script based on you and me, and a friendship greater than both of us. And there were three notes from three different producers to Cal, each of them praising it but passing on it, all of them dated the year before Cal's death.

I read the whole plot this time. Every page. Why not? Cal was dead. You were gone. Maybe you had changed a few scenes, but it was the same story about two girls, a rich girl and a poor girl, who become improbable friends. Together, they run away from home and launch their lives in a frontier city. They find jobs in a hotel, rent rooms, and gleefully torture an array of hopeful suitors—it's all quite charming, until the poor girl gets the Spanish flu. For once, the rich girl can do nothing to save her. All her wealth cannot stop death. Do you want to know what the producers said? You assumed they would love it."

Edith blinked. Her eyes were shiny.

"The producers said it was 'heartwarming' and 'smart,' but a bit too 'experimental' and 'emotional,'" said Lacey, "and they all wondered if Cal could add a stronger male part, perhaps a soldier on his way home from the war, or a cowboy in search of an old enemy. They thought the women's relationship might work as a backdrop, while the foreground could be a good vengeance plot. Something 'scorching' and 'iconic,' they said. Cal was, after all, known for his Westerns."

There was a muffled burst of conversation in the hallway, someone passing the room. Edith looked startled by it. She grabbed for her wine and drank. "I guess that's not surprising," she said.

"You must have found out I burned the original," said Lacey. "Maybe from Cal, maybe from Bruno. Maybe you came here yourself and saw the ash. But for all you were done with me, and done with Cal's child, and even done with Cal, you were still willing—desperate, even—to sell a fantasy of us to the highest bidder. You didn't want to stay in that freezing hamlet with your fake husband and your underling job." Her scorn surprised her; her fury had chosen the words. She heard the Czech army captain from long ago. *You are a child with a child's desire.* "You wanted to come back in glory and show us all."

"How many people have had true friends?" Edith's voice rose.

"More than you think," said Lacey. Papi had Bruno's father. Mutti

had her Prague confidantes. What if Edith's one naivety was not knowing how ordinary it was to love hard when you were young? Lacey
wanted to laugh, a harsh, knowing laugh, but it did not come.

"And anyway, if you wanted to dwell on my tragic helplessness,"
she said, "you could have just visited me. All my wealth didn't stop
Papi from dying a slow, painful death."

"My name would not be on it," mumbled Edith. "I refused to be
paid." She gestured at the envelope. "I didn't even want to know if it
sold." She hesitated, then added, "You and Cal could have had it all."

You and Cal could have had it all. The declaration might have
shocked Lacey earlier. Not now.

"It didn't sell," she retorted. "Cal never got a dime for it. But he
tried to throw away my money, to impress you. Threw away our marriage, too."

She saw Cal running through the Agoura stream again, running
for Edith, who was falling from the sky. One night, nearly a year after
Cal's plane accident, after the investigation had closed, a police officer
brought Cal's favorite bomber jacket to Lacey. It had been recovered
from the crash site. Cal couldn't have been wearing it on the flight—
his body had been smashed to pieces—but the sheepskin collar still
smelled of him. When Lacey slept with it that night, tucked against her
ribs, she felt their old love pass through her, Cal's vitality and passion,
the tenderness of their early years. She felt that era separate and pull
away—thread by thread—from the bitter drunk he had become. It
was only then, paradoxically, that Lacey allowed herself to weep over
missing Edith, her friend and blood sister. Only Edith would have understood her pain.

"You thought you would just walk into a dark theater one day, and
see us two there, larger than life," said Lacey.

Edith blinked. "That was the daydream, I suppose. Do you blame
me?"

"Of course I blame you. You chose the daydream over me," said Lacey.

"And you burned that copy, too?" said Edith, an edge in her voice. She couldn't hide it. She'd cared about that pointless story. The perfect friendship.

"It's gone," said Lacey.

In truth, Lacey wasn't sure what had happened to Edith's script. There had been so many boxes to move when she cleared her parents' house. So many papers to file or shred. All that Lacey had kept was this letter of Cal's. The letter to Edith, the one meant only for Edith.

"Do you want to read it now, what Cal wrote?" she said. "You didn't expect him to die. Perhaps inside the envelope is the answer to our last remaining mystery: whether Cal thought of you as the mother of his lost child, or the muse he couldn't live without. And also, if, in the end, he thought most of you, dearly and passionately of *you*— while leaving me, his lawful wife, destitute."

She held up the envelope. "We could find out together."

Edith shook her head.

"Speak," said Lacey.

"No," said Edith.

Lacey threw the envelope back in the desk drawer and slammed it closed. She felt damp all over, and covered with a grainy residue that could have been the smoke, but felt older and dirtier, like the soot of the ancient city in which she had been born. Without another word, she rose and went to the bathroom, flicked on the haranguing fan, and sat on the toilet with the seat down, slumped forward over her bloated middle. *Whir-whir-whir* went the fan. In the mirror, she looked like a doll with its eyes and mouth stitched on, the lashes too black, the lips too red. A doll that has sat on a shelf for ages, its owner grown up. A relic that ought to be tossed out.

She stayed in the bathroom so long, summoning the strength to return, that the busboys had finally come and left; they'd cleared the desk, brought the two glasses of cognac on a silver tray. Lacey half expected Edith to be gone, too, when she emerged, but Edith had merely put her valise by the door and was at the bookshelves again, doing her infuriating inventory.

"You didn't leave," said Lacey.

"Not this time," Edith said, her fists balled. "For once."

The cognac filled the room with its heady scent, apricot and vanilla.

"A little taste of spirits?" said Lacey. "It's a marvelous brandy."

20.

"THANK YOU," SAID EDITH. SHE DIDN'T PICK UP her glass.

"How long will you stay?" said Lacey, walking up behind her. The smoking and drinking and sadness made the carpet feel very far away. A tickle on her bare toes.

"I fly back tomorrow," said Edith. "I'll get the morning flight."

Lacey lifted her snifter of cognac, swirled the amber liquid. The bouquet hit her nose again; this time, she smelled honeysuckle. *Should we toast?* she thought of saying aloud, but she didn't know what to toast. Edith had come three thousand miles to see Lacey only, and just tonight? She didn't believe it.

"All this way, and no sightseeing?" Lacey asked.

"I'm too old for sightseeing. I just get lost," said Edith. "Or I want to take a nap and I can't."

"But the city has changed so much. I thought you'd want to see it." Lacey held up the cognac. Perhaps they could toast the city. How it had altered, how it had stayed the same.

Edith's eyes went to the drink, but she didn't move. "You don't seem particularly inclined to see it yourself," she said drily.

"I see it from my windows," said Lacey, setting her cognac down. "That's enough."

Edith's lips twitched but she did not respond.

"Besides, the moment I stepped outside, I'd require a facelift and an entirely new wardrobe," Lacey said.

"Please. You look perfect," said Edith.

"Do I?" said Lacey in a hollow voice.

"Always," Edith said. And, as always, it was the thing Lacey needed to hear.

They stood close to each other now. She was still barefoot and she had shrunk in recent years, while Edith appeared taller, more solid. Even after hours together, Lacey could not stop studying her friend's face, searching for the old resemblances. The slight uplift to her nose. Her wide, high brows, now whitened and coarse. Her sardonic mouth. She felt Edith's gaze devouring her back. Oh, Edith.

Lacey forced her next words to remain steady. "So you'll go back to your hut in the snowy forest and wait out the rest of the tale?"

"I don't have anywhere else I want to go," said Edith.

"But at the end, who will look out for you?"

"I have my friends," said Edith. "And I know the nurses at the local hospital. I've seen them often enough. They've pumped the stomachs of dozens of my students. And mended an unbelievable number of broken bones."

It wasn't hard to picture: Edith on her deathbed in a sterile white room, surrounded by unflappable women. No fuss, but no fear or desperation, either.

"Well," said Lacey. "I hope you'll have safe travels." Were they supposed to embrace, wave, shake? She held out her hand. There was a flash of panic in Edith's face.

"Clever Elsie. That's the one I was thinking of," Edith said suddenly. "Did you ever read that tale?"

The name sounded familiar. "From Grimms'?" Lacey had a copy of the book somewhere on the shelves.

"The Grimm brothers got the credit for it, of course, but a tailor's wife told it to them," said Edith.

Lacey didn't recall the story. She had the impression that *clever* in the fairy tales usually meant the opposite. "Is she some kind of fool?" she said. She didn't want to hear about a fool.

Edith didn't appear to notice. "Clever Elsie is a maid," she said, walking away from Lacey, to the window again. She looked up this time, up the hill, toward the bank tower, its unreachable height. "She's ready for marriage, but she attracts only one suitor, a fellow named Hans, from far away," Edith continued, her face tilted skyward. "And he has a condition: if Elsie is truly as smart as her name, he will marry her. So they throw a big feast for Hans, and afterward, her mother sends Clever Elsie to the cellar to fetch more beer. When Elsie is watching the beer pour from the keg, she spots a pickaxe on the wall. She imagines what will happen if she does marry Hans."

"He'll turn into a lumberjack?" said Lacey.

"They'll have a child," said Edith. "They'll send the child one night to fetch the beer. And the pickaxe will fall on the child's head and kill him. Elsie is so overcome with fear for this unborn son, she stays in the cellar weeping. One by one, the whole dinner party goes down to check on her, and one by one, she tells them her fear and shows them the pickaxe, and she is so persuasive that they join in her grieving and wailing. Finally, the suitor, Hans, is the last one upstairs, alone, and he tromps down to the cellar to find all five people howling over what could happen to Elsie's imaginary child. The pickaxe is still hanging on the wall. For whatever reason, this demonstration impresses Hans and he marries her."

"I really don't remember that story," said Lacey. It sounded odd for a fairy tale, all that sobbing and hysterics. "Why would they believe her? It's just a silly fear."

"Isn't that the worst fear of loving, though?" said Edith. "The abrupt finish to it all?"

"I suppose," said Lacey. "But you can't let fear dictate your choices."

Edith regarded her.

Lacey made an impatient noise. "Anyway, it sounds incomplete." Her legs hurt and she longed to sit, but she didn't want to give Edith the impression they ought to carry on all night, not if Edith was going to teetotal and monologue.

"It's not finished," said Edith. "It gets stranger. Elsie doesn't bear children, or at least the story doesn't say so. But one day, Hans sends her to the fields to cut the grain. Elsie takes some soup with her, and when she gets to the field, she decides to eat, and then to sleep, before setting to work. Why not?" Edith gazed up the hill again. "Her husband, waiting at home, thinks Elsie must be devoted to her task and taking her time. Obviously, he doesn't understand Elsie. Not yet. When night falls, Hans gets worried, and he goes to find Elsie sleeping, and the soup eaten, and the grain untouched. So he hangs a set of bells on her. When Elsie wakes up, whenever she moves, she hears jingling. It puzzles her. Elsie never jingled before."

"Can't she see the bells?"

"Apparently not," said Edith.

"Why can't she?"

"Perhaps because they're right in front of her," said Edith. "I don't know."

"Where's the husband?"

"He went home."

"Without her? He just left her there?"

"Yes. There's more."

"Go on, then," said Lacey. She was feeling sick to her stomach again, but she fought it down.

"Elsie is so confused, she wonders if she is herself, if she's Elsie at all. So she decides to run home to her husband to ask him. But Hans has locked the door. She knocks and asks if Elsie is inside. Hans says yes, Elsie is inside. So the woman who rings can't be herself. She is not Elsie. She runs to the next house and the next, and no one will let her in. Finally, she runs away, out of the story. The end."

Lacey waited.

"That's really the end?" she said.

Edith nodded.

"How bizarre and unsatisfying," said Lacey. "I rather hoped Elsie would get smart finally."

Edith turned from the window. "And what?" she said softly. "Become the drudge and mother she was expected to become?"

Now, wasn't that pure Edith: casting Clever Elsie as a heroine, smashing the shackles that enslaved women. Too bad Elsie came across as a weepy, lazy idiot. Lacey pointed this out. "I'll admit, the husband doesn't sound like a prize, either," she added.

"I don't know," said Edith. "Maybe he set her free."

"Or maybe the storyteller ran out of ideas for her," said Lacey. "And had to conclude somehow."

Lacey's legs were starting to go numb. Now she truly wished Edith would leave.

"How about you?" said Edith, returning to stand across from Lacey. They were two feet apart now, unbearably close.

"What?"

"At the end." There was an intensity to the words. As if Edith had been waiting to say them.

"They'll take care of me here," Lacey said, gesturing to the walls around her. "This is my home." The word sank through her like an iron weight. *Home.* Was she home? Didn't she have somewhere else to go, something else to find, before time ran out? These rooms were so small, so confined. Her eye fell on the paintings, and her energy revived. "Do you suppose you could get these to him?"

Edith cleared her throat. "What?"

"These three." She pointed. "I never liked them, but they're worth a lot of money."

"I bet they are."

"You picked them out, I'm sure," said Lacey. "Cal was ever so good at gifts. He knew my taste to a T." She regarded the spokes of the flower, its jarred center. "So I never understood his wedding present. Why would he give me these? You must have advised him. I realized that much later, after you left. This art, if one can call it that, is something you would love."

"They're magnificent," said Edith.

"So I was right." Lacey folded her arms.

"You sent me to distract Cal one Saturday when you were in the flurry of wedding preparations," said Edith. "We drove to Beverly Hills and stopped in some art galleries. Cal wanted to buy you a land-scape painting, something European, like your mother and father preferred, but when I saw these, I told him they would be the greater investment. That one day most landscapes wouldn't be landscapes anymore. That these flowers weren't flowers at all, but a depiction of the geometries of desire. As you said, Cal was a sucker for a bet. Once the gamble was in his mind, he couldn't let it go. We went on to look at more pictures of sleepy castles and waterfalls, like he'd originally intended to buy you, but his mind was made up. We went back and paid full price. I'm sorry you hate them, though I thought you might have."

"I've detested them for forty-six years," declared Lacey. "Now I'd like to let them go. Is there any way to give them secretly to Daniel?"

"To Daniel?" said Edith. "Oh." Her face fell.

"He must need money for something," Lacey persisted. "He probably has a family of his own by now. What is he, mid-forties? What if he doesn't inherit?"

"But I wouldn't know how to reach him."

"You wouldn't know, or you wouldn't tell?" said Lacey.

There was a fraction of a second before her friend shook her head. "I wouldn't know."

A lie. Maybe the Stan story was all a lie. Maybe Edith had raised Daniel, after all. Her son. Cal's son. Her "life of bondage." No. Edith hadn't, or she wouldn't be wearing that stricken look, the one she'd worn in the woods after Vaudeville Night, when they'd held hands so tight, on the dark path back to Lacey's parents.

"You take them, then," Lacey said gently.

"Too bulky for me to carry."

"I'll have them shipped to you."

"I don't have the space," said Edith. "This isn't my life anymore, Lace." She flicked a hand at the desk, the books, the window, but then the panic flooded her face again, almost a horror, and her palms were on Lacey's shoulders, seizing her close. Her warm cheek leaned in, next to Lacey's cheek. The heat and scent of Edith's skin, so familiar and from so long ago. "I have to go. Goodbye, my dearest."

"Goodbye," Lacey whispered, leaning back, closing her eyes. In the quickest flash she saw the pond, the sunlight, her girlhood arms extended around Edith, both of them dunking underwater and bursting out together, newly hatched, and then she felt a peck on her cheekbone and Edith pulling away, walking to the door. Edith had a red wine stain on her skirt, a fleck of ash on her blouse, and her face looked older and plainer than ever, but not her eyes. Her eyes shone with their eternal brightness. She picked up her suitcase, then turned back.

"Should I tell you I've made it home safely?" she asked. She sounded like she dreaded another conversation.

Lacey hesitated, then shook her head. "Tell Bruno," she said firmly. "He'll let me know."

Edith nodded and let herself out. The door made a heavy, final *thunk*.

"This isn't my life anymore, either," Lacey said to the silence and the paintings. "It isn't," she added, as if there were someone there to contradict her. As if someone would come back to contradict her. She stood in the middle of the outer room for a long time. Then she blew out the candles and moved them to a side table, along with the two full glasses of cognac, the ashtray, the wine bottles. She pulled off the tablecloth, leaving the shining, polished desk, and collapsed against it, her breasts smashed on the wood, her head in her hands.

21.

I T WAS DAWN WHEN LACEY WOKE ON HER BED, STILL
fully clothed. She wiped the crust from her eyes and went
through her rituals for hangovers: a long drink of water, three
aspirin, a piping-hot bath, an icy shower. She left her blue dress, her
hose, her girdle, and her brassiere in heaps across the tile floor, tow-
eled off, and limped naked into the outer room, which stank of ash and
booze.

The two glasses of cognac gleamed in the corner, a pool of dark
liquid in each. Together, they'd cost more than the entire meal. Blear-
ily, Lacey regarded them. All that preciousness poured out but untouched. Whatever had spurred Edith to come yesterday, she never
said. And yet there had been some urgency in the letter, in Edith's
insistence on seeing Lacey—an urgency that remained a mystery.

The cool air prickled Lacey's damp skin, touching the sags and
age spots, the bulges of her once shapely knees. Her hair hung wet
and heavy against her cheek. Her eyes fell to Cal's desk, to a small
dimple in the wood on the right side where the finish had blistered in
the heat of a fire. Edith's script had burned slow, then hot, pages curl-
ing, flames leaping, and Lacey had run to the bathroom and soaked a
towel to put it out. She'd left the sodden lump on the desk, and when

the desk came into her possession, after Cal's death, she saw the permanent scar her act had made. Sometimes, her eye would land on the dimple, and she would think, *That's Edith. That's the piece of Edith I will always carry in me, the part of me that is her.* A dark mark, but pure. It was the Edith inside her who asked Cal for a divorce, who locked the door and hung up the phone on his protests. Who insisted that Lacey couldn't live a lie anymore, even if it meant giving up on love. It was the Edith inside her who refused another marriage, even to a good, faithful man, because it meant binding herself forever to his dreams. It was the Edith inside Lacey who admitted now that she'd been waking more tired every day, that her frequent nausea might be more than just hangover or nerves. She had pulled it together for last night, but at a cost.

Lacey touched the ridge in the finish. Her body shivered, then shook. She stood, fragile and stripped, barely holding herself upright. She hadn't fooled Edith. No one fooled Edith. The whole time, even before she came, Edith knew. She came brimming with knowing and never spilled a drop. And then she left. Gone. Again. *This isn't my life anymore, Lace.*

After what could have been seconds or hours, Lacey felt the paintings watching her and marched to her bedroom, threw on a robe, and called the front desk.

"I'd like the room cleaned up," she said. "A deep cleaning. I'll pay the extra fee. No, just the second room. My bedroom is fine." She picked at her cuticle. "And I want to get rid of the desk. Yes. That's right. It can be donated, or someone on staff can have it. It's a valuable antique. In its place I'm going to order a gate-leg dinner table. It's about time I had one. Yes. I'll have Bruno manage it. I'd like the cleaning and the removal to be done as soon as possible, though. Today."

She closed the bedroom door. They would come soon. It was early enough in the day. Housekeeping could fit her in before the guests left in the late morning and the rooms changed over. The outer chamber wasn't that dirty, and *deep cleaning* only meant getting the rug shampooed and the baseboards dusted, but it was a satisfying phrase. She ordered a hearty breakfast and dressed carefully, in bone trousers and a long-sleeved coral blouse with a darling scalloped collar. She sat by the bookshelf and looked out the window as she chewed her French toast. Though everything on her plate tasted good, it was hard to swallow. Her stomach heaved and roiled. Her books seemed disordered, but when she scanned the titles, everything was in its proper, alphabetical place. She would not read today. She might take the record player out of the closet and relax to some Smetana or Vivaldi. She might make a project of a long afternoon nap.

An hour later, the staff began banging around in the other room, doing her bidding. There was a volley of conversation in Spanish, something about a letter, and then a white envelope slid under her door.

"No," she said aloud. "I don't want that." But when she bent down to pick it up, she saw that it wasn't the same envelope. No *RETURN TO SENDER* written on it. No seal either. Instead, there was Lacey's name in Edith's hand. She lifted the flap and pulled out two tickets and a folded piece of paper with her name again in rushed ink, beneath which was written: *Read this after you go.*

"Wait," said Lacey, and burst through the door on two men hefting the desk in their arms. They stared at her, surprised, their foreheads creased with the strain. "Put it down, please," she said in Spanish. "Please."

With resigned looks, they lowered the desk slowly and she flung open the drawers, empty, all of them now. The letter from Cal to Edith was gone. "Where did you find this?" she asked.

The younger man pointed to the desk. "Top drawer," he said. The drawer where Cal's letter had been. She looked at the new one in her hands. The tickets inside were to a movie screening that night. A movie called *Days of Gold*, directed by Daniel Fallada.

"Tonight," she said faintly. She recognized the theater. A small arthouse on the West Side, if she remembered it right.

"So?" said one of the men in English. "Stay or go?"

"Go," said Lacey, her head spinning. "Go."

* * *

She called the Hotel San Marco, but a guest named Edie or Edith Morgan had never arrived. Nor Edie or Edith Holle. Nor Crane. She asked the front desk if Edith had ordered a cab anywhere, but she hadn't. "She must have just strolled out to the taxi stand herself," said the manager. "Or strolled anywhere, really. I don't remember her leaving."

Lacey called Bruno. He had not heard from Edith.

"Are you sure?" she said. "She said she'd call you when she made it home."

"So she's not home yet," said Bruno. "Long way to the great north."

"I need you to take me somewhere tonight," said Lacey.

"Somewhere?" Bruno said after a moment.

"You said you walk for miles all day. Why can't you take me somewhere? To a movie."

"I can. But you. Are you sure? Last time—"

"Last time was different. I wasn't ready. Besides, that was just a fanciful idea."

"Visiting your parents' graves was a fanciful idea," said Bruno.

"I couldn't do it anymore."

"And you can leave now? What is this movie?"

She told Bruno about Edith and Cal's birth son, about the tickets to a movie he had directed. "It must be the same Daniel." She said that Edith had left the tickets for her. "I assume she thought we'd go together," she said. "She and I."

"Of course she did," Bruno said gravely.

"So why leave them behind for me, after all that?" Her voice wavered, surprising her.

"Maybe she's already seen it," said Bruno. "She wants you to see it, too."

"Or it's a trick. To get me to leave the hotel." Lacey's hand tightened on the receiver. She wasn't going to let herself be sad. "Edith always thought she knew what was better for me."

"Complicated trick," said Bruno. "Why not just pretend Elvis is outside to see you."

"Elvis has been dead for ages. Besides, I never liked Elvis."

"First time you ever lie to me," said Bruno.

"I don't know why you find this funny," said Lacey. "Edith just did another one of her mystery moves and left me to interpret it."

"So don't," said Bruno.

"Don't what?"

"Don't interpret."

Through the phone, she could feel his shrug.

Don't was an option. Don't interpret. Don't go. She fingered the tickets. The trouble Edith must have gone through to purchase tickets from a theater in a distant city! She must have written to the cinema. Sent them a check. So premeditated. To see the film by Daniel Fallada. His name was as clear as day, and he had evidently earned some fame now. How did Edith find him? It wouldn't be so hard. How many immigration lawyers were there in New York, how many with a son named Daniel, and Daniel's exact age?

Don't go, said the voice inside her, but the voice was weary of solitude, of hiding. The tickets were so light in her hand, barely the weight of feathers. Daniel Fallada. A movie director, like his father. Cal would have been proud. No matter his faults, he'd badly wanted a son. That was the hard truth of it, how much he and Lacey had longed for children, had often spoken of it in courtship and after they first married. "We'll have a huge family," Cal had predicted. "The hugest," promised Lacey. "They'll fill every corner of our enormous house." And then they'd laughed at the image, its giddiness and greed.

"So it was a good visit?" said Bruno. "You have made up?"

"I don't know," said Lacey. "We talked for a long time. I suppose it was good to talk. I won't see her again."

"No?"

The truth deflated her: she would never see Edith again. Edith had made that choice, for both of them, by stealing Cal's letter to her, by leaving the tickets in their place.

Or maybe this was Edith's final test. A last measure of friendship. A fragile blue bottle, carefully wrapped. *This will cure you.*

"Can you get here by six thirty?" Lacey said.

"For a seven o'clock screening? On the west side of town? Miss Lacey, you don't know the traffic these days."

"I don't want to be early. If Edith does go, I don't want her to catch me there beforehand. She'll be looking smug, as if she's the one who got me to leave this suite. You know she judges me for it. You all do."

"You will leave?" said Bruno.

"Yes." She was sure of it.

"You really will go," said Bruno in a wondering voice.

"Six thirty," said Lacey. "Now, stop acting like the sky is falling."

"I will be in the lobby at six," said Bruno. "In case you decide to believe me about the traffic."

* * *

Lacey couldn't bear another day of excruciating waiting for evening, especially now that her sitting room looked raided, a stage set without its main piece of furniture. The desk was gone, the rug dented and vacant where it had stood for years, and the couch looked absurd sitting there by itself. So she booked a complicated set of treatments at the salon—hair, nails, makeup—and told the astonished stylist she was coming downstairs for it. Usually, she hosted the hairdresser in her room, and skipped her nails. The salon would kill three hours if Lacey combined it with dinner at the restaurant. She wasn't hungry, but she could pick at a steak tartare and recall all the times in her twenties she'd ordered it hungover, because Marlene Dietrich herself had whispered to Papi that it was the perfect cure.

To Lacey's surprise, it didn't feel strange to hear her door click behind her, to walk to the elevator. She didn't feel ill, either. Just faded and frail, cautious of stumbling on her way out. Papi's maze of hallways was still his maze of hallways. The carpet still a plush dark blue. The elevator doors still a burnished brass. The painting by the mirror across from them was new: a bunch of triangles and cones, but somehow it expressed Papi anyway: his elegance, his devotion to quiet and ease, a luxury that didn't shout but beckoned. Relieved, Lacey checked out her reflection: the crisp coral blouse, slimming pants, sandals with a platform heel. Better than the overbearing formality of last night. With some polish and color, she would manage in public.

The last time Lacey had tried to leave the hotel was a chilly, windy New Year's Day five years before. At Lacey's request, Bruno had come to escort her on her annual visit to her parents' graves. Each year, she had done it, kept this one tradition while other outings faded, as friends died and invitations dried up. But since the summer, Lacey had been bothered by her view. A scattering of drunks now slept on the library grounds below her window. She could see their bodies down there, curled, sometimes rolling and writhing. From the thirty-eighth floor, they looked a bit like war casualties and a bit like worms. As winter came and more men crowded in, Lacey finally called the police, who told her the rules had changed. They couldn't arrest and prosecute inebriates anymore. The paddy wagon wouldn't swing by and take the men to the farm outside the city to dry out. They might hold them in a cell for a few hours, at most a few days, and then they'd be released. "The only way for a drunk to get free of his vice now is dying," said the policeman, a weary cynicism in his voice. "We had triple the number of fatalities this year."

"Can't a patrol be arranged?" said Lacey. "Some police presence would help, wouldn't it? No one will want to vacation downtown."

"Ma'am, I hate to say this, but I'd rather our tourists stay elsewhere," said the policeman. "And watch your purse if you go out. The drunks are easy marks, so the pickpockets follow."

The instant Lacey had set foot outside the hotel on that New Year's Day, she'd known that she wouldn't make it. She wasn't safe on these streets anymore. Her heart had seized so hard, and her breath had come so short and quick, she was only at the valet stand when she asked Bruno to take her back in. Bruno had been swift and considerate, holding her arm, steering her away from a cab's open door. All day, she stared at her windows, still sick with nerves, unable to move from the couch, her skin too clammy and sensitive for blankets, her mind too frantic to nap. The world: It was rotten. It had burned Mutti's family to ash, and now it was drowning Papi's dream. The hotel would fail. She would lose her sanctuary. By evening, it felt like her parents' gravestones had found her, had climbed the hotel's walls, crawled in her window, their cold stone faces pressing against her cheeks and mouth.

Within weeks, Lacey had sold most of her shares cheap to an investor who promised to pay for the expensive renovations and who grandfathered her into free rent forever. The loss of responsibility had been a mistake; Lacey no longer had the reason or will to depart her room. But it was also a gift. Freedom from fear again. She had grown to love her own lonely tower. To treasure its remoteness and peace.

She could leave today, though. Tonight. Holding the tickets, seeing that name, filled Lacey with determination. Daniel. Daniel lived. Forty-three years old and a filmmaker. A director. Admittedly, forty-three was a little old for career breakthroughs, and an arthouse film was an arthouse film, not a major production. Cal had directed his first movie at twenty-nine. But maybe Daniel had bounced around as a young man, like Cal should have, or maybe his plots were slow and thematic, like Edith's. Maybe Daniel's tastes were old-fashioned or strange because he had been unloved, given up, raised by strangers. Maybe he'd had to raise himself, because his adoptive family had finally conceived a child after all—a usurper, a precious son.

She would indeed like to give Daniel a mysterious present of the art Cal had bought for her. The paintings were the only thing he'd left her worth a dime; that was the irony of it. She'd even had to sell her old LaSalle to pay off his debt collectors. But she didn't want the paintings anymore. And she didn't need them. Papi and Mutti had made sure she would always be cared for. She would update her own will to include the anonymous bequest. She would call her lawyer tomorrow.

Inside the elevator, Lacey punched the floor for the salon. Straight down she would go and save her perambulating for later. The new renovations had waited a year. They could wait a few hours longer. At the brightly lit salon, the stylist was young and sweet, the mani-pedicurist silent and thorough. The woman who did her makeup wore too much eyeshadow herself, but she adorned Lacey with the deftest of strokes. In turn, Lacey found herself quite capable of small talk. She saw herself smile in the mirror and laugh at the right intervals. She saw her blue eyes crinkle and shine. Her years out of the sun had preserved her face, and her tailored sleeves hid the crepe on her arms. She was a crone, all right, but she might never reach hideous. Never a drooling ruin.

None of the young people had heard of the movie *Days of Gold*, but they knew the theater and they recommended bars and nightclubs nearby as if she were twenty-five years old and wanted to spend her evening in a shouting match with her conversation partner. It was fine, being in public. Only the glare of the salon bothered her after a while, all those lights and reflections, all the empty, shining counters and metal sinks. In her day, people had liked their living spaces dark and intimate, dens and caves, and now they preferred to pretend they inhabited a sand dune, or the moon. She tipped the staff all lavishly and tried not to notice how curious they were about her, the heiress who hardly ever left her room.

The restaurant was in the former men's club. They had painted a rustic fishing village across one dark-paneled wall to lighten the room's once dim, secretive mood. "Who likes to eat with seagulls," Bruno had grumbled about it. Who indeed. Lacey's dinner was a disappointment. The server was too chummy. To recite the dinner specials, which Lacey did not want to hear, he insisted on crouching by her table, a grown man shrinking himself to the height of a dog. His aftershave gusted over her, and she had to watch his Adam's apple bob. Her steak tartare was late and unpleasantly chewy. Her cola was diet and had too much ice. The old Corinthian columns still graced the decor, but the new furniture was bolder and slimmer. Her chair seat was hard white leather. It was like sitting on a car door. The tabletop was stone, hefted by a thick iron pole at center. Lacey didn't feel like she was touching the past, not with her arms and legs resting on cold slabs, her feet brushing a girder. She couldn't hear the murmur of her own youth inside the brash exclamations of her neighbors. They had the nerve to wear their baseball caps inside and ask where the TV screen was.

Lacey didn't linger after the check came but picked her way down the galleria to review the other updates. More than three hundred feet long stretched the hotel's original hallway, every inch of it adorned. Thick coils twined up terra-cotta columns, a fresco of Roman gods radiated overhead like a giant clock, and satyrs lofted a coat of arms over the gilded gates to each ballroom. The galleria's colors were ivory and gold now, and the marble floor bare. Lacey's footsteps echoed. She could have been touring a tomb. Long ago, tints of soft blue and rose marked the hall, with wall-to-wall carpet that evoked lattices of ivy. Lacey missed the tapestries, the plants, and the sofas that lined the sides in Papi's day. They made the place feel cozier, strollable. So many celebrities liked to be seen here, lounging and promenading, that Bruno had to hire a bouncer to scare away gawkers. Now it was just a corridor, an on-the-way instead of the destination. A bridal party clacked past Lacey, giggling, their lilac dresses shining.

She stopped at a ballroom to cheer herself up. There, the renovation team had preserved all the fixtures and used buttermilk to wash the hand-painted ceiling free of smoke stains. She walked up the steps and across the green carpet, to the center of the chamber. The cupids overhead glowed again, fresh-faced, saluting Ceres looking down from her heaven. For decades, Ceres had blurred to a faint cloud, but now Lacey could count each billowing fold in the goddess's gown, the slender stalks of wheat she clasped. Balconies glittered below, draped with a dusky pink satin, hiding chips of glass in their railings. The paired pilasters looked mightier than ever, lining the walls like dancers waiting for the music to begin. The chandeliers, those twelve-foot parasols of light, were sparkling clean. They would blaze over brides and grooms for decades to come. So Papi's dream did persist in tiny pockets, little eddies in the river of time. It might outlast Lacey, too. She twirled slowly once, lifting her arms to an invisible partner, then hurried on before any staff members caught her. Lacey Weber Crane, out of her room and acting sentimental. She preferred the employees to think of her as a fragile harpy, or they might lose their compulsion to please her. The old Palm Room was next. Papi liked to sit in there with a scotch and stare at the gold-painted ceiling.

By the time Lacey ascended to her suite, satisfied that the hotel had not been entirely savaged by modern notions of beauty, she had only fifty minutes left to prepare. She sat on the couch and hovered over the tickets, the folded piece of paper. *Lacey: Read this after you go.* Typical Edith, keeping her secrets to the last. Implied in the message was the assumption that Lacey *would* go to the cinema. That Lacey *would* wait to read the folded letter. Why shouldn't Lacey skim it right away and skip the movie? She opened the crease, then stopped and put the paper back in the envelope beside the tickets. She didn't want to know about Daniel before she saw the film. Better to observe him for herself, without Edith's arch opinions. *Days of Gold.* It sounded romantic. It sounded regretful. You didn't know you were living "days of gold" unless they were over. Was Daniel a cynical man, like Cal at the end? Lacey tucked the envelope in her purse. Forty minutes left. She debated about a drink and had a smoke instead. Then another. Tomorrow she would throw the pack away. She could already feel the sting in her lungs, and deep below it, a different but increasingly familiar feeling, more absence than pain, that she might never take a deep breath again.

* * *

Half a minute before six thirty, Lacey appeared in the lobby. At her arrival, Bruno stood slowly from a blue armchair, his expression dazed. He looked handsome and distinguished in his dark suit. Men could do that—glide from being young to middle-aged to an elder state that accommodated their grayness and wrinkles without making them one bit uglier. The heavy bones of their faces showed more, as did the angles of their torso, and Bruno had good bones and good angles. He stood a little crooked, favoring his left side, and with the same slight hunch, as if hung from his spine, but in his eyes was the wary, resigned affection she remembered so well. Her first kiss.

"Shall we?" she said, taking his proffered arm.

"You are all loveliness tonight," said Bruno.

"Thank you." She felt the eyes of the clerks and managers and the barkeep upon them. The heiress who never left her rooms was leaving. Leaving in style. Her papi's daughter. It should have felt slow, crossing the lobby, passing under the wooden ceiling and skylight, by the stone angels, the bar, the plush couches and chairs, but it was over before she knew it. She swept as grandly as she could on her sandals toward the glass doors. Her last sight before they left the building was the lion's-mouth fountain that Papi had adored, the water rising but never quite reaching the marble brim.

22.

Lacey and Bruno did not speak after seven o'clock passed and they were still at least fifteen minutes from the theater, but Bruno's expression grew beakier, like a tortoise. He peered out the window at the slowly passing blocks, as if searching for an escape route that would take them faster to their destination. Lacey declined to cave in to Bruno's anxiety. She had far too much to do, observing the changed city. It had to be eight years since she'd gone anywhere but the cemetery or the synagogue. Everything was taller now: the buildings, the billboards, the trucks. The amount of neon, it astounded her. Each bar, restaurant, and store sign glowed with lines and bands of color. Streetlamps, too, poured their hazy gleam. Trash overflowed the cans. Plastic bottles swarmed against curbs, sluices of soda left in them. Graffiti splashed metal security doors, the windows girded in iron bars. Everywhere looked dangerous and watched.

A crowd materialized outside a club, clustered like ants at a splotch of jam. Lacey pressed her face to the window, hoping to catch the eyeliner and tattoos that Edith had been salivating over. Instead she saw girls in slip dresses with chunky black boots, their boys in cargo pants and plaids. Everyone pale, pouting, and slouching. Their hair uncombed. A pajama party crossed with a meeting of hicks. At least some of them still had the decency to smoke. No mustaches, no waist-length ironed tresses, though, all the flair of the seventies gone. The cars, too, no longer cruised, low and boat-like, but bounced along, boxy and higher, like everyone was primed for a jungle adventure. Lacey had seen these vehicles from above, but on the street level it astonished her how much they blocked the view ahead. The beefier the car, the more likely you could see over your neighbor. A new competition was on.

"Well?" said Bruno.

"It's taller," she said. "And dirtier than I remembered. But I like it. I do."

"I can't remember the past," said Bruno. "Except I had more hair personally."

He was lying, of course.

"I can't either," Lacey lied, too. She did remember the last day before she moved into the hotel. She'd been at a café by the beach, sipping Cinzano, wearing a hat to hide the line of gray at her scalp. The Cinzano had tasted refreshing but made her thirsty. She ordered an ice water. After a few sips, her pants felt tight. So she drank nothing and watched both glasses sweat and bead, running her painted fingernail through the rivulets. She was trying to distract herself from thinking about the party the night before. All the women her age had either talked about their children or their gurus or their interior decorators. They all seemed to be seeking a life inside someone else's desire, someone else's vision, and if they found their own days interesting, they never said so. Lacey was fifty-six years old, both her parents dead, their house finally cleared out, and she had booked a plane ticket to Paris with no return. It was finally time to enjoy herself, she'd announced to her gals, and they'd hugged her and agreed, knowing only a fraction of Lacey's last decade, after Mutti died and Papi lingered, having survived cancer, but not old age and its relentless breakdowns. For these, there was no remedy: no chemo, no radiation, no jewelweed. or goldenseal. Only time and death.

Go live, Papi would urge Lacey as she hovered at his bedside through another bout in hospital (gall bladder, vertigo, minor strokes), but she was terrified of the wards neglecting him, of the busy personnel deciding Papi was not beloved, not precious above all, so she wore her finest clothes and engaged in bright conversations with every doctor and aide who came in. *Isn't it a lark*, she hoped to imply, *that we're here today? Tomorrow we'll dine at the Chateau. Don't you know my father once danced with Ginger Rogers, in the grand ballroom he owned?* Season after season passed that way. By the end of it, by the last days, Papi couldn't hear her anymore. Her charming comments scraped the silence, and she felt plucked of every feather she'd ever grown.

Now it was time for Lacey to make her own adventure, but as she stared at the glittering Pacific, a voice entered her head, one she had not heard in a long time. It was Edith's voice, and it said: *You have nowhere to go.*

Lacey sipped and posed in a mint linen suit. *Of course I have somewhere to go*, she retorted in her mind. *Paris.* She had a new set of mauve suitcases, already packed with clothes.

Yet as Lacey watched the young men and women flaunt their bodies in skimpy tops and cutoffs, she felt a mounting dread. What was there to see in Paris, anyway? Better fashion? More strangers? The beachgoers didn't seem to care anymore that two great wars had been fought, or a devastating Depression overcome, just that their hungers and lusts would be sated. Their skin glistened with oil and their eyes were drunk and corrupt.

You have nowhere to go. The statement wasn't accusing or insulting. It was the truth. Lacey didn't yearn to tour castles and cathedrals in the half of Europe not closed off by the Iron Curtain. She didn't long to reconnect with Papi's distant relatives, or to revive her rusty German. She didn't want to build a new life or find a great cause like her mother. Seek a new love. She just wanted quiet, and time to think, to dwell. To *dwell*, she thought, savoring the word.

She had paid her bill and walked back to her car to find her driver's-side window smashed. Glass scattered all over her leather seat. Wires spilled everywhere: yellow, red, and white. Snarls and loops. Like guts. A gutted body. Someone had yanked open the dashboard and tried to hotwire the car. To steal it. In broad daylight. It was a sky-blue Oldsmobile, her father's car, his pride and joy. Her head began to pound.

You have nowhere to go, repeated the voice.

That night, Lacey called the hotel and told Bruno she was moving for a few weeks into the old apartment on the thirty-eighth floor. She took the suitcases she'd packed for Paris and two boxes of Cal's books and began reading. For the first time in years, her head felt clear enough to sink into the stories, and she found herself blissfully absorbed. At night, while the city glowed, she stayed awake and turned the pages of other worlds, sinking back into the Lucie Weber who first arrived in America and dived into books to become Lacey. She had read all her life, but not with this feverishness, this intent. She had no system but pushed herself through the dry intelligence of a history, followed by a sweet simple novel, then a tragedy, then a mystery. She read the florid books by young authors, now forgotten, that Cal had bought with an eye toward producing them, and then his college philosophy text, and then the handsome, embossed *Song of Hiawatha* that she had bought for their unborn son or daughter. She ate in the restaurant a few times but found she preferred the serenity of her suite. Soon, she sustained herself on one hearty meal a day, ordered from the kitchen, and a bottle of Benedictine, brought by a delivery boy. Not since her father's death had Lacey felt so safe. And not since the party after the Danube, long ago, had she felt so deliberate about choosing her own future.

After a month, she had finished twenty of Cal's books and had the rest delivered. The boxes lined up before her like stepping-stones. Half a year's work, and meanwhile she could ask the librarians across the street to loan her more. Lacey told Bruno she was staying. For good. "This is my home," she said, and made arrangements for the remainder of her possessions to be sold or brought to her suite. Bruno got the repaired Oldsmobile, a gift that pleased him immensely. He unpacked the books himself and helped her fill the recessed shelves. Bruno never questioned her choice; after all, the hotel was his second home, too. Instead, he stayed on working long past his retirement age, just to keep an eye on Lacey, his boss's daughter. That little minx in the ermine-lined cloak who'd once begged him for smokes.

"I do remember your hair," she said now. "I always loved it, even when you were a teenager and it was constantly falling in your face."

Bruno kept a stern expression at this, but his upper lip twitched, and she could tell he was pleased.

"Weren't we both beautiful when we were young," Lacey said dreamily, leaning back.

"Yes," said Bruno. "And unforgivable, how stupid."

"Oh, I forgive us," said Lacey. "You and me."

She gazed out the window and tried to remember what Edith had said about a "youth energy." It wasn't youth that Lacey felt, looking at the city. The theater row that was now swap meets and Hispanic churches hadn't looked any younger or older than the Hollywood scene she had known, but it had been altered, the way seasons change a year, though the year always stays the same. Green light, yellow light, red. Stop and go. Cycles, revolutions. Now the downtown belonged to someone different from Cal or Lacey or Edith's people. One day, a new generation would replace them.

Bruno was tortoise-faced again, peering down the side streets as the cab stalled at another light. "My son Robin, now Rob," he announced, "got another DUI." He stressed each letter, *dee-you-eye*. "He needs a ride to his meetings, so I have to drive him."

Robin was Bruno's firstborn. Bruno's wife, Viv, had insisted on the name, despite Bruno's objections that it was better for "fairy dust than a boy." Robin-now-Rob was also the drummer on welfare, bearded and long-haired and slightly fat, according to the last photo Lacey had seen.

"How awful." Lacey shifted toward Bruno, but her curiosity seemed to prickle him, and he eyed her warily.

"No matter what he does, I always see him the way I saw him for the first time. Little helpless baby. Who needed me. For everything," he said to his window. "You asked me the first time I saw Edith. You maybe think of the first time you saw her, too."

Lacey sank back in her seat.

It was camp, of course, but all the first days had blended until the morning Edith had woken to Lacey crying and asked what was wrong. In that memory, Edith wasn't bruised. She wasn't singing onstage. She was listening. To Lacey. A trembling began in Lacey's legs. What if Edith was waiting at the theater for them? What would they say to each other now? She swallowed hard.

"Her camp uniform was too small," she said. "On account of her mother being gone. Poor thing."

Bruno appeared to be waiting for more. When it didn't come, he made a big production of checking his watch. "Show's started," he said.

The words burst from Lacey: "Why did you always take her side? You knew about her and Cal. Why didn't you tell me?"

Bruno stared straight ahead. "I took only one side all my life." His voice came from somewhere distant inside him. "I would not be the one to break your heart."

In the pained silence that followed, Lacey lifted her palm, wanting to touch him, but touch him where? A pat on the arm? Bruno would hate her for that. Nor could she lean into him and kiss his cheek. She would have to unbuckle and unstrap. Across the cab, Bruno would see her puckering like an ancient fish. She couldn't tell him how much he'd always meant to her, either. If she did, he would hear the truth in her voice, and see the fear in her eyes. So she pretended she was searching for something in her purse, jingling the loose change around, tissues, a spare lipstick, until a familiar amused exasperation suffused his face.

"What?" he said. "We need to go back?"

She held up the tickets. "They'll let us in," she said. "Two old codgers, and in this traffic?"

"Only one codger here," Bruno said. His gaze on her was safe again.

"I dare them to turn us away," Lacey declared, and distracted herself by preparing to play the queen. She had a lifetime of practice, and she wasn't going to lose it now. She kept her head high and her eyes straight ahead as they disembarked from the cab and negotiated their way past the ticket booth and into the darkened theater, where the film was already playing. It was a small place, nothing grand like the Court, but it wasn't the Danube, either. This venue was red-carpeted and clean. It smelled of fresh popcorn. The screen was the size of the side of a cabin. Their seats were good seats, reserved in the center. Unfortunately, this meant they had to climb down the row, past people's scrunched knees and rolling eyes. There was no way to look for Edith without tripping. If Edith was here, she would see them come in, but they wouldn't know she was there.

Twice Lacey paused, her heart racing, but she kept her breath even and did her best with the obstacle course of legs. She and Bruno made it to their chairs, which sank so deeply, her body buckled in half, and she doubted she would ever rise again. Soon it didn't matter, because there was a field on the screen, a yellowed field under a vast sky, and a man lounging in the middle of it, his shirt open at the neck, one suspender loose and the other hitched over his shoulder, and he was the spitting image of Cal. Or he was Cal with Cal's grace, but with Edith's green gaze, and his own ranginess. He was just lying there, on his elbows, but you couldn't look away from him. He possessed something mysterious in his expression, and when a young woman appeared at the edge of the field, calling for him, he cocked his head, and you saw that the mysteriousness had a humor and laziness to it, like he knew the world all too well, and he was conserving his energy to confront it.

The movie proceeded in images like this, rich and lush, the plot minimal, but the screen itself a canvas of color and mood. The lead actor made it so. Lacey felt Bruno shifting restlessly from time to time, extending his legs, popping his ankles. She heard wrappers crackle and popcorn sift, straws punch deep in cups, and ice slide and settle. She sat silent, stilled to her core. Daniel was the center of every scene, but also the lord of their making. The star and the director in one. His father could have never created a film like this. He'd come of age in a world in which a man chose his one role and stuck with it.

When Daniel walked shirtless out of the shadows of a barn, Lacey's breath caught. Daniel had Cal's shoulders. For years, she'd tried to forget the perfect curve of Cal's deltoids and biceps, to bury her affections for a disappointing, faithless husband, but there they were, the shoulders she'd loved despite the man. The shoulders that had once held Edith, too, that had lifted Edith from the creek bed. The bare gold hue of them. Their supple roundness and angles of an easy strength. Lacey felt Bruno's eyes on her, and she wondered if she had gasped aloud. She pursed her lips and tried to look disapproving at the display.

She had a good time admiring Daniel until about an hour in, when the movie's plot thickened, a shadow overtaking the bright tones. The man and the wife began to struggle with bad weather, spoiled crops,

thieves. They made mistakes. They went hungry, and the wife begged
to leave and return to the city, but the man refused. He had committed
a violent robbery back there, and he didn't want to get caught. Besides, he was too attached to his land, to his dream of a rebirth. The
panoramas' dazed grandeur became complicated by sadness. The wife
lost her baby, and the couple grieved together at the bare dining room
table. With each blow of fate, Lacey felt more swallowed by her chair.
Why? Why did so many stories lead to dissolution and entropy, the
slow falling apart of a future? Two futures.

"This farmer I knew as a girl," the woman's character was saying.
"He had it all, a big spread of fields. Five sons. A wife he loved more
than anything. But twice a year he'd leave and go the city. When he
died, sudden, a heart attack, they found out he had another family,
a wife and a daughter, from when he was a young man. Those two
women were always just scraping by. Those two came in their cheap
clothes after the funeral and told the truth about him." The actress
paused. She was a pretty woman, bony and big-eyed. "It broke everyone to know it. The whole good family went bad, and by the time
I left, the five sons were selling off the land to pay off their habits and
debts." She reached forward and clasped Daniel's hand, her stringy
blond hair falling in her face. "We can live any way but one, Jamie.
We can live poor. We can live sick. We can live always fighting for our
next meal. But we can't live a lie."

Daniel, playing Jamie, looked off. "What's the lie?" he said. "You
know where I got my money."

"The lie's that you care about anything but this." She gestured at
the farm.

Daniel hung his head. He toyed with a bridle on the table, untan-
gling the leather straps.

"What if the farmer knew he could never make her happy? The
first wife," he said to his hands. "What if he knew it was no use?"

The woman winced as if he'd punched her. She touched the belly where the child had been. Lacey felt her face soak with tears.

Down the row, someone slurped their soda. *Now you'll have to barge through to the restroom,* she thought accusingly, and then she wondered if she should go herself. A preventive. Suddenly she wanted to go. To leave the theater before the climax. To have Edith see her leave, if she was there. But the seats were so deep, and Lacey would need Bruno, and then they'd both be making a scene, with her weepy face and her old mincing steps. She sat cupped and folded by the tilt of the chair. She watched the film with growing dread and sorrow. *Not this,* she thought. Secretly, the man made a plan to sell his property after the next harvest. The wife ran away before she found this out, abandoning the man. He walked his land, tearing at the stalks of grass. The sun shone on the fields. It was no longer the same sun. But it was the same sun.

Lacey's cheeks went so slick that her tears collected beneath her chin. She felt something soft shove against her hand, and accepted, for the umpteenth time in her life, Bruno's handkerchief. His eyes shone in the dark, and he gave her one of his rare, wincing smiles. She cradled it inside her as she watched the last scene, of the man, Daniel, arriving in the city and committing another armed robbery, more violent this time. A blaze of gunfire ended the film.

The credits rolled and no one got up. They sat there, as if bolted to their chairs. Lacey felt too desolate to go anywhere, either, especially not across the path of bright wrappers and yellow buckets, the sugary spills of cola, to the enormous, indifferent city. She turned and scanned the audience in the dim light. A sea of faces, but no Edith. So Daniel had made Cal's movie after all. Not his mother's. Not the one where the love between people outlasts their suffering. But was everyone really too depressed by Daniel's bombastic ending to move now? She glanced at Bruno. He shrugged and cracked his knees.

A couple of young men in black jeans and T-shirts sped to the front. They set out tall stools and microphones.

Daniel was here tonight, Lacey thought with a jolt. That's why his name was on the ticket. *Directed by Daniel Fallada.* He was here to talk about the making of the film. Edith knew. She'd known. She'd flown across the country so that she and Lacey might behold him together, just once, a sighting and a letting go. So what had changed Edith's mind? Why hadn't she said anything? Why had she left the tickets in the desk like a hidden treasure?

That's your problem, Lace. You think everyone makes mistakes the same way.

The woman who rings can't be herself. She is not Elsie.

What choices do you think I had?

The houselights came up. Lacey grabbed Bruno's hand. "He's coming," she whispered.

Two people walked up the aisle: the actress who played the wife, and a stout older fellow, who looked unfamiliar. Not the actor/director. Not Daniel. They sat on the stools. The man tested the microphone with his finger. It made a dull, popping sound. "Well," he said, and then looked at the actress.

"You go ahead," he said.

The actress took a breath. "Naturally, Daniel wanted to be here," she said, her voice full of emotion. "He was so excited for this screening, his first in Los Angeles." Then she hesitated, as if overcome, staring out.

Lacey felt Bruno's hand tighten on hers, and heard whispers behind them, too low to discern the words. Something was wrong. The worst had happened, and that was why Edith had traveled so far to see her. No one else in the world would know how much it hurt.

No, she thought fiercely. *You didn't surrender all you did, just to lose him.*

The actress's face split into a hopeful smile. "But as some of you know, two days ago, Daniel became the father to a beautiful baby girl. He felt it was too early to leave mother and child. The birth was hard, but they are both doing fine." She turned to the man. "What's the baby's name again? It's an old-fashioned one. They let Daniel's mother choose for them."

When the man said, "Lacey," Bruno gave a grunt of surprise. Lacey felt disbelief, then loneliness gouge her, so deep that her whole body shuddered. Cal's grandchild was named Lacey. This was too much of a coincidence. The news and Edith's testimony could not both be true. Or could they? There was more to the story, and she needed to hear it. If there was still time for that. Lacey hadn't wanted time in so long, but she wanted it now.

The blond actress and the man kept talking about *Days of Gold*, about Daniel, about cast and crew, but Lacey floated alone, gripped in Bruno's strong fingers. She was recalling the day in Agoura again, sun beating down, sweat in her eyes as she stared into the shadows of the canyon, where Edith lay and Cal bent over her. She was recalling how Edith's pale arm reached for her, how her mouth called out, *Wait*, and Lacey had turned away.

Once there were two girls in a dark forest and they pledged to care for each other, no matter what came.

The theater lights flickered.

"Thank you all," said the actress, sliding her mic back into its hook. "I think it's time we let you go home."

23.

BRUNO SAID GOODBYE TO LACEY IN THE HOTEL lobby. His voice was reluctant, and his eyes were tender and grave. In the late hour, Lacey could see now where the stroke had swept through him, stripping his fullness, leaving a winnowed man. He had faced his own end and fought it off. Afraid, defiant. It was visible in the lines of his neck, in the muscles around his mouth, the denial they shaped. He who had lost his father so young would not abandon his sons. Dear brave Bruno.

He would not take his wet handkerchief back, either. "I will call you tomorrow, as soon as I hear," he said. "She is fine. She is home by tonight. I know it."

Lacey tried to sound certain: "I know it, too."

Bruno continued to hover, appraising her. The whole taxi ride back, she had sobbed silently, and he had held her hand. At the hotel, he came around to Lacey's side of the cab and helped her out. He lifted her by the elbows until she straightened for the slow walk back in. Bruno hadn't asked about the baby. The girl named Lacey. Maybe he thought Edith had raised the child, after all. Maybe she had. All of last night, a falsehood. But why?

"You want me to take you to your room?" Bruno said.

Everyone was giving them the side-eye now, the night manager, the bartender, a young couple with their hands on each other's knees.

Lacey shook her head, and pressed the damp cloth to her mouth, an unconscious gesture. Her lips left a red smear on the cloth. She dropped her hand, clamping the sogginess in her fist. "Thank you, Bruno," she said hoarsely. "But you'll miss your ride."

He looked over his shoulder, through the glass doors, at the line of yellow cars. "He can wait. Or I can find another."

Did he want to stay? Did she want him to? It was too much tonight.

"I know Edith's fine," Lacey insisted. "And just as stubborn as I am. Thank you for the lovely time." Before she could hesitate or he turn away, she stepped close and kissed Bruno's cheek. She planted a big one right on his gorgeous cheekbone, felt the brush of her lips against his stubble, and her breasts nudge against his chest. Let them ogle.

Bruno blinked. "Whenever you need me," he said. "Tedious movies, cemeteries, I am your man." His eyes twinkled, but his voice was scratchy and solemn.

"Oh," she said, and lost her way trying find a light reply. She felt her eyes fill again. "I appreciate that."

She stood straight and still, unable to meet his gaze, until Bruno finally kissed her back on her forehead, a firm, gentle kiss, and limped away to the waiting taxi. After he left, she could not bear to go up to her stale, quiet room. Ignoring the curious stares, she chose an empty chair, the one Edith might have waited in, for Lacey, for hours, and sat down with her purse on her lap. Beyond the rug, the old, tiled floor shone. Long ago, Lacey and Edith had swept over that floor in the arms of young men while a live brass band played. Lacey and Edith, circling the crowd, but always in sight of each other. Edith had been an excellent dancer, quick on her feet. No one could shimmy like her,

her whole body a wriggle, her red-gold head chucked back, her hands snapping. One day, tipsy on punch, the two of them had danced together, rib to rib, then twirling out. At first, it had been fun and free, but then an expression closed Edith's face, a possession in her lidded gaze, and that had made Lacey want to go faster. She had gone faster and faster, until they were both spinning and kicking madly. Then Edith suddenly stopped, and the room swam, and the sweat stung Lacey's eyes. "You'll fall," Edith scolded as Lacey banged against her, still in motion. "Don't fall." But there had been fear in Edith's voice as well as anger. Even then, there had been the deepest dread.

The desk phone rang, a low bleeping toll, and the clerk picked it up, his greeting fake and cheery. His fingers tapped an empty beat as he talked. This chamber hadn't been the Music Room in years. Young people didn't dance their afternoons away in sky-lit atria, under the eyes of chaperones. They could escape the confinement of their bodies, their age, into a thousand different lives. The room wore a new atmosphere as the lobby, but it was still a threshold. A portal. Suitcases and check-ins. People coming and going. Going, mostly. You didn't arrive at a hotel to stay.

She ought to retreat upstairs to read Edith's letter. If she had any tears left to cry over it, Bruno's sodden handkerchief would hardly dry them. If the letter drained every shred of pride she had left—forcing her to accept that Edith had triumphed at motherhood, too, and in that final hollowing out, Lacey decided it didn't matter, it had never mattered, what mattered was they still needed each other, always— the clerk would have to help her rise, hobble to the elevator. If it was Edith's promise to stay in touch, to resume where they left off, to invite Lacey to get to know Daniel and the baby as a kindly aunt, she might mutter aloud, *Why didn't you just tell me? She's going to be different from us. She'll have so many opportunities.* Or she might want to open a drawer, pull out some stationery, and write back to Edith that very instant, just like in the old days, in the autumn after their camp ended. *I may not have much time,* she might begin. *I suppose you knew that, deep down, and that's why you came.*

All of this would unfold better in Lacey's room—hidden, aloft, alone—with her shelves of books, her view, her midnight-blue dress in the wardrobe still scented with smoke.

But Lacey didn't go. She stayed. She stayed in the low, puffy chair, a stranger among strangers. Not a queen. Not a monster. Just a muddled being of hope and fear and waiting. A fool in the field, waking alone. She opened her purse and took out the paper, bracing herself.

The note was long, the words flowing across the page. Edith must have dashed it out the night before, when Lacey was in the bathroom:

> *I can't do it after all, kid.*
>
> *I thought us watching Daniel together might finally help you and me make sense of everything we both gave up. But I can't bear to say goodbye to you again. I can't be in the same room with him, either.*
>
> *Now that you've seen Daniel for yourself, I have one last confession. I didn't go by my own name when I met Daniel's parents. I went by yours. They knew me as "Lacey" and I carried him to term as Lacey, too. The only way I could stomach becoming a mother was by being you, the one who wanted a child, and then fleeing afterward as myself again. As Lacey, I bore a son, so that as Edith, I could let him go. I didn't know that, for the rest of my life, I would miss you both terribly. Especially you.*
>
> *The Falladas seem like good people, though. Eventually, I deciphered who they are, and Daniel, too. And he's a star, isn't he? I hope he lights up Hollywood so bright I can spot it from the plane. I won't ever see him face-to-face.*

But I know that you would want to. That somehow you are
meant to, instead of me. That this might finally give you
peace.

All my love,

E

The letter seemed to fold itself again, back to the rectangle with Edith's note at the top. Edith wouldn't know about her granddaughter's birth yet. She could be told. She could be given the chance to hope and speculate and, yes, to grieve her heart out if she wanted, with a willing listener. She might be home by now, orbiting her phone, wondering if a call would come. The paper rested in Lacey's hand, thin and light. The song changed on the lobby speakers. Something faster, brighter began. Lacey didn't recognize the evening soundtrack anymore. It was all pop tunes from the seventies and eighties, massaged to easy jazz. But if she closed her eyes, she could pick out another sound, of the water falling from the lion's mouth into the basin of her father's favorite fountain. Or she thought she could hear it. Her left ear was rather deaf now. Lacey knew the noise so well, perhaps her mind was remaking it for her. That gurgle and splash, the ripple lapping the stone. Her father once claimed that the fountain's sound reminded him of spring in Prague, when church bells rang from every spire in the greening city. At the time, Lacey humored him with a smile. She thought, *Church bells are big and loud*, but tonight she understood what Papi was saying. The sound was like the feeling of throwing off winter, defying death again, and knowing that spring would come and go, all your life, even when every inch of your skin had stained and crinkled, when your hair turned to wisps and your teeth to stumps. The feeling would come as a comfort. It would come as a sorrow. It would pour clear and cool into itself while you stood at the rim, gathering your courage to live.

Afterword

When Sándor Márai's classic novel, *Embers*, appeared in English translation in 2001, my husband, Kyle, and I were living in Hollywood, both employed in downtown Los Angeles. I worked at an art museum, and Kyle worked at an old luxury hotel, the Millennium Biltmore. On lunch breaks, we sometimes met at the fountain above the public library steps, and Kyle would take me through the back doorways of the hotel, up and down its inner staircases. The Biltmore was a majestic building with many secrets—the speakeasy hidden behind a long mirror, ghosts who haunted the corridors, the rumor of a woman who had lived in her suite for years and never left. The hotel's ballroom had hosted eight Academy Awards ceremonies and was the site of the luncheon when the MGM art director first sketched his idea for the Oscar statue on a linen napkin. The thirty-five-story building remained when urban renewal razed the Queen Annes around it and replaced them with half-empty apartment blocks, when the rise of suburbs and decades of urban crime hollowed American cities. The hotel also survived the threat of a sale to convert it to low-cost senior housing, and finally major renovations in the 1970s and 1980s restored its beautiful interiors to their original glory.

When Kyle and I couldn't meet, I read books in a little park under the skyscrapers. One of them was *Embers*. It told the story of two men, two old friends, a general and an officer, reuniting at a castle in the Carpathians in 1941. They had not seen each other in four decades because of an event in the past that had split them apart. After some backstory on their devoted youth together, the rest of the novel is their tense conversation, scouring the past and examining what broke them both. *Embers* reads a bit like a play, a bit like a fable, and a bit like a riddle, and naturally at the heart of that riddle is a woman. Proud, beautiful, enigmatic Krisztina was the general's wife and the officer's lover, and she is not quite real. Instead, she is the emblem of their greatest passions—to love her as she was—and their most colossal failing: to love each other.

That same autumn that I read *Embers*, hijacked American planes plowed into the Twin Towers in New York City, and the twentieth century ended, for the first time. Several ideas fused in my mind during the traumatic post-9/11 period: a plot about two women's friendship, a contemporary castle inspired by the Biltmore, a recluse who has retreated inside it, and the death of an old century. I knew that one day I wanted to write a female-centered story using the structure of *Embers* but also that I was not ready, and might never be.

If the twentieth century died with the events of September 11, 2001, the COVID-19 pandemic buried it completely. In the spring of 2021, in the lingering shadows of an oppressive year and the sense that we had truly, finally turned the page from the America of my childhood, I began to see a plot, a story of female friendship and isolation, with a sudden clarity. It would be set in 1990, the waning years of the millennium, in a fictional grand hotel. It would be the story of Lacey and Edith, but it could also be the story of many twentieth-century American women, the explosion of our freedoms, the evolution of responsibilities and possibilities, the lingering of old archetypes, and the ways we have sometimes divided against ourselves in order to claim safety and power. The first draft emerged in six weeks. I wrote every day, and on many days I felt like I was not composing a story, but racing to transcribe voices that already knew what they wanted to say.

Sándor Márai authored forty-six books but died, mostly forgotten, in San Diego in 1989, from suicide, his diminished reputation a casualty of his exile from his native country and his insistence on writing in his mother tongue, Hungarian. This book owes an immense debt to him, and to another figure rendered nearly anonymous by history. Her name was Dorothea Viehmann, and she was the aging wife of a tailor and the mother to seven children, who told the brothers Grimm dozens of stories in the early 1800s. Many of the Grimms' sources were young women of privilege, who gathered folk stories on the brothers' behalf, but Dorothea Viehmann was different. She was poor and old, and she had grown up in a tavern, where she must have heard many travelers regale their companions by the fire. In exchange for a silver spoon and a few coins, Viehmann related her tales with such writerly exactitude that she dazzled the brothers; they attested that they could almost copy down her stories verbatim. She also told them narratives that did not quite fit their canon of helpless, isolated females saved by marriage and motherhood, and her fables like "Clever Elsie" and "The Lazy Spinner" and even "The Goose Girl" continue to stand out to this day for their subversions. As for Viehmann herself, the Grimm brothers commissioned a relative to draw her picture for their subsequent editions—highlighting her wrinkled and careworn face, her modest bonnet and gown—and rhapsodized to their readers that "she was probably beautiful when she was young."

My thanks go to several readers who helped me immeasurably

with the early drafts: Glori Simmons, Melanie Finn, and Rita Mae Reese, and to my generous and visionary agent, Gail Hochman, who helped me grow *Goldenseal* from there. I also owe a great debt to my colleagues in the UVM English department, AED, and Humanities Center for supporting me along the way. Thank you and cheers to the Peach Palace. Thanks also to the Los Angeles Conservancy for their useful historic guides to downtown Los Angeles and to my long-ago teachers at Charles University.

Many thanks to the crew at Counterpoint/Catapult/Soft Skull for their multitude of talents at bringing books into the world, and especially to my infinitely wise editor Dan Smetanka, who carries the map and compass for every book I've done with him and reminds me of the way. My mother and my brothers and their wives and children have been a constant inspiration in my life, along with all my beloved extended family. This book would not be possible without Dearie, Manfred, Erika, or Ilsa, all voyagers of their times. Finally, always and ever, my deepest gratitude to Kyle, Bowie, and Bruce.

© Karen Pike

MARIA HUMMEL is a novelist and poet. Her novel *Still Lives* was a Reese Witherspoon x Hello Sunshine Book Club pick, Book of the Month Club pick, and BBC Culture Best Book of 2018, and has been optioned for television and translated into multiple languages. She is also the author of *Lesson in Red*; *Motherland*, a San Francisco Chronicle Book of the Year; and *House and Fire*, winner of the APR/Honickman Poetry Prize. She has worked and taught at the Museum of Contemporary Art, Los Angeles; Stanford University; and the University of Vermont. She lives in Vermont with her husband and sons. Find out more at mariahummel.com.